ABOUT THIS BOOK

MOCCASIN TRAIL
Eloise Jarvis McGraw

It had been eight years since Jim Keath ran away from his family
into the wilderness of the great Oregon territory. Rescued by the
Crow Indians from a near-fatal battle with a grizzly, Jim spent
six years living with and learning the ways of the Crow Indians.
Then Jim received a desperate message and learned that his
brothers and sister were journeying west to take up land. "Jim,
if you're still alive, come help us!"

But regaining his family's trust would be as difficult as the long
journey through the frontier. His brother Jonnie was caught
between his suspicion of Jim's Indian ways and his reliance on
him for survival. Sally, filled with resentment of Jim for running
away from the family, was fearful of his growing influence on
little Dan'l, who had come to idolize his brave and adventurous
brother. This is the story of Jim's long, hard journey back to
civilization and the difficulty he has trying to fit in with the
family he hasn't seen since childhood. It is also the story of the
death of one era and the birth of another—of a new land in
the making.

MOCCASIN TRAIL

by Eloise Jarvis McGraw

Puffin Books

PUFFIN BOOKS

Viking Penguin Inc., 40 West 23rd Street, New York, New York 10010, U.S.A.
Penguin Books Ltd, Harmondsworth, Middlesex, England
Penguin Books Australia Ltd, Ringwood, Victoria, Australia
Penguin Books Canada Limited, 2801 John Street, Markham, Ontario,
Canada L3R 1B4
Penguin Books (N.Z.) Ltd, 182–190 Wairau Road, Auckland 10, New Zealand

Published in Puffin Books 1986
Copyright Eloise Jarvis McGraw, 1952
Copyright renewed Eloise Jarvis McGraw, 1980
All rights reserved
Printed in U.S.A. by R. R. Donnelley & Sons Company, Harrisonburg, Virginia

Library of Congress Cataloging in Publication Data
McGraw, Eloise Jarvis.   The moccasin trail.
Reprint. Originally published: New York, N.Y.: Coward-McCann, 1952.
Summary: A pioneer boy, brought up by Crow Indians, is reunited with his family
and attempts to orient himself in the white man's culture.
1. Crow Indians—Juvenile fiction.   2. Indians of North America—
Juvenile fiction.   [1. West (U.S.)—Fiction.   2. Crow Indians—Fiction.
3. Indians of North America—Fiction]   I.Title.
PZ7.M47853Mo   1986   [Fic]   86-4855   ISBN 0-14-032170-5

FOR PETER AND LAURIE—
MY OWN LITTLE WILD INDIANS

MOCCASIN TRAIL

Chapter I

Silently, in the hour between sunset and dark, young Jim Keath moved upstream, his flintlock in one hand and his last trap in the other. He walked with an easy, almost careless gait, yet not a twig snapped under his moccasins, not a branch swayed or a pebble rolled to show he had passed.

His appearance was unusual, even for the time, which was 1844, and the place, which was the wilderness of the great Oregon territory. He wore the leggings and fringed buckskin shirt of a white trapper, but his long dark hair was braided like an Indian's, and an eagle feather was stuck into it. His eyes were not black, but so light a brown they looked almost golden against his bronzed skin; yet they had the Indian's wild, unsettled, wary look in them.

One highly skilled corner of Jim's brain was furiously busy, receiving and digesting the information sent to it by his alert ears and constantly moving eyes. That magpie sounded off key. Why? What had scared it? How far away was it? Was it flying toward him or away from him? There was a broken limb bobbing on the current of the stream. What had broken it? Wind? Indians passing? Animal? What kind? How long ago? Yonder was a gnawed sapling—beaver sign. That made the third. Was it time to take to the water now?

But all this noticing, remembering, judging, interpreting,

3

deciding, took place swiftly and automatically, without his ever giving it a conscious thought. Even as he changed his course in obedience to that gnawed sapling and moved soundlessly through the leafless underbrush to the stream's edge, his mind loafed among thoughts of food and a warm fire, his horse and mule nibbling bunch grass back at camp, the moccasin he must mend tonight, the good taste of beavertail.

Jim stepped into the icy water, swearing inwardly as the bitter cold penetrated the strips of old blanket he wore for leggings. It was as good as winter already, here in the mountain meadows above the Powder River, though it was only October.

Likely snowed up higher yesterday, he thought, and from the look of that sky it'll snow here tomorrow. Time fer Tom and me to git movin', less'n we aim to winter here. Wisht I could talk him into stayin'. If he heads back to Taos, ain't nothin' fer me to do but go back to Absaroka, on back to Crow country.

The thought made his brows knot, sent the familiar restlessness creeping over him. Was it really meant that he go back to the Crows and settle down once more to be an Indian? He'd run away from them little more than a year ago, lonesome for his own kind, crazy for the sight of a white man. What had gone wrong?

He waded on upstream, plagued by the uncertainties that had dragged at his life for weeks now, ever since Tom Rivers had said he was quitting the fur trade, come fall. What would he do after Tom left? What would Tom himself be doing? Plenty of trappers had gone back east to the States, or taken to guiding wagon trains, or set up trading posts on the Plains somewhere to sell meal and powder and calico to bourgeways heading for Oregon. Tom might do one of those things, but Jim couldn't see himself doing any of them.

He shoved the matter out of his mind and swerved toward

the bank, for his trained eye and that ceaselessly busy corner of his brain had together selected the best spot for his trap. It was there near the beavers' lodge, where a slide came down the bank into the pool created by the dam. He cached his rifle in a low branch and stooped to sink his trap, glancing as he did so toward the mud-plastered structure looming there in the fading light—a big lodge, it was, six feet high and twice as broad. He smiled briefly, remembering the night he had once spent in a beaver lodge, listening to the footsteps and sullen grunts of three Sioux warriors prowling about outside, looking for him. A lodge made a good hiding place, more comfortable than many another, though of course, its only entrances being underwater, you had to get soaking wet getting there. But what of that if you kept your scalp?

The trap was placed now, in the proper depth of water. A stout, dry limb hacked from a nearby cottonwood made a good enough trap pole, and Jim drove it hard through the ring at the end of the five-foot steel chain, into the gravel at the bottom of the stream and through that into mud and the solid stuff beneath, putting all his strength behind it. He tested it, and nodded. It would take a man-sized beaver to yank that free. Still, they sometimes did it, dragging the trap after them onto the bank, and you'd be minus a plew—a pelt—unless you reached them before they could gnaw off the imprisoned foot.

As an added precaution Jim cut a small branch for a float stick, to show him the position of the beaver's body should it yank free but drown before it reached the bank. Then he splashed water over every place he had stepped on the bank, and on the trap pole itself. When all was finished, he arched a small willow shoot over the surface of the water just above the trap's trigger, fastened it, and smeared it with castoreum, that powerful medicine made from the glands of other beavers, which he carried in the plugged horn slung from his belt.

The strong, pungent smell of the stuff filled his nostrils as he straightened up, corking the horn. That oughta fetch 'em, he thought, if they's any left to fetch.

He turned away, automatically touching for luck the string of blue beads and bear claws that hung around his neck. By gor, I need some luck, he thought. We all do. Country's nigh trapped out.

Retrieving his rifle, he waded back downstream, once more turning and twisting the problem in his mind. That was the whole trouble, the beaver were all but gone. With plenty of beaver, a man could live content day by day, needing neither bourgeway wagons to guide nor Indians to live with, needing no plans and no future, but only the broad land—the mountains, the streams in the high meadows, the good, wild country once choked with beaver dams but now trapped out. Trapped clean out. The Humboldt, the Snake, the upper Green, Pierre's Hole and Jackson's Hole, Wind River, the Clearwater—all were finished. Even the Powder, where he and Tom had prowled for the past month, with only a few plews to show for it. Lifting empty traps every morning made a kind of emptiness inside you too.

He ran a hand back through the tangled lock of front hair that always escaped from his braids. As he did so, his fingers touched the four thin, slick scars that ran from his hairline down to his right eyebrow.

That grizzly done a sight more than just tear me up a little, he thought. He wondered, as he had wondered so many times, how things would have turned out if it hadn't been for that bear's catching him. He'd never have grown up in the Crow village, that was sure. He'd likely have gone back to the States after Uncle Adam died; or even if he'd gone on trapping it would have been with white men, and he would never have got so mixed up as to which world he belonged to.

He turned toward the bank and waded ashore at the same place he had first entered the stream. As he reached out to

6

splash water over his trail, his buckskin sleeve hiked up, revealing the other scars, the bad ones, on his forearm—twisted, cruel furrows blazed white on his brown skin—four of them, running diagonally across the underside of his forearm. There were others under his shirt, sweeping down over his chest and belly in that same vicious curve.

He moved into the forest and on downstream with his soundless tread, remembering the bear crashing into the camp on Wind River that evening more than seven years ago; remembering the yells of his uncle and the other trappers as they scattered, the shots, the screaming horses, his own paralyzing fear. He was only eleven then, and a greenhorn—it had been less than a year before that he'd run away from home to follow his uncle. And like a greenhorn, he'd floundered away upwind, through underbrush and over boulders, every move he made bringing his scent more clearly to the wounded and infuriated grizzly, roaring in pursuit.

Within minutes it had been all over. The bear hurtled through a last thicket just as his own legs gave out with fear and exhaustion. His heart knocking wildly, he swung about and raised his rifle. For a fraction of an instant he stared through the gun sights into a red and glaring eye, then squeezed the trigger. As the gun roared, the bear was upon him. He flung up his right arm, felt the claws tear white-hot down his forehead, through the sleeve and the flesh under it, then into his chest. He pitched backward, the bear a suffocating weight on top of him, into spinning blackness.

When he woke at last it was three days later. He was in a Crow lodge, and all around him were the sights and sounds and smells of a strange new world—one which was to become his own.

Jim's thoughts broke off abruptly as an alarm sounded, back in that always vigilant corner of his brain. He froze. Finding his eye riveted on an angle of hill and sky visible between two

7

branches, he knew that he had seen a split second of what might have been movement there.

For perhaps a count of sixty he stood motionless, bringing every faculty of his mind to bear on the matter. An animal that far away and upwind need not concern him. It was not a white man—seasoned mountain men were the only whites who would be wandering this country in mid-October and still alive, and they would be heading away from these mountains toward the Plains and winter lodge. That left Indians; by the end of his sixty seconds Jim had arrived at the probable location of every tribe in the northwest, modified their positions with regard to the season, the present threat of snow, the probable state of their larders, and the last reports of their activities and mood.

He moved on, puzzling over why a lone Digger Indian, or at the most two, should be scouting so far from their village on the banks of the Snake at this time of year. When Tom got back from setting his traps on the other fork of the stream, he'd mention the matter.

Jim reached camp before full dark. A quick glance told him that all was well, even before his gaunt wolflike dog, Moki, who always slept with one eye open, came wriggling out from beneath a bush to greet him with a flurry of tail wagging and panting. There was Tom's horse, Tucky, and Buckskin, his own half-wild cream-colored Crow mare, both standing half hidden behind a clump of willows near the stream. It took longer to locate the mule, whom Jim had named Wah-Keetcha, Bad Medicine, for a very good reason. There was not the slightest sign of him. Jim stood quite still, scratching Moki's ears and whistling tunelessly under his breath, searching the nearby thickets. He stared for seconds at an irregular dark spot between two clumps of leaves before he realized he was looking directly into the mule's long-lashed and inscrutable eye.

He grinned, walked over to the cache of firewood he and Tom had collected earlier in the day, and selected four small logs, which he arranged like the spokes of a wheel. With a handful of dry twigs, flint and steel, he soon had a blaze going. Still whistling softly, he took a kettle from his pack, which like all mountain men he thought of as his "possibles." Filling the kettle at the creek, he set it simmering over the fire on an improvised tripod. A good chunk of buffalo hump, a handful of the dried wild onions he always carried, and a section of beavertail went into the pot. Then he sat down and stretched his legs to the fire, feeling the warmth slowly creep through the soaked leggings and moccasins.

Moki padded toward him, yawning, and dropped down at his side, stretching his nose out on his forepaws but keeping his yellow eyes on the boy.

"You lazy good-fer-nothin'," Jim said.

Moki's tail thumped ingratiatingly. His eyebrows moved as his yellow gaze went briefly to the fragrant steam starting to come up out of the kettle, then back to Jim's face. He began to drool.

Jim grinned, stood up and turned his backside to the flames, holding up first one foot and then the other to the comforting warmth. "*Wagh!* Too lazy to hunt, even," he drawled. "Whar's all the rabbits? Rabbits, Moki?"

Moki emitted a low, enthusiastic growl but didn't move, except his tail thumped a little faster. Jim reached down and rumpled his ears, then walked over to rummage among his possibles for his other pair of moccasins, his awl, and a length of deer sinew. He also dug out a chunk of meat which he threw to the dog.

"There, you thievin' coyote. Tomorrer you hunt fer yourself or go without, by gor!"

Taking the heavy-bladed knife from his belt, he hacked a tab of fringe off one of his sleeves, and settling down cross legged by the fire, began to mend the split moccasin with the tab of deerskin and the sinew. As he worked his low, tuneless whistle mingled with the dog's snarling and slavering over the meat.

Lonesome, thought Jim. Wisht Tom'd git back. What'll it be like when he's gone south? Here I'll be, with only Moki and Buckskin and that cussed mule, and never nobody to talk to. Didn't use to get lonesome. What ails me? It's 'cause the beaver's all gone, that's what's done it. Makes a body feel like the ground's cavin' in all around, like ever'thing's slidin' away and there ain't no solid place to step no more. I best go home to Absaroka and git busy fightin' Sioux.

He jabbed the awl through the tab and through the moccasin until he had a row of holes, then began to thread the split sinew through them, binding the patch in place. The smell of meat cooking and the sight of his fingers handling the sinew made him think of Red Deer, his Crow mother, whose seamed and cheerful face was the first thing he'd seen when he woke up in the new world of the tepee that morning.

All he'd really been conscious of at first was the pain in his body, the strange stiff feel of the muscles in his right arm, and the smell of meat and herbs simmering over the fire in the center of the lodge. Then he'd noticed other smells, too—dog smell and smoke smell and the smell of fresh-scraped hides and blood. And something else, very pungent and strong, that he realized finally was the odor of the wet, sticky poultice somebody had bound around his naked chest and his arm. It was made of some kind of leaves he had never seen before. He looked again at the old woman in the vivid skirt crouching there by the fire, and her face crinkled suddenly into a thousand seams as she smiled at him and nodded, her black eyes bright as a sparrow's. She was working at something in her lap. In a moment she finished and held it up—a necklace of blue beads and long, curved, yellow-white claws, strung upon sinew. He gazed at it, uncomprehending, as she rose and came toward him. She was still nodding and grinning, pointing first to the necklace and then to his chest, and all the time repeating something over and over in a language he did not understand. Gradually it dawned on him. Those cruel ivory curves dangling among the beads were the claws of the grizzly—the same claws that had ripped open his flesh and all but taken his life. Revulsion swept him, and he jerked away from the woman, pressing his cheek into the rough hair of the buffalo hide under his head. The sudden movement sent flame and ice streaking through his wounds, and for a moment he sank once more into blackness. When he came to himself the woman was fastening the necklace around his throat.

He lay there rigid, fighting off nausea at the feel of those talons, cold and heavy against his flesh. After a moment, as they warmed to the heat of his body, he lifted his left hand and touched them. Slowly his fear evaporated; a kind of triumph took its place. The bear was dead, but Jim Keath was alive, very much alive. He turned his head again, looking at the woman. She was watching him closely, and her brown, crooked finger pointed across the tepee to a fresh hide stretched over a frame. The fur was rough and black in color, each hair tipped with silver. So that was all that remained of his enemy! The brute had come to a sorry end, for all his might—all because of eleven-year-old Jim Keath, who had killed him with one shot through his red and wicked eye.

He looked back at the woman and suddenly laughed aloud, gripping the necklace and feeling a fierce joy spurt through him. He was glad the bear had died, glad he had killed him, gloatingly proud of that splayed hide and the talons dangling from his neck, and his own valor. That joy was his first step toward savagery.

He took many more, in the months and years that followed. During the tranquil, shadowy weeks of his convalescence the

11

lodge became home to him. He lay on his bed—buffalo hide stretched on a willow frame—drowsing or watching the fat, furry puppies, one of whom was Moki, tumble over each other in the sunshine near the entrance, or listening to Red Deer's tales of the Little Men or the warriors of long ago and the great medicine dreams they had dreamed. He had soon learned her guttural language, learned too that when a Crow hunting party had discovered him barely alive under the grizzly's body and brought him to their village, she had claimed him in place of her dead son.

Sometimes in those first months he had been lonely, and longed to run away back to his uncle. Then he would turn a deaf ear to Red Deer's stories, and talk English aloud to the puppies or even to rocks and trees, from pure homesick craving to hear it once more. And Red Deer, half jealous, half compassionate, had named him Talks Alone. But as his wounds healed his life grew more active and his memories less so. He joined eagerly then with the other boys in their rough and dangerous games, tugged constantly at his hair to make it grow long and luxuriant like that of the proud warriors about him, who often worked switches into their braids until they trailed the ground, and had to be doubled back in glossy, coalblack loops.

Scalp Necklace, the graven-faced old chief who was husband to Red Deer, had also accepted him as his son, and saw to it that he learned all a chief's son should know. How to pull a bow, how to bear pain or joy if necessary without the quiver of an eyelash, how to steal a horse from under an enemy's nose and ride him as a feather rides the wind. How to hunt, how to stalk, how to drum his heels in dances, how to keep his scalp.

And in his fourteenth year he achieved the first goals every Crow boy must achieve. He counted coup—won honors in war, earning the right to wear the eagle feather—and dreamed his own medicine dream. After that no memories ever plagued him; he talked only Crow and thought only Crow and was only Crow.

Then one day in his sixteenth spring—nearly six years after the bear's attack—a group of warriors rode back to the village telling of a party of Long Knives—white trappers—they had found camping without gifts or palaver or permission in Absaroka country. Three Crow braves had gone under in the hostilities that had followed, but here were two of the Long Knives' horses, their rifles, and their scalps.

Something happened inside the boy as he watched one of the warriors curvetting proudly on his beautiful cream-colored mare, waving his coupstick from which a blond scalp dangled. It was no longer Absarokee Talks Alone but white-born Jim Keath who stood there, shaking with sudden anger. His own mother's hair had been that color, and her face, lost to memory for years, now filled his mind.

After that all was changed; it was not enough to win coups and paint himself and be a Crow. As the weeks passed he grew thin with longing to see white faces like his own, and hear a civilized tongue, and sit again by a trapper's campfire while the stars came out over Jackson's Hole or the Popo Agie.

He thought about it until he could think no longer, and had to act. One night he crept alone out of the lodge that had been his home for six long years. He took only a few treasures, his weapons, and Moki, and ignoring his own horses, counted coup one last time by cutting the beautiful mare, Buckskin, from the very lodge of the warrior who had flaunted the blond scalp. She had carried him southward over the Plains and the wild hills, back to Taos and the world of the white trapper—a world which now, two years later, he knew was crumbling under his feet.

Jim jerked a sinew through the moccasin. As he did so he saw Moki's ears go up briefly, then down again. At once his every sense snapped alert; he began to grin. Though his fingers never stopped their calm work on the moccasin, with one elbow he loosened the sheathed knife at his belt, and his muscles gathered. The tiny rustling of a leaf gave the signal. One lash of his supple body brought him to his feet; his wrist flicked and the firelight glinted on the flying steel blade as he melted into the bushes.

Tom Rivers' familiar laugh rang out from the clump of cottonwoods by the stream's edge. He emerged, his shoulders shaking, and yanked Jim's knife from the tree trunk one inch above where Tom's head had been a second before.

"It was a tie agin, you knife-throwin' coyote! I ducked afore it hit." He walked toward the fire as Jim, still grinning, went back to his scattered sinews. "By golly, I'll sneak up on you someday yet!" Tom went on, tossing Jim his knife. "Done pretty well this time. Got to within thirty foot of you afore you heerd me."

"*Wagh!* I set around five minutes waitin' fer you to come in range. Yer gettin' old, Tom."

"Say, listen, hoss. I was strollin' in and out of double-guarded Blackfoot camps afore you'd cut yer teeth. I'll git old when I git ready, and not afore, you hear? What's in the pot?"

He leaned over to sniff the steam, grunted appreciatively, then settled to the business of drying his soaked legs. He was a tall man, gray at the temples, slow smiling and easy, but dangerous as a rattlesnake, as plenty of Blackfeet and Sioux had found out, and as quick moving as any man needed to be. Even aimed to kill, that knife would never have hit him. Jim liked him better than any white man he knew. You could trap and ride and hunt alongside Tom Rivers and never say a word from sunup to dark if you didn't want to, and still you never felt alone. The fact that Tom was in his fifties and Jim barely nineteen had mattered to neither of them these months they'd traveled together, though the amiable bickering about it was a nightly ritual. The camp would be mighty lonesome soon, Jim thought, with the night closing down like this and the fire brightening and the pot bubbling, and no Tom standing there angling his long legs one way and another while his leggings dried from wet dark red to faded scarlet.

As if he had read Jim's mind, Tom said, "Reckon I'll be headin' south tomorrow."

Tomorrow! Jim's heart sank as he fastened the last sinew on the moccasin. "*Wagh!* You best git them old bones into warmer weather!" he murmured. As Tom grinned, he added, "Goin' to Taos?"

"Mebbe, mebbe not. Kinda hankerin' to see Californy fer onct. Anyways I'll happen by the Nez Perce country fust to git my squaw loose from her relatives. Tired mendin' my own shirts. Never marry a Injun, boy, they got too many relatives."

Jim got up to toss the moccasins back into his pack, concealing his surprise. He'd never known Tom had an Indian wife. But then he and Tom had never asked questions of each other, and there was no sense starting in now. Instead, he remarked, "I reckon that meat's done."

He ripped two slabs of bark off a nearby cottonwood and they piled stew on them. Tom filled his mouth with beavertail and spoke around it. "Lookee here, hoss. Why don't you come on with me?"

"To Nez Perce country? Not much."

"Why not?"

Jim jerked a thumb toward the eagle feather stuck in his hair. "I earned that stealin' Nez Perce horses."

"Shucks, ain't nobody gonna scalp you fer a little thing like that. I thought it was Sioux you was so unpopular with."

"Sioux, Blackfoot, Nez Perce—all the same."

Tom laughed. "All right then, meet me in Californy."

15

Jim hesitated, then shook his head. "I reckon not, Tom."

"By golly, yer a stubborn—"

He broke off, his eyes snapping with Jim's toward the thicket, where Bad Medicine had suddenly scrambled to his feet. The mule was facing south, his long ears cocked forward and trembling slightly, every muscle tense.

"Digger scout, I think," Jim muttered. "Saw somethin' earlier."

He set aside his bark plate and reached for his rifle, as did Tom. As they rose silently, Moki stiffened and growled, and Buckskin raised her head, muzzle dripping, from the creek. The mule was always the first to be aware of danger.

"Moki, guard!" snapped Jim quietly. The dog bounded out of the circle of light to crouch threateningly in front of Buckskin, blocking her way. Tom had already faded into the trees where Tucky was tethered, and Jim leaped for the thicket at the other side of the clearing, turned the mule half around, and got behind him. He was not seriously alarmed; Diggers were nothing when you were used to Sioux and Blackfeet, and if he had been right about that flash of movement on the hillside earlier, there were only a couple of them. But live trappers were careful ones.

"What in tarnation are them coyotes doin' so fer from home?" came Tom's annoyed mutter. "I wanta finish my meat."

"Dunno. Ain't nobody on the war trail that I've heerd of."

The whole thing was puzzling. Well, no matter, they'd find out soon. Jim primed the flintlock's pan, cocked it, and filled his mouth with extra bullets. Then he slanted the gun barrel over the mule's back and waited.

16

Chapter II

A long five minutes later, bushes on the southwest side of the clearing rustled. Jim's rifle swung to cover them, then dropped, as a white rag at the end of a stick pushed through the branches. He reached far to his left to make an answering rustle. Since no bullet immediately crashed into the twig he had shaken, he spat his own bullets back into his pouch and grunted, "Reckon it's all right, Tom."

"Friend," came immediately from across the clearing.

"Come out then," said Tom's voice.

Two Indians stepped from the bushes some six feet away from the white flag, holding their rifles above their heads.

"All right, fellas, what's on yer minds?" drawled Tom, appearing from the trees. "Well, it's old Big Bull, ain't it?"

The older Indian, hearing his name, bobbed his head and grinned. Jim felt disgust as he pushed out of his thicket and joined the group. Diggers were poor excuses for Indians. Look at them. Bandy legged, grinning like skinned coyotes, stinking of the fish they lived on.

Big Bull turned and saw him, and his eyes sharpened. Darting a glance at the eagle feather in Jim's hair, he made the sign for "Crow," moving his arms up and down like the wings of a great bird. "Talks Alone?" he said.

Surprised, Jim nodded. He'd never set eyes on this Indian as far as he knew, though Tom seemed to recognize him.

"What do you want?" he asked in the Crow tongue.

Big Bull shook his head and shrugged, glancing at the bubbling pot. "Only savvy white talk."

"Yeah," chuckled Tom. "I'll bet you savvy enough white talk to ask fer meat, anyways. Looks like we split our grub, Jim."

Jim was thinking uneasily of Scalp Necklace and Red Deer and all the others back in Absaroka. Had one of them sent word to him by this skinny-legged old man? It didn't seem likely. "What d'you want with me?" he demanded.

The two Indians merely looked bland and kept their eyes on the pot.

"Keep yer shirt on, Jim," Tom drawled. "They ain't gonna tell us nothin' till we feed 'em."

He tore off a couple of bark strips and motioned the Diggers toward the pot. When they had eaten most of its contents Big Bull produced a long pipe, stuffed it with kinnikinnick and lighted it, puffing smoke to north, south, east, and west before handing it on to Jim.

"Makin' a lot of fuss about this, whatever it is," Jim growled. He puffed at the pipe and passed it on, then with a grunt of impatience got up and moved to his pack, returning in a moment with a small sack of gunpowder, which he tossed at Big Bull's feet. He made the sign for "on the prairie" by brushing one palm quickly over the other, to signify it was a free gift.

Then Big Bull picked up the sack and began to talk, using grunts and signs and bits of English. As the long, confused tale emerged, Jim became more and more puzzled. There was no mention of Absaroka. Whatever Big Bull was talking about had all happened about three or four weeks ago, apparently, somewhere on the Snake River. There was something about wagons, many of them, and trading for dried salmon, and a lot of white people and spotted buffalo, which meant cattle. A Long Knife had given Big Bull a fine present of blue beads to find Talks Alone who wore the Crow coup feather. But the Long Knife was not with the wagons, he was a beaver man known as Black Jaw.

"Ol' Bill Hervey!" exclaimed Tom. "He was trappin' up north of here a while back, remember? Musta run into this wagon train on his way back to Taos. But what's it all got to do with us?"

Big Bull had caught the gist of his words and was nodding excitedly. Reaching into his tangled braid, he drew out a crumpled and very dirty bit of paper, brushed a few lice off it, and handed it to Jim.

"Well, by gor!" exclaimed Jim disgustedly. "All that palaver about nothin'! What'd I give that coyote good gunpowder fer?"

But Tom was staring at the piece of paper. "Let's see that thing, hoss. Lookee here, it's got writin' on it."

Jim frowned and took another look as Tom smoothed the paper out on his knee. There were words crowded close all over it.

"By golly, it's a letter!" Tom exclaimed. "You say Black Jaw give you this, Big Bull?"

Big Bull nodded again, but pointed to Jim. "Talks Alone," he insisted.

"He's crazy," Jim said. "Who'd be writin' me a letter?"

Tom scratched his ear reflectively. "Not Bill Hervey, that's sartin. He can't write no more'n I kin. You reckon it was somebody in that wagon train?"

Jim suddenly felt queer. "Couldn't be, Tom."

"Many wagons," Big Bull repeated. "Plenty spotted buffalo." He gathered up his pipe, the gunpowder, and his rifle, beckoned to the other Indian, and in a moment they disappeared through the bushes, leaving Jim staring uneasily at the piece of paper. He was wishing, for the first time in his life, that he could read. Once he'd known how to read print a little, even how to spell out his name and a few other words in block capitals. But this was writing, and besides, all that was so many years back.

He raised his eyes, finally, to meet the shrewd, curious ones of Tom Rivers. "What's it say, Tom?" he muttered.

"Hoss, you know I can't read wuth a Piute's underbritches. But I'll make a try at it if you want."

"I want."

"All right, then, let's see how I make out." He dropped down cross legged beside the bright flames and Jim squatted beside him. Both squinted at the mysterious letter. "Well, it's fer you all right," Tom said. "Fust word is *Jim. Jim, if you*—no, that ain't right, I don't think. Lessee. Here's *dead*."

"Dead!" echoed Jim.

"Yeah, I'm pretty sure of that one. D-e-a-d." He scratched his ear thoughtfully. "Hoss, I ain't gonna git fer with this. They's a lot of little words that don't mean nothin' till you hitch 'em with big ones, and I can't do much with the big ones."

"Can't you figger out who's dead, even?"

"No-o—'ceptin'—lessee, ain't this a name? This here word at the end. J-o—" Tom squinted at the word doubtfully. "J-o-, I reckon that's a *n*. J-o-n-n-i-e. *Jonnie*, that's what it says. Know anybody called Jonnie?"

Jim turned slowly to stare at Rivers. "I—I reckon I did, onct."

"Mebbe it's him that sent you this."

"No! That just ain't possible." Jim ran a hand shakily through his forelock and said, "See what else you kin read, Tom."

"Well, lemme see now. S-t-i— That's *still*. Here's one down here looks like *valley*. And lessee, C-h-a—"

Jim's fingers and toes had begun to tingle strangely. *Still*, and *valley?* His eyes widened as he stared at the paper. Those words were part of his own medicine song, part of the dream itself! Were the spirits that Red Deer used to tell him about suddenly beginning to take an interest in his affairs? He peered cautiously around the edge of the clearing into the darkness that shrouded the woods, feeling the little hairs rise on the back of his neck.

"Go on, Tom!" he muttered.

"I got part of it now, hoss. Listen. *All that's left* . . . *bound for the* . . . *valley* . . . then somethin' else, and then *it's our only chanct*. Then that name, *Jonnie*. Any of that mean anything to you?"

Jim didn't answer. He snatched the paper and stared at it, then shoved it back at Tom and was on his feet with one swift movement. His heart was beating like the drum of old Many Horses, the Wise One, as he knelt beside his pack, found his medicine bundle, and tied it with trembling fingers behind his left braid. He hesitated a moment until he could be sure the muscles of his face were under rigid control, and would not disgrace him by betraying emotion. Then he went back to the fire and took the note in his own hands, staring at it unblinking until his eyes watered. But still the words held their secret; he could read them no better than before. Perhaps the powerful grizzly teeth in his medicine bundle were helpers only in battle.

He started convulsively as a log crackled, sending up a stream of sparks.

"Say, what's up, hoss?" exclaimed Rivers softly. "Yer jumpy as a treed painter."

Jim looked at him, then back to the paper, wetting his lips. "Tom, I got to know what that says! All of it."

21

"Better hunt you up somebody as kin read writin', then.

"How, though? Where?"

"T'wouldn't be hard, hoss. Take 'er down to Laramie or Fort Hall—"

"Too fer! I wanta know soon."

"Well, The Dalles, then. That ain't but a few days ride, the way that Buckskin of yours skitters."

Jim folded the note carefully and tucked it into his pouch. Tom was right. This was white man's medicine, it would take a white man to unravel its meaning.

He moved restlessly across the little clearing, every nerve in him as tight as a bowstring. The wind had risen; a wolf or two skulked out there just beyond the circle of firelight, drawn by the smell of meat. Jim suddenly picked up a pebble and hurled it at a pair of shining gold eyes.

"Hoss, you want to tell me who that Jonnie is?" Tom said quietly.

Jim was silent a moment. The dark out yonder seemed lonesomer than ever without the golden eyes, and his thoughts kept going back, and back. He turned abruptly and returned to the fire. Tom was his friend, and a thorough white man. He'd tell him. Maybe it would help. He dropped down beside Tom.

"I reckon it's my brother Jonathan," he said.

"Yer brother! What the devil? A Crow named Jonathan?"

"He ain't Crow, he's white like me."

Tom stared at him, his eyes traveling from the braids to the coup feather, from the claw and bead necklace to the medicine bundle dangling below Jim's left ear. "By golly, hoss," he said slowly. "I thought you was a half-breed. Didn't you grow up Crow?"

"Yeah, but I come from Missouri afore that. Long time ago."

"What happened, Injuns steal you?"

22

"No. I run away from home. It's nigh nine year back now." Jim hesitated, letting the past drift over him. "Tom, you ever know a trapper called Adam Russell?"

"Russell. Yeah, sure. Tall, git-out'n-the-road lookin' feller, warn't he? He turned up missin' at rendezvous way back in '35 er '36, though. I heerd he got rubbed out."

"He did. Blackfeet tuck his hair. Old Bill Hervey told me that soon's I hit Taos last year. He was with him when it happened." Jim hesitated, then went on. "Russell was my uncle."

"By jiminy!" Rivers stared a moment, then eased back on his elbow and stretched his legs to the fire's warmth. He took a red clay Indian pipe out of his pouch and slowly began to stuff it with kinnikinnick. "Go on, hoss, if you want to."

Jim nodded. He watched Tom's fingers working the tobacco and tried to sort out his thoughts. He might as well tell all of it, now he was started. "Uncle Adam was my mother's brother, but she never seen much of him. He'd been out west here in the mountains fer half his life. I never seen him at all till one day he come to our farm in Missouri. He'd been back in the States spreein' and spendin' his beaver, and he was headin' fer the Plains. I reckon I was about ripe fer bustin' loose from my tether anyways when he come walkin' in, that afternoon. Seemed like it was the fust time they'd ever been any fresh air in that house."

He remembered that vividly enough. Tall, hawk eyed, and swaggering, Adam Russell had seemed a being from another world, a strong, exhilarating wind that could blow a boy's smoldering wanderlust into flames. While Pa sat grim and disapproving, while Mother fluttered excitedly, and the other children stared like a row of owls from across the kitchen, Jim crept close. He listened, dazzled, to his uncle's talk of Indians and prairies and the great sky and snow-capped mountains far to the west. He took in every detail of Adam Russell's

23

dress and speech, tingled to his boisterous laughter, drank in the wild smell of castoreum that clung to his buckskin shirt.

"Seemed like I couldn't stand stayin' put any longer, onct I'd seed him," Jim murmured. "I never said nothin', but when he left at sunup next mornin' I follered 'im off. Had to stay so fer behind, to keep him from catchin' me, that I come near losin' him twict. But I stuck with him somehow, till we was away out 'crost the frontier and he had to take me on west with 'im. I ain't never been back since."

Rivers swore softly, his keen eyes searching Jim's face. "So yer a farm boy from Missouri. By golly, hoss, that takes some believin'!"

"I never tuck to farmin'. I allus wanted to git away. Do somethin'—bigger."

"A kid eleven year old is mighty young to run that fer, Jim. Warn't you ever homesick?"

"I reckon I was at first." Jim smiled faintly. "Like when Comanches was chasin' us, or we'd git our horses stole and have to git arrers in us stealin' 'em back agin, or we didn't dare show a f'ar and have to eat our meat raw. Fust time I eat raw prairie dog, by gor I wisht fer my mother, and felt mean I'd ever run off and left her. I missed her other times, too, and I missed Jonnie mighty bad. But I was skeered to go back 'cause my pa'd of beat the daylights out'n me. My pa, he was a great one fer beatin's."

"He couldn't beat you now."

"No, but I couldn't go home now, neither."

"Why not? You're young—"

Jim's smile twisted. "Tom, kin you see me plantin' corn in Missouri?"

Tom was a realist. He took one look at Jim, laughed shortly, and said, "No." Then he added, "What'd you do after Russell went under?"

"Oh, we was split up afore that. I'd only been in the mountains about a year when the grizzly got me, and after that I lived with the Crows."

Tom puffed in silence for a moment, and Jim could hear the familiar night sounds—Buckskin's hooves clopping daintily over the gravel to the stream's edge, the wind rustling in the cottonwoods, the fire hissing. Finally Tom said softly, "Hoss, it ain't any of my business, but I'm wonderin' why you ain't still with them Crows."

That was hard to answer. Jim reached out and scratched Moki's ears, digging his fingers into the dog's coarse fur. "I run away from them too, Tom. I—somethin' happened that put me in mind of my mother. I—just got to feelin' *white*." Rivers nodded, as if he had expected to hear just that. Impulsively Jim went on. "I figgered if I come back amongst white men mebbe ever'thing'd turn lucky fer me, I'd git plenty beaver, and— Well, I was wrong about that." He got up, suddenly restless again. "I've been thinkin' lately mebbe I was wrong to leave at all, and oughta head on back to Crow country. But now that paper's come—"

"Reckon yer brother sent that paper?"

Jim shook his head. "Clean from Missouri? Ain't likely. But what if Jonnie's dead?" His voice dropped to a whisper, the whites of his eyes gleamed in the firelight as he turned back to Rivers. "Remember the 'dead' in that paper, Tom? When Jonnie and me was kids, we—" The phrase came to Jim's mind in Crow, "*We knew each other's heart.*" He did the best he could with it in English. "We was—close to one another. Mebbe—mebbe his spirit's around somewheres, tryin' to tell me what to do, now the beaver's all gone and yer leavin' the mountains."

Rivers flashed him an odd look, but covered it quickly by pulling a twig out of the fire and relighting his pipe from the blazing tip. The silence urged Jim on. He hunkered down beside Tom again.

"It ain't meant I should go to Absaroka but to some valley. That word 'valley,' that's part of my medicine, it was in my dream! You—you know about medicine dreams, Tom?"

"Not much about 'em, hoss."

Jim's hand crept up under his left braid to finger the medicine bundle, and he could feel the grizzly's teeth moving against each other inside the buckskin. "Well, ever' Crow boy, he's got to have one, so's he'll have helpers on the war trail. They's always some kinda animal in it, a fox or a otter or a wolf or somethin'. And when you wake up the Wise One tells you what the dream meant, and you find you a fox or whatever it is and make a medicine bundle out'n its skin, or maybe its teeth or somethin'. Then yer safe, long as you've got it with you. It turns arrers and bullets away from you and helps you shoot straight."

Tom's eyes went automatically to a deep arrow scar on the side of Jim's neck, but he only nodded and said nothing.

"It's mighty hard to have a good dream," Jim went on huskily. He was staring off into the dark woods, remembering. "You take a long sweat bath and go afoot to a high mountain all alone, and don't eat nor drink nothin' and sometimes you have to hurt yerself with a knife to make the dream come. I was pretty old afore I managed to have one—fourteen. It took me three days atop Crazy Mountain afore I fell down amongst the rocks and the world got all black . . ."

The words trailed to silence as Jim thought of that most important sleep of his life. In that blackness had come the dream. Three times in the whirling dark the old grizzly had loomed up again, alive and savage, all claws and teeth and glistening red eyes as before, but now wearing moccasins and a coup feather like a warrior. And each time Jim had shouted words at it, words like an incantation, which seemed to spring into his head from nowhere—or perhaps from that far corner of his heart where the past lay buried, for the

words were not Crow but English: "*The lord is my shepherd
—he makes me lie down in green pastures—he leads me beside
still waters—though I walk through the valley of the shadow
I will fear no evil—*"

So he shouted three times, wondering how he knew those
words and what they meant, and as he did so the bear faded
away, bit by bit each time until at last there were only his
great teeth scattered on the ground, and the coup feather beside them. Then, in the dream, Jim thrust the feather into
his hair, gathered the teeth into his pouch, and fell into a deep
and comforting sleep.

He took a long breath, bringing his thoughts back with an
effort to the fire-lit clearing and Tom Rivers. "They was
white man's words in the dream. Many Horses, he said they
was big medicine and never to fergit 'em. Now here they turn
up in this paper. You see how the stick floats, Tom? They're
tellin' me what to do."

It was a long time before Rivers said anything. He lounged
there and puffed his pipe, and gazed with half-closed eyes
into the flames. Jim began to think he wasn't going to speak
at all, and moved uneasily over to his pack, half frightened at
having revealed so much of himself. Never had he talked like
this to anyone, except old Many Horses. Maybe his helpers
would be angry?

Then Tom spoke, softly and calling him by his Crow name.
"I'm wonderin', Talks Alone, if you wouldn't be happier in
Absaroka than anywheres else. I'm wonderin' if that ain't
what you oughta do—go back."

Jim turned to look at him in astonishment. It was the last
thing he expected to hear. "Tom, can't you read signs no
better'n that? I'm white. My medicine's white too, with
them words in it. I bet you six plews my luck'll turn if I hunt
up some valley where they's white folks, and live amongst
'em agin."

"That's a risky bet. Lookee here, Jim, you ain't gonna find trappers and such settin' in no valley, yer gonna find bourgeways! You sure you savvy how to live amongst bourgeways?"

Jim stared at him, suddenly uneasy. Then he shrugged it off. "Savvy, *wagh!* You show me a bourgeway I can't out-hunt and out-ride and out-trap and—"

"That ain't quite what I mean." Rivers heaved a long sigh and straightened, knocking out his pipe. He looked up, his keen blue eyes gentler than Jim had ever seen them. "Hoss, I hope that medicine of you'n is thunderin' big. I'm thinkin' this ain't gonna be no easy trail fer you to foller."

"I ain't never whined fer things to be easy!"

"Well, I know that, hoss." Tom studied him a moment longer, then with his usual slow grin got up to fetch his buffalo robe. "All right, you knife-throwin' coyote, go at it. I reckon you'll make out."

Jim grinned back at him, feeling relieved. He pulled the grizzly-hide robe from his pack and they lay down with their feet to the fire, wrapping themselves against the cold of the coming night. Jim took a long look at the familiar humped shape of Tom's big shoulders under the buffalo robe beside him, then rolled to his back and watched the stars prick out one by one until they spangled the whole sky.

It's the last time, he kept thinking. Tomorrer we'll be goin' different ways, and I'll never lay here like this again.

Long after he thought Tom was asleep he heard his voice from the depths of the robe. All the humor was gone from it now. "Anyways, hoss, I reckon there jest ain't no easy trail leadin' down out'n the mountains. With the beaver all gone, the good old days is about over fer you and me both."

Chapter III

Jim slept fitfully. At daybreak next morning he was off upstream to lift his traps. As if to underscore Tom's bleak words of last night, five of them were empty. But as he came to the place near the big mud-plastered lodge where he had set the sixth one, he saw that the trap pole was gone. He swore under his breath, then splashed into the water and peered about him in the gray half-light for the float stick. To snare one finally and then have it get away—! It was an anxious few minutes before he spotted the stick bobbing in a little eddy between two rocks, several yards downstream. By the time he had explored the bottom of the stream for five feet around it and finally located the trap, he was soaked from head to foot and all but frozen. But he was grinning as he hauled his beaver to the bank. It was a prime catch. It weighed sixty pounds if it weighed an ounce and had the finest pelt he had ever seen. A good omen! He made short work of skinning it, and hurried, shivering, back to camp.

Tom was there ahead of him, roasting buffalo ribs for breakfast. "Any luck, hoss?" he drawled.

"One. A good 'un. How about you?"

"Six empties."

Jim bent to tousle Moki's ears, feeling unhappy. Tom should

have got one too, this morning—just for a good sign. "Listen, Tom, you take that plew."

"*Wagh!* Not much! I got too much to pack around as 'tis. Come git some grub, you coyote."

With an uncertain smile, Jim did as he was told. He felt a little embarrassed in Tom's presence after all that talking last night, and he ate in silence. But Tom paid no attention to that; his eyes were as bland and his drawl as careless as ever. While Jim set about rough curing the beaver pelt he gathered his possibles and began breaking camp as if this were the same as any other morning in the world.

Jim's clothes were dry by the time he had the plew stretched on its willow hoop. He left Tom to quench the fire and went to free Buckskin from her stake. She was eager to be gone; she had been stamping and snuffing the wind restlessly, and tossing her wild white mane. Murmuring under his breath to soothe her, he strapped on the apishamore—the buffalo-hide blanket he used for a saddle. With a last caress of her sleek neck he whistled Moki to guard her while he dealt with the mule.

Rivers watched out of the corner of his eye, grinning as he tightened Tucky's cinch.

Bad Medicine had already emerged from the thicket and was standing with apparent docility beside the pack. But at the first touch of Jim's hands, he flattened his long ears, buckled his middle, and aimed a kick that would have broken a man's leg had it landed. Tom's laugh burst out as Jim, used to the ways of mules and of this one in particular, merely leaped clear, muttering a few remarks in the Crow tongue that would have singed holes in anything less tough than mule hide.

Tom strolled over, still shaking with laughter. "Here, hoss, I'll blindfold that there primer donner for you this mornin', seein' as it's the last time I'll git to see the show."

30

He did so quickly and efficiently with a strip of old blanket. By some mysterious mulish logic this convinced Bad Medicine that he was a pack animal instead of a spoiled beauty, and he stood quite still while Jim cinched the pack in place.

"I'm gonna miss that critter," Tom chuckled.

"By gor, you kin have him, then!"

Jim grinned and whipped the blindfold off, then with a last look around, vaulted to Buckskin's back. She was in swift motion almost before he was seated, and Bad Medicine, who loved her with that mad devotion possible only to a mule's heart, kept close behind as they started down the mountainside toward the Powder River.

"Good day fer huntin', if we was to spot a elk," Tom remarked. "Lookee there, Moki's at it already."

Jim glanced down at the dog running along in front, tail aloft and nose to the ground. "Go find us a elk, Moki," he urged. "Go on, git at it."

Moki looked up absently out of his yellow eyes. His mind was on rabbits.

"Oh, well, I'm full anyhow," Tom drawled, and laughed.

It was so much like any other day—and yet it was the last. With every hoofbeat the final minutes of this good, familiar life were running out, the parting with Tom was drawing nearer.

They feigned indifference, both of them, until they descended the last slope and pulled up on the flat stretch beside the river. "Best let the hosses breathe a minute," Jim mumbled. He was feeling oddly short of breath himself.

"Yeah. Tucky's plum winded."

They sat in silence for a while, looking at the river, the wind in the treetops, the rumpled manes of their horses—anywhere but at each other. But finally Tom turned.

"Hoss, this is whar I head south."

"I reckon so, Tom."

"You sartin you don't want to come along with me?"

Jim hesitated, in spite of himself. Then his hand crept to his pouch, in which rested that powerful paper. He shook his head.

"Well—" Tom wheeled Tucky close to Buckskin's flank and thrust out his hand. Jim gripped it with all his strength. "Hoss," said Tom very softly, "take good keer of that medicine of your'n, you hear?"

Then he was gone, trotting swiftly through the leafless underbrush and yellowed grass, the familiar jingling of his traps growing fainter, his straight back and battered old hat smaller and smaller with distance.

Jim watched until a wooded bend in the river hid him from view. Then he swung Buckskin's head northwest, toward the Blue Mountains—beyond which lay The Dalles and, with luck, some white trader who could read writing. It took all his will to bring his heels back against the mare's flanks in the kick that would commit him, once and for all, to this strange new course. But once he was in motion, it seemed as though he could not go fast enough.

Something over a week later—it would have been less had he not been forced to stop and hunt—he reined Buckskin in on a promontory overlooking the dalles of the Columbia. There below him boiled the mighty river, thrashing and foaming between its towering black walls as it plunged into the cleft it had carved for itself through fifty miles of solid rock. This was the Columbia Gorge, most used passageway through the Cascade Mountains to the broad and fertile land bordering the Willamette River on the other side.

Close at hand, to the west, rose the Cascades themselves— shining with snow, impassable except at the gorge even for horsemen this time of year, difficult enough last summer when Jim and Tom had wandered over briefly in a vain search for new trapping grounds. And back to the east stretched the two thousand man-killing, beast-killing miles wagons must travel to reach this spot from the States.

There were wagons here now, many of them. Jim could see them clustered there far below him, in the last nook short of the actual rapids. Crowded about the dark spots that were the few buildings in the settlement of The Dalles, they looked like stubby gray grubs around chips.

Jim started down the timbered slope, half eager, half frightened at the sight of those battered canvas tops.

In another half hour he was threading his way among them through a light misting rain, toward the largest of the log buildings—the trading post. As he rode, hands busy with his nervous mare, his eyes darted among the crowds of emigrants who were everywhere he looked; huddled over campfires, tending oxen, clustered in groups to look fearfully at the thundering river. Jim found himself breathing hard or else forgetting to breathe at all. So many people! Not mountain men or Indians or Mexicans like at Taos, but bourgeways from the States, folks dressed in fabrics instead of skins, wearing shoes and coats instead of moccasins and blankets and furs. Families. Women and children. He stared at them with sudden hunger, his pulse racing with the half-forgotten, half-familiar look of them. He had not seen a white woman or child for nine years.

They were staring at him, too, curiosity briefly erasing the lines of weariness from their faces as he passed.

Outside the trading post he tethered his animals to the rail and spoke sharply to Moki, who was bristling with suspicion and trying to keep an eye on all two or three hundred of the nearest bourgeways at once. Jim shared his uneasiness. His mouth was dry and he was sweating in the grizzly cloak, which had barely kept off the bitter wind ten minutes before. He shucked it off and flung it over Buckskin's back. Then

33

with a last hesitating glance around, he tucked his rifle into the crook of his arm and stepped into the post.

There were bourgeways here, too. The place was full of them. He flattened himself against the door as a group of three hurried past him—a sandy-haired young man and a woman, accompanied by a snub-nosed boy of about eleven with a mass of blond ringlets. The child stumbled as he went by and half fell against Jim, turned to pipe " 'Scuse me," and stopped short to stare with great, wondering, gray-green eyes. Jim stared back, fighting a purely Indian impulse to touch and finger that unbelievable yellow hair.

Then the boy was gone, darting after his companions. Jim stepped inside, dodged another couple, and moved slowly toward the wooden counter. One quick glance located the trader, the same one who had been here last summer.

"Hello, Harris," Jim said in a voice that shook a little in spite of his best effort. He felt all these people were staring straight at him, though his common sense told him they were busy with their own affairs. He swallowed, and forced carelessness into his quiet tone. "I was wonderin' kin you read writin'."

"Yep, good as a perfesser." Harris, busy measuring out a length of calico for a huge, red-bearded man, didn't look up. "But I only trot out my learnin' fer them as makes it worth my while. You got any—"

Then he did look up, and stopped dead, his coarse, beefy face twisting with surprise. "Well, if it ain't Injun Jim!" he roared, dropping the calico. "Say, you ain't come back to finish off pore old White Bear, have you?"

"Who's White Bear?" muttered Jim. He was rigid with self-consciousness. At the man's bellow every head in the room had turned in his direction.

"Why, my old Chinook, White Bear! He's been a tol'able good Injun since you drapped around to teach 'im his manners last summer, and he's the best canoer I got. Leave 'im keep his hair!"

Jim didn't like the trader's laughter. He remembered the incident now. The old Chinook had tried to steal Buckskin, and he'd put an arrow through his hat by way of discipline. "*Wagh!* I ain't after no hair!" he mumbled. "I want—"

He stopped, as his sharp ears picked up the familiar ominous sound of Moki's snarl. He grunted, wheeled, and was out of the room before the surprised trader could open his mouth.

The instant he hit the open air he was conscious of danger. He had cocked his rifle even before his eyes focused on the scene before him—Moki crouched with bared teeth beside Buckskin and the mule, holding at bay one frightened little boy with curly blond hair. Behind the child stood the couple Jim had encountered in the doorway. The man, white faced, held a pistol leveled at Moki's head.

With a yell of rage Jim sprang forward. He seized the man's wrist and wrenched it upward as the pistol roared in his ear. Half deafened, he barely heard the woman's scream, the sound of shouts, and running footsteps.

The fellow was struggling angrily in his grasp. "Let go of me, you fool! It's a wolf!"

"Wolf, *wagh!*" Jim flung down the wrist he held, sending the pistol clattering to the ground. With a moccasined toe he flipped the weapon out of reach. "Yer the fool," he remarked. "That's my dog."

There was a moment's silence as the man's pale eyes shifted from Jim to Moki and back again. "Dog?" he echoed.

"What's goin' on?"

"What's wrong here?"

The crowd was gathering. Jim glanced up, snapped his rifle to his shoulder, and saw the first arrivals stop in their tracks and then fall back a pace. At the same time he gave the low whistle that released Moki from his duty. As the dog came trotting forward, wagging his tail and whining a relieved greeting, the astonishment on the faces before Jim suddenly struck his boisterous Indian sense of humor. He grinned broadly as he lowered the gun. To his surprise, an answering grin spread over the face of the golden-haired little boy.

"Say!" breathed the boy. "He *is* a dog, ain't he? I guess I made him mad, but I never meant to. I only tried to pet that horse there. Is it your horse? My, but she's pretty. I—"

"That'll do! You get on back to your folks now, d'you hear?" The woman's eyes flashed suspiciously at Jim as she reached for the child's collar and hustled him through the crowd and away. The man retrieved his pistol and stood a moment, glaring at Jim.

"Dog or wolf, the critter's a menace," he said. "Oughter be tied up."

"By golly, you're right," muttered somebody else. "These wild Injuns and their hounds—!"

"Y'ask me, they *both* oughter be tied up!" said a louder voice. " 'Ja see him aim that rifle point blank at us a minute ago? Why, he blame near—"

"Leave 'im be, folks, I know 'im, it's jest Injun Jim." This was the trader's rasping voice from the doorway of the post. "Yer hair's safe if you don't touch that horse of his'n."

He went back into the building and the men scattered reluctantly, casting hostile glances over their shoulders as they lumbered away in their cracked and broken greenhorn's boots. Jim turned to quiet the nervous mare, glaring scornfully now at the wagons and their owners. Bourgeways! he thought. What've they got to be so git-out'n-the-road about? Ain't got the sense to know a dog from a wolf, tucker their-selves out wearin' factory boots in moccasin country . . . He felt his anger dissolve into a nagging uneasiness. "Injun Jim!" He was as white as these folks, even his medicine was white—

He frowned, his mind suddenly full of that unread paper. Where was this mysterious valley, and how did one get there? He had to know. He must go back to the post.

He dug one of the smaller pelts out of his possibles, wondering what Harris would consider "worth his while." Everything in him bucked and shied at the idea of entrusting his magic paper to that peddler. Under ordinary circumstances he would no more have showed it to him than he would have revealed the contents of his medicine bundle.

To quiet his uneasiness he took the bundle from his pouch and tied it under his left braid. It calmed him a little, but he had felt less vulnerable prowling among enemy lodges, a stolen horse trailing from each hand.

Back in the post, the big red-bearded man was paying for his calico with a bag of gunpowder. He looked around, and so did everyone else in the place, as Jim tossed his beaver on the counter in front of the trader.

"I want somethin' read to me," Jim said quietly.

"You back agin?" Harris dropped the bag of gunpowder into a drawer and propped his elbows on the counter, grinning. "Awright, where's yer pay? This here plew? Why, shucks, that ain't enough fer *my* readin'. I—"

"I reckon it's enough," Jim said, very softly.

Harris glanced at his face. "Awright, awright. It's enough this time." He flipped the plew to one side and reached across the counter, winking at the man with the red beard, who stood nearest. "Le's have yer piece of writin'. What is it, a billy-doo from some little Digger squaw?"

"No it ain't!" Jim felt the hot blood climb to his hairline. He drew the paper from his pouch. There would be specific directions in it—rivers named, mountains identified; perhaps a promise of much beaver. Did he want to share it with all those bourgeway eyes and ears behind him?

37

But Harris already had the paper. He opened it with careless fingers and began to read loudly. *"Jim, if you're still alive come help us. Pa's been dead three year and mother—"*

"Mother?" Jim gasped. "Wait, that's private—gimme that—"

Harris only bellowed louder *"—and mother died two months ago. We buried her by the—"*

Something exploded in Jim's head. Before he knew he had moved, his knife was at Harris' fat throat. *"Gimme—my—letter,"* he breathed into a sudden dead silence.

The trader's body went rigid, his eyes glassy as they clung to that poised brown fist and the steel that glinted from it, then moved upward to meet Jim's stare. Abruptly his face was bathed in sweat. Slowly, careful to move nothing but his hand, he extended the paper. Jim snatched it and turned a face like stone to that roomful of alien eyes and ears. Blindly he pushed through them and was gone.

A stir rippled over the room as people let go their held breaths and shot glances at one another. "By golly, Harris," muttered somebody. "You nigh got what you asked for that time!"

Harris said nothing. He was sagging on the counter, mopping at his white face. But the big red-bearded man, darting him one look of contempt, moved quietly through the crowd and out the door.

The trampled mud was under Jim's moccasins, the cold wind on his back, his hands moving over Buckskin's warm, muscled neck in a pretense of adjusting her halter. Even when the worst of his outrage had passed, he stood sick and empty. He raised the crumpled note and stared at it hopelessly. Mother dead. Buried. He had to know the rest. But how? Fifteen armed Sioux couldn't drag him back to that post.

There was a footstep, then a slow, quiet voice at his elbow. "Son, I reckon you must be Jim Keath."

He wheeled to face the huge, red-bearded man who had watched it all. For a moment he stared into grave but gentle blue eyes. Then the man said, "My name's Rutledge, son. I knew your mother. Will you let me read that to you?"

A great, painful knot untied itself in Jim's chest. Wordlessly he handed the paper over.

Rutledge smoothed it, his eyes clinging for an instant to Jim's braids and coup feather before they turned to the message.

"*Jim, if you're still alive, come help us,*" he read. "*Pa's been dead three year, and mother died on the trail two months ago. We buried her beside the Sweetwater. Now me and Sally and Dan'l is all that's left. We are just across the Snake bound for the Willamette Valley, and none of us old enough to claim land after we get there, except you. If you ever cared anything for mother or any of us, then come. It's our only chance. Jonnie.*"

There was a silence in which even the roar of the river seemed to recede into a far and dreamlike whisper. Then Rutledge's big hands folded the note, carefully and slowly, and handed it back. His face was troubled but kind.

"They're here in The Dalles now, son," he said softly. "You want I should take you to 'em?"

Jim nodded. His breath was deep and hard, his whole mind full of awe. He knew now which valley he must go to, and why everything had happened just as it had. He was to find Jonnie again, that's what the paper meant. He was to go home. His medicine was more powerful than he had dreamed.

Chapter IV

Dusk was gathering over the broad sloping area between river and hills where the wagon train was encamped.

There was a curious disheveled air about the place. Wagons angled this way and that under the dripping trees; oxen and cattle bawled mournfully; campfires sparked here and there through the gloom; and people moved about them wearily.

"It's ever' family for itself now," Rutledge was saying as he led the way over the muddy, uneven ground. "The train's busted up. Folks got to tackle this gorge the best they know how, ain't no way to go it together. Jonnie and me's been plannin' to team up on our raft—build it big enough for both families, if we can. I reckon we'll find him at my wagon now. We was gonna talk about it some more this evenin'—"

Jim, moving silent as a shadow at his side, with Moki close at heel and Buckskin and the mule clopping behind, was grateful for the quiet, steadying rumble of the man's voice, though he only half listened to the words. His mouth was dry. Would he know Jonnie, after all these years? He groped after fragments of memory—a tousled dark head in the next cot, loud arguments about chores or beanshooters or who broke the window, low-voiced talk after the candles were out at night. But Jonnie's face remained blurred and featureless, save for black eyes with thick black lashes. How far away it all was.

". . . been a mighty hard trail for Jonnie—for all of 'em—since your mother died," Rutledge was saying. "They're fine kids. I've raised three myself and I know. Ain't a soul in the wagon train wouldn't stake his last ox on Jonnie Keath. And Sally—well, she's got more grit than many a man I know . . ."

Sally. A seven-year-old with a mop of yellow curls, a childish treble, "Mama, them boys! They've woke the baby."

Jim stopped walking. Baby? Yes, Dan'l. The letter had mentioned him: "Me and Sally and Dan'l is all that's left." The three of them on their own from the Sweetwater to the Cascades! A sense of guilt, powerful as it was unexpected, filled Jim suddenly. It alarmed and bewildered him. His fingers tightened on his rifle, his glance flashed over trees, sullen sky, mud, and trampled grass, then lit on Rutledge's burly figure half turning to wait for him a few steps ahead.

"Somethin' wrong, son?" came the deep quiet voice.

Jim shook his head. Nothing was wrong, he was just jumpy. He moistened stiff lips and moved forward. "Let's git on with it. How much further?"

"Just yonder. That's my wagon by the pine trees—now don't let that bunch of people bother you none. Looks like a crowd but it ain't nobody but my family and a few folks from our train. Just neighbors dropped in, likely to borry somethin'."

Jim hardly heard the low, reassuring flow of words as they neared the wagon. A snatch of melody drifted toward them on the chilly wind and Rutledge chuckled.

"Yep, he's there, all right. That's Jonnie, son, that's him singin'. Hear the banjo? I tell you, that banjo's seen the lot of us through some rough times . . ."

The melody came and went, half lost in the noise of the river and the spurts of conversation coming from the direction of the wagon, winding in and out among the other sounds like a bright thread of embroidery. The voice was lusty and careless, interrupted now and again by little flurries of laughter; Jonnie's voice, deep as a man's. He'd be seventeen by now.

Jim tied his animals to one of the pines, his eyes on the fire crackling over there, on the figures moving back and forth or lounging under the pine trees. He could smell food cooking, hear scraps of talk. "Now where's that clasp knife? La, I had it right here—" "It's the cattle worries me, Ned. *They* can't ride no raft, we'll hafta—" "Sam, gimme a lift with this—"

Then Jim felt Rutledge's hand on his shoulder as they pushed through a stretch of low bushes, and a few minutes later he stepped full into that blaze of firelight. Heads turned, talk trailed off, the music died. Dazzled by the glare, Jim flung a confused glance around the ring of faces, seeing only blurs.

"It's your brother, Jonnie," he heard Rutledge saying. "Your brother. He's come."

The fire snapped, sounding like a gunshot. Then a tall boy rose slowly to his feet and stood there, the banjo trailing from one hand. For an instant Jim forgot to breathe. He could have sworn he was looking straight at his long-dead uncle, Adam Russell.

He stared at the long legs, wide shoulders, tumbled black hair. They were Uncle to the life. So were the jutting nose and straight dark brows. But the furrows of forty years of hard living were absent; these cheeks were smooth with youth. And instead of Uncle's hawk eyes, here were those thick-lashed black ones he remembered. They were going over him slowly, numbly, from coup feather to moccasins.

"Good lord a'mighty," said Jonathan.

Something in his tone killed the eager greeting on Jim's lips. With an effort he got one word out. "Hello—Jonnie."

He took an uncertain step forward, stopped, then took another. Jonnie suddenly dropped the banjo. "Jim—" he said hoarsely. "*Jim!*" Then he was moving, too, kicking aside a heap of brushwood that lay in his path, somehow conveying the impression that had a mountain stood there, he would have kicked that aside too. His hand reached out; it was square and muscular and bony like the rest of him, burned dark by months of travel. In another stride Jim was beside him, gripping it.

For a moment they stood silent, taut as two bowstrings, staring at each other. Jonathan spoke jerkily at last.

"Jim, by all that's holy! Never reckoned to see you again in this life. Ain't sure you're real— What's the matter? You're shakin'."

"Well, thunder, you gimme a turn. Yer the spit of Uncle."

"Oh. Yeah, I've heard that. Mother used to say so . . ."

The words trailed off. Suddenly neither could find anything to say. Jonnie freed his hand and wiped both palms on his shabby jeans in a gesture Jim found vividly familiar. Jonnie used to do that as a child, whenever he was wrought up, crammed full of something he couldn't handle.

He exploded into speech. "Mean to tell me you got that letter of mine? Or did you just happen to turn up here?"

"Got the letter."

"Crimeny! How? All that country—I figgered that trapper'd never find you, even if you was still alive. How'd he—"

"Sent Injuns with it. Hervey knowed whar I was, within a hundred mile or so."

"A hundred mile!" Jonathan laughed nervously. "You talk like they was a signpost on ever' mountain."

"Is, onct you git to know 'em." We'll start feelin' easier pretty soon, Jim thought. We just got to git used to each other agin, that's all. "Did—was it a rough trip out?" he asked.

Jonnie shrugged. "We got here. Wagon turned over onct, comin' down Windlass Hill. Nearly lost a ox crossin' the Snake."

"Some river, that Snake."

"Yeah, dunno a worse ford anywheres. That ox of mine, the blamed old goat, he . . ."

Jonnie's voice went on jerkily, but Jim lost track of what he was saying because Jonnie's glance was going over him, this time clinging to his braids and his medicine bundle and his claw necklace with a fierce intensity.

"By the almighty, you've done some changin'," Jonnie said slowly. "What in the name of—" But he didn't say what he'd started to. Instead he stirred, darted a sidewise glance at the ring of faces around them, and muttered, "Say, let's get out of here."

His words produced an awkward flurry among the watchers. Women began to bustle toward the cook pots, men became absorbed in the examination of wagon wheels and their own muddy boots. Jonathan strode off to fetch his banjo, moving with that brusque, shoving gait of his. He walked like a man up to his knees in swift water. Jim, watching every move, noticed that he was limping. On the way back Jonnie stopped beside Rutledge.

"We'll have that talk of ours later, shall we?"

"Sure, sure. I'll come around after supper, Jonnie."

"Yeah, do. Bring Ned." Jonathan moved on, beckoning Jim with a jerk of his head. "Our wagon ain't far, just over yonder a piece. Sally's there."

Jim nodded, his mind a ferment of unfamiliar emotions. This young brother of his had grown up into somebody, all right. He thought of Rutledge's words, "Ain't a man in our wagon train wouldn't stake his last ox on Jonnie Keath." And Jonnie's own grim "Well, we got here." Jonnie would get where he set out to get, you could tell that from his walk and the set of his chin. There was a streak of iron in him that hadn't been there when they were youngsters, and there was something else, too, something that made him look less like Uncle at

44

times and more like Pa. Jonnie could throw a look at you that was like a blow. Maybe it wasn't going to be easy, this coming home.

The thought took root and grew disquietingly, all but blotting out Jim's familiar world of sensation. The river's thunder, a pine branch that caught at his rifle, the shape of a twig under his moccasin, all had a curious remoteness, as if his body and mind had temporarily parted company. He was almost surprised, when they stepped past the wagon into the chilly dusk, to find that busy corner of his brain functioning as usual, automatically reporting a north wind and the scampering passage of a squirrel.

He frowned. Running into Jonnie after all these years was kind of a shock, that was all. They'd both changed, sure. Nothing so queer about that. It'd been a thunderin' long time.

"You got any belongin's?" Jonathan was asking as they started back through the scrubby bushes.

"Yeah. Tied my critters to a tree over this-a-way. I'll fetch 'em."

Jim swerved to the right, where Buckskin's pale shape loomed ahead in the dusk. But he slowed and then stood still. One of many unasked questions was pounding too hard to be delayed. "How'd it happen—with Mother?" he blurted. "Injuns, or—"

Jonathan shook his head. "She was sick back in Missouri, Jim. One reason we left. She kept havin' this fever. Seemed like she was better for a while, crossin' the Plains, but then—I dunno. I guess it was just too hard."

"It's hard country," Jim muttered. After a moment he added, "Wisht I'd a been there."

"So do I," Jonathan said grimly. "She couldn't talk about nothin' else."

"She wanted to see me?"

Jonathan turned slowly and looked at him as if he couldn't believe what he was hearing. "Yeah," he said at last. "She wanted to see you. She never quit wantin' to."

They stared at each other a moment. "Well, I wisht I'd knowed that," Jim mumbled at last. "I didn't know." He cleared his throat roughly and started walking again. "How come you to head out here, anyways?"

"Oh, a lot of reasons." Jonnie shoved along beside him, swinging the banjo. "We lost the farm when Pa died, three year back. And—"

"Thunder! You did? Whar you been livin'?"

"Here and there, anyplace I could find work. Council Bluffs, St. Louie—I loaded river boats a while there, done farm work up around Independence. Kept hearin' Oregon talk, free land, mild winters and all—sounded mighty good. We finally just packed up and started."

"By gor, I'll say you got nerve."

Jonathan smiled one-sidedly. " 'Bout *all* we got, now. Broke, clothes all wore out." He halted and turned, the smile gone. "Can't even get the land, now mother's gone. You gotta be eighteen to sign them papers, and I lack six blasted months." He hesitated, then burst out, "Jim, you aim to get that land for us?"

"Why, sure. If that's what you want."

The depth of Jonnie's relief showed in every line of his body. "It's what I want, all right. By golly, it's all I need, just that land. I'll do the rest without no favors from nobody. Come on, come on, let's get movin'. I wanta tell Sally."

Jim led the way, wondering at such enthusiasm for a job he wouldn't touch with a ten-foot pole. Farming! Starting from scratch, too. Clearing land. He wondered if Jonnie knew how thick the trees grew in that valley. Then he decided it wouldn't matter if they grew three to the inch—not to Jonnie. it wouldn't.

46

Preoccupied, he forgot to warn Moki as they stepped around the last thicket. The dog glimpsed a stranger lurking behind his master, and drew his own conclusions. With a snarl he lunged straight at Jonathan's throat. Jim swung an arm violently backward, sending Jonnie staggering; next instant he had Moki by the scruff. A sharp swat and a sharper command restored discipline.

"What the devil?" Jonathan grunted. "You keep timber wolves for pets?"

"It's a *dog*. Stay there, Moki." Jim brushed past, suddenly irritable, to yank the mare's bridle free. He'd had about enough remarks about Moki today. But he could hardly blame Jonathan. "Moki ain't used to so many people around," he said by way of apology. "He'll be all right onct he gits to sniff you."

"Well, suppose we get it over with right now. I'd as soon keep my skin whole."

Jim smiled briefly. "All right. C'mere, Moki."

With a firm grasp on the coarse fur, he allowed Moki to investigate Jonathan's hands and clothing, talking softly meanwhile in Crow, and waiting until the dog's bristling died down and the plumy tail began to thump amiably.

"He'll be friends now," he said, straightening.

"What was you sayin' to him?" Jonnie demanded.

"Oh, just calmin' him down."

"That was Injun talk, wasn't it?"

Jim suddenly wished he'd used English. "Yeah. Crow."

He waited uncomfortably, but Jonathan turned back to the dog. "Guess he's decided I'm all right. Let's go." He took a step, then stopped. "What about Sally? He gonna jump at her like that too?"

"Naw, I'll watch him." The doubt in Jonathan's expression made Jim add, "*I* won't bite her neither."

Jonnie laughed and turned away hastily, but the flush that

47

crept up over his cheekbones told Jim he'd struck home. Jim knew that look, he'd had it turned on him many times, not always by bourgeways. Usually it amused him and suited his purposes. This time it was wrong, all wrong.

He tugged on Buckskin's bridle and they headed southeast, away from the river. As they walked along in the gray half-light he let his eyes travel covertly over the threadbare shirt and jeans, the wide shoulders and flat belly that belonged to this grown-up Jonnie. How much of that iron had been in him before he started west? There was a lot of country between here and Missouri; you forgot what it could do to people until you saw its mark on somebody who wasn't used to it. If it didn't make wolf's meat out of them it whittled them down to bone and muscle like this. And all because they fought it like an enemy instead of learning to live with it. You had to give in, fit yourself to it. Injuns knew how, they'd always known. Mountain men found out mighty soon. But bourgeways were too stubborn—or too proud—to change their ways. They had nerve, all right, but they were fools to make so much extra trouble for themselves.

Looked like Jonnie had extra trouble all right, foot trouble. Jim shot a glance downward. Factory boots! Broken and half gone. Jonnie was limping bad and trying to hide it. Still fighting.

"What's the matter with yer feet?" Jim grunted.

Jonathan gave a short laugh. "What *ain't* the matter with 'em!"

"You got oxen to haul you, ain't you?"

"They haul our stuff. We mostly stroll alongside."

Some stroll, thought Jim. Two thousand miles. "Why'n't you ride horseback?" he demanded.

"Don't own a horse." Jonathan's eyes strayed to Buckskin, as they had often in the past few minutes. "I see you got yourself a good 'un! Where'd you buy her?"

"Buy?" repeated Jim. He almost laughed. The Crows—himself among them—were the most talented horse stealers on the Plains. "You can't buy no horse like that one."

"Where'd you get her, then?"

"Stole her, a-course."

Jonathan stopped in his tracks. "You *what?*"

Now then, by gor! thought Jim with satisfaction. That impresses him! "Why, I stole her. From a Crow warrior," he added, in case Jonnie might underestimate the coup. He waited, with an eagerness that surprised himself, for dawning respect to break over his brother's face. But something was wrong.

"What about the mule?" Jonnie said. "Did you steal that too?"

"No. Give thirty plews fer it, Taos Valley."

"Thirty what?"

"Plews! Beaver." Don't he know *nothin?* thought Jim.

"Oh, beaver." Jonathan continued to stand there, studying him with that peculiar expression. Maybe Jonnie hadn't heard about the Crows. Jim elaborated.

" 'Taint as easy as it sounds. Tom Rivers, he used to say it took a Crow to steal a Comanche's horse, and there warn't Injun nor white could steal a Crow's. Well, I done it. Cut her right off'n his lodge while he was settin' inside."

Still no awed admiration dawned on Jonnie's face. "Who's Tom Rivers?" he murmured.

"Trapper I know."

Jim turned and started on again. Why, he didn't know Jonnie at all, any more. They were strangers. What was Jonnie thinking, anyhow?

Jim was suddenly and desperately homesick for Tom, and for the old, drifting, uncomplicated life, and the smell of beavertail bubbling over the fire. His stomach twisted with hunger and he realized he was smelling food from all directions. He could spot three or four wagons among the trees nearby and each one had a pot of something cooking. Not beavertail, not anything he recognized, though the odor nudged something far back in his memory. He glanced around, about to ask Jonathan what it was, and felt a twinge of sympathy. Jonnie was sniffing hard. He looked nigh starved, all right. Likely the others were too. The others— Would Sally stare at him that queer way? He wished he could think what that baby looked like.

He turned, struck by a sudden thought. "By gor. The little one—Dan'l—how old is he, anyway?"

"Eleven."

Eleven! And Sally would be—fifteen? Jim made another hasty mental readjustment and found himself staring once more into the yawning gap of those nine years. It seemed to be getting wider all the time.

"What's he look like, Jonnie?"

"Oh, just a young 'un. Growin' out of his clothes—got yaller hair like Mother's."

Jim slowed, his mind full of a sudden clear image—the little golden-haired boy at the post. At the same moment Jonathan swung around. "I bet you seen him a'ready. He was tellin' us earlier about some tangle with a wolf and a Inj—"

There was an abrupt, strained silence. Jim stood there grimly, watching a dark flush spread over Jonathan's face. All right, it was out in the open. Best get it cleared up once and for all.

"A wolf and a Injun, is that it?" he said.

"Yeah," said Jonathan. Suddenly he burst out, "The kid made a mistake, but I can't blame him. You do look Injun, blamed if you don't! More Injun than white! What's happened to you, anyways, Jim? I don't know you no more. Where you been? How you been livin' all this time? Crimeny, you just dropped outa sight and never even said good-by. I thought you was dead long since. I just knew you was, 'cause you never come home nor sent word nor nothin'. Why don'tcha *tell* me?"

"Ain't much to tell, Jonnie."

"They's plenty, from the look of you. Let's have it. You run off with Uncle, didn't you? We figgered out that much."

"Yeah. Up the Missouri into Blackfoot country, then acrost into Absaroka and out agin—we trapped about a year, I reckon. Bill Hervey was with us, and some others. We was workin' up along Wind River when we got separated—"

"Separated? How?"

"Well, a grizzly busted up our camp one night. Uncle and the others got away, and—I didn't. I killed the critter, though, and after while some Crows run acrost me layin' there, lucky fer me. They tuck me home with 'em, and made some big medicine, and I got well. Tuck a while, though. Most all summer."

"Crimeny, Jim! You lived with them devils a whole summer?"

"What'd'ya mean, devils?" snapped Jim.

Jonnie's eyes widened, then gradually went expressionless. He murmured, "Sorry."

"I lived with 'em six year," Jim said.

Jonnie didn't move or answer, but he looked as if he'd been hit in the face.

Jim took a long breath and went on. "Well, then a couple year ago I run away from them too, and started trappin' agin with Tom Rivers. But it warn't like it used to be, there ain't no beaver noways, the trade's done fer. Tom and me, we was breakin' camp fer good, and I didn't know whar I was headin'. Then yer letter come and I lit out down here to git it read to me, and—"

"Read *to* you?" exploded Jonathan. "Good crimeny, Jim, Pa taught you to read!"

"I forgot. Thunderation, Jonnie, there warn't no books whar I was!"

Jonathan's shoulders sagged. He muttered, "Go on."

Ever'thing I say is wrong, Jim thought. He shrugged carelessly. "That's all," he grunted.

After a while Jonnie turned away, rubbing his palms on his jeans in that old gesture. "Yeah. Well, it's quite a bit, ain't it. Like I said. Well, let's get on."

He started walking again, toward a wagon half hidden in a clump of straggly pines. It had a big triangular stain on its top, and in the silence of the short walk Jim memorized every dreary dip and curve of its outline. When they were almost there Jonathan stopped and spoke in a strained voice.

"I think I better go first, Jim. Kinda warn Sally you're comin'. She don't remember you at all, y'know, and—"

"Go ahead," Jim snapped.

He stood there waiting, mechanically noting the scurry of a lizard, a couple of blurred and stubby footprints near an overturned stone, the strong smell of oxen. He fingered his braids, wishing he had switches to work into them so they'd hang looped and glossy to his knees like a warrior's ought to, since Jonnie kept staring at them anyway.

The devil with Jonnie, he thought restlessly. I don't care what they're sayin' over yonder.

One of the footprints had a long, wiggly indentation across the heel, and there were a number of slits in the earth nearby, as if a knife had been repeatedly jabbed in and pulled out. Jim thought, I only come here 'cause the medicine said to, anyhow. I don't need to worry about no bourgeways. I'll git 'em in shape and through the gorge and claim their land like I said I would. Then after that I'll lift my own traps and they kin lift theirs. Don't matter to me what Jonnie thinks.

Yonder, in that bare space, was where the oxen had been grazing. Somebody had moved them around the wagon not five minutes ago; there was mud still crumbling into a deep hoof track. Jim made an exhaustive study of it, burying far, far down in his heart the knowledge that what Jonnie thought might matter more than anything had ever mattered before.

Chapter V

Jim's defenses were built high and double thick by the time Jonathan appeared around the wagon. He flipped Buckskin's bridle over a branch and leaving Moki on guard, moved past the high, battered wheels. Sally was just another stranger; let her look him over as much as she liked. He was prepared for it.

But he was not prepared for the attack of shyness that laid hold of him the instant he saw her. She stood alone and tense beneath the gloomy pines—a tiny, fair-haired figure, straight as a ramrod. Her hair, like their mother's, framed her face in crisp, sun-bleached tendrils, then fell in a honey-colored cascade. She wore a sky-blue dress whose shabbiness Jim never saw. One look at Sally, and all the bead-bedecked Crow girls in Absaroka seemed gawky and overgrown, homely as mud.

My sister, he thought incredulously.

He moved toward her, noting the level brows, the firm, almost fierce little chin, the wide eyes— He halted abruptly. Those eyes were looking straight into his, and they were bright with hostility. She was his enemy before they'd spoken a word.

Jonnie stepped past him. "Sis, ain't you gonna say hello?"

She must have heard the nudge in his tone, for she managed a brief and unconvincing smile. "Of course. Hello, James."

"*James?*" gasped Jim. She couldn't have staggered him more completely with a war club.

"Why, ain't that right? It's what mother always called you."

"Yeah," Jim said through his teeth. By gor, the place was full of ghosts! First Uncle, then Pa, now Mother—the most disquieting one of all. "I ain't heard the name for years. I'm Jim now."

"Oh."

Her look took in his braids and feather, the buckskins greasy from many wipings of his knife. Her nostrils quivered slightly, and for the first time in years Jim was conscious of the wild, animal odor of castoreum that always clung about him. He edged downwind of her, under the pretext of examining the wagon.

"Pretty beat up by this time, ain't it?" commented Jonathan. "But I reckon it'll hold out till we reach the valley. Say, sis, you got no fire. Run out of wood?"

"Dan'l's fetchin' some," Sally murmured. Was she afraid of him, or only distrustful? Trying in vain to guess what might go on in the mind of a small, golden-haired, white squaw, Jim paid scant attention to Jonathan's questions about the rapids in the gorge, and his own mumbled replies. This was all wrong—everybody stiff and uncomfortable, miles from understanding each other and not even knowing how to start trying. Maybe Jonathan and Sally didn't want to try.

He heard a light footstep and turned to find Sally at his side. Her erect little head barely reached his shoulder. "I hope," she said, "our letter didn't interfere with no plans of yours."

"No."

"Where do you—live?"

He shrugged and nodded vaguely toward the continent east of them. "Anywhere they's beaver. Right now that means nowheres."

"James, what happened to Uncle?"

"He got scalped." It sounded blunter than he'd intended, but every time she called him "James" it rattled him. Hurriedly, he added, "He didn't feel nothin'. He had a arrer in his brain."

His awkward attempt to smooth things over took the remaining color from Sally's cheeks. "Injuns!" she said. "My stars, I can't see how—" She stopped abruptly, drawing a long breath. "Jonnie says you're gonna go clear to the valley with us, and claim our land."

"That's the idee, I reckon."

"We lost the old farm. Did you know that?"

"Not till today."

She looked at him a moment, clearly stifling a dozen questions she didn't quite dare ask. "You sure been gone a long time," she murmured resentfully.

Jonnie stirred, and said, "Sis—"

"Well, it's true, ain't it?" She whirled back to Jim. "Why didn't you ever come home to see Mother?"

He didn't know the answer to that, so he kept still. But Jonnie broke in brusquely, "Look, sis, the main thing is, he's come now. Let's get some supper goin'. Blast it, where's Dan'l? He go to Jericho to get that wood?"

"He'll be here directly," Sally mumbled. She turned in a little swirl of blue skirts and started to climb into the wagon, but hesitated. "We're much obliged to you—for comin' now," she said, civilly but as firmly as if she were marking a line on the ground and daring him to cross it. Then she disappeared into the wagon.

Jim said, "She thinks a heap of me a'ready, don't she?"

"Give her time, Jim," muttered Jonnie. He turned and walked over to a log that lay beside the ashes of last night's fire, dropping down on it with a grunt of weariness.

Jim followed him. "What makes her call me 'James'?" he burst out.

Jonathan shrugged. "She's heard about you all her life by that name. Mother always called you James."

"Well, thunder, you never did!"

"I never talked about you," Jonathan said.

So that was that.

In a moment Sally emerged from the wagon with her apron full of something, peering off toward the south. "Well finally!" she exclaimed. "Yonder comes Dan'l."

Jim turned. If Dan'l were that nice little kid at the post. . . . Yes, here came the same boy, his head like a spot of sunshine in the dreary tangle of trees and mud and wagons.

"'Bout time!" Jonnie grunted. He got up again and started around the wagon, no longer able to hide his painful limping. "We'll have a fire goin' soon, at any rate. But I better move them oxen first."

Jim made a sudden decision. "No," he said. "You better git off'n them feet, that's what you better do. I'm gonna fix the f'ar. And the oxen got plenty grass right where they're at."

"That's right," Sally said slowly. "I moved 'em a few minutes before you come. But—how'd *you* know it?"

Jim thought of that hoofprint—plain as day and twice as obvious—and wondered how anybody could help knowing it. But he said only, "Stay off'n them feet, Jonnie," and strode past the wagon and into the trees to tether his animals for the night, and unload the mule. It was clear to him that there would be no happy home-coming yet a while. Jonathan and Sally had each other. He meant little to them except a means of getting their land.

All right, he thought, giving Bad Medicine an unnecessarily rough push. Want him or not, they needed him. They needed him to claim that land, they needed him to help them through the gorge, and they needed him to get them in shape before they could start. They didn't even know how much they needed him.

But he was going to show them.

When he came back, carrying his possibles and clutching Moki firmly by the scruff of the neck, he found Dan'l there.

"That's the one!" cried the boy. "That's the dog I was tellin' you—" The rest trailed away as he gazed up at Jim. "You really our brother?" he inquired softly.

"Yep." Nothing to dread here, that was plain at once. Jim dumped his pack. Now for a start on all that had to be done. Better settle Moki first. "Come over here," he told Dan'l. "You kin pet the dog now."

Dan'l and Moki took to each other as readily as Dan'l and Jim had done. Sally's turn came next, and though she eyed the big beast with suspicion, she showed no sign of flinching. Jonathan had taken Jim's advice and was sitting beside her on a flat stone near the wagon, his feet stretched out gingerly in front of him, his hands busy splicing a length of rope.

"You notice I ain't arguin' with you on who'll build the fire," he remarked with a grin. "I feel like I got stumps instead of feet. Sally'll have the grub ready by the time you get it goin'. Dan'l, let's have that wood."

The boy ran to get the wood he had dumped. Jim followed to the fallen log, where the old ashes were, conscious of Sally murmuring something to Jonathan as he moved away. They began to talk in low tones, too indistinctly for him to hear.

The boy staggered back with the wood. Jim tossed half of it aside and began arranging a few sticks like the spokes of a wheel. "Say, is that the way you build a fire?" asked the boy in surprise, squatting down nearby. "Jonnie allus piles on a whole lot, so's it'll burn up bright."

"White man's fire," grunted Jim. "So big you can't git near it to warm yourself."

He moved a little distance away and came back with a handful of dry bunch grass, which he twisted into a little nest, the

58

boy watching every move and chattering eagerly. "We had *real* big fires at night on the trail. And guards to watch for Injuns. Jonnie was a guard lots of times, and I pertected sis. That was after—after Mama went away. Jonnie took care of both of us, and the oxen and the wagon and ever'thing, all the way from the Sweetwater. He can play a banjo, too."

"Jonnie's quite a guy, ain't he?" Jim murmured.

"Yeah, I'll say. Hey, where'd you get them scars on your forehead?"

"Grizzly slapped me."

"Cr-acky! What'd you do?"

"Killed 'im." Jim had filled the nest with bits of punk from his pouch, and now was striking sparks into it with flint and steel. When it began to smolder he waved it in the air until it burst into flame, then thrust it into the pile of twigs underneath the logs.

"Jonnie killed a wolf onct," Dan'l said thoughtfully. He peered again at the scars. "They ain't new, are they? Look all healed up."

Jim answered absently, his mind half on the low-toned conversation behind him, half on the wood, which was too wet to catch well. "No, they ain't new. I was just a young'un when that happened. 'Bout yer age, little older."

There, it was burning all right now. He started to rise, and caught sight of Dan'l's face. "What's up?" he inquired, startled.

"You fought a *grizzly?*" cried the boy. "When you was just *my* age?"

An unfamiliar warmth flowed through Jim. He grinned and shrugged. "Well, it was him er me." A notion struck him suddenly. "Lemme see yer shoe. The left 'un."

Dan'l looked at him in surprise, then obeyed. There was a deep, wiggly scratch across the bottom of the worn leather

59

heel—the same as had showed on those footprints behind the wagon. Jim squatted down again, smiling. "What'ja find under that big rock this afternoon? Grubworms?"

Dan'l's eyes widened to twice their size. "Beetles," he answered mechanically. "Say, how'd you—"

"What was that knife game you was playin'?"

"Mumblety-peg," gulped Dan'l. He fished a clasp knife out of his pocket. "You take a-holt of the blade, see, and—" He demonstrated, producing a series of slits identical with the ones Jim had noticed earlier.

"Want to learn a new trick or two?" Jim asked him.

"Sure!"

"Look. Hold it this-a-way. See that bug crawlin' up the tree yonder?"

"Yeah, I see 'im. He's— *Cracky!*" Dan'l stood frozen. The small black bug was sliced exactly in half by a quivering blade. Slowly he turned back to Jim. "Could *I* do that?"

"I'll teach you."

"I'd as soon you didn't!" cut in Sally's emphatic voice. She was standing beside Jonathan. Both of them were staring from Jim to the knife. He rose, his face settling into its impassive mask.

"F'ar's ready fer cookin'," he remarked.

Sally came forward, carrying a skillet full of white knobby objects that must be supper. "What's that?" he demanded.

"Spuds. It's all we got."

He smiled at her defiant face. "Throw them things away!" he said. "I got meat, plenty of it."

Potatoes! he thought as he moved toward his pack. That's what he had smelled cooking all around the encampment. He dug a bulky, hide-wrapped bundle out of his belongings and came back to the fire. Jonathan walked over and faced him.

"Now listen, Jim. We ain't gonna take your grub."

"Not take it? Want me to set and eat it by myself?"

60

"If you want. We got the spuds, and they'll do us. We don't need—"

"You need plenty, from whar I sit," Jim said.

"All right, mebbe we do. But we ain't aimin' to live off you. That ain't why I wrote the letter."

"I don't keer why you wrote the letter! You gotta eat, by thunder!" Exasperation flared up in Jim as he saw the stubborn pride only deepen in both their faces. "You ain't got no more idee than a beaver kitten what you're up agin!" he roared. "How fer d'you think to git with a raft to build and the gorge to run, and you half froze fer grub and plum crippled? Start shootin' that river yonder on a empty belly and yer a gone beaver afore you hit the first rapids! Long as I got meat we all got meat, and we all eat it, understand? I'm takin' over around here till I git you in shape. Now *set down*."

He turned his back to them, and in his usual quiet, husky tones, said to Dan'l, "Fetch me two sticks. Forked ones. High as my knee."

The sudden burst of temper had been as unexpected to him as to them. But at least it had the desired effect. Jonathan and Sally dropped down on the fireside log in strained silence, and after hastily obeying Jim's order, Dan'l joined them.

Jim stooped, unrolled the bundle, and set to work. The knife slipped in and out of the slab of meat with swift precision.

He rigged a spit across Dan'l's two forked sticks and in a matter of moments a haunch was sizzling there. The ribs he slanted over the flames on a sharp stick thrust at an angle into the ground. When the heady aroma of roasting meat began to blend with the smoke, he turned and looked at these strangers who were his family. Sally sat close by Jonathan on the log, her arm linked tight through his, the set of her chin stubbornly at variance with the tender curve of her throat. They looked alike, those two, in spite of her delicacy and Jonnie's gaunt strength, though Jim could not tell just why. Perhaps it was the angle of jaw and brow, perhaps their identical expressions of forced carelessness. Only Dan'l, huddled on the other side of the fire, his eyes glazing with hunger, gave any sign of noticing the aroma that floated upward from the haunch. Jim knew the others must be turning faint inside from the smell of it.

Still fighting.

He turned away, shaking his head. He moved back and forth from his pack, bringing the grizzly robe to throw around the shivering Dan'l, producing strips of blanket and a curiously shaped root which he pulverized by pounding it between two stones. He found a bucket of water beside a wheel of the wagon and filled his gourd, then went back and splashed water onto his mortar stone, mixing it with the powder already there. Then he stood up and turned to Jonathan.

"Take off them boots," he ordered.

"What?" Jonathan stared up at him. He looked half drunk with the smell of meat.

"Them boots. Git 'em off."

Jonathan obeyed mechanically. Next instant Jim had flung them into the fire.

"Wait!" shrieked Sally, and Jonathan exploded into profanity.

"Never mind them things," Jim told him calmly. "Nothin' but a nuisance in this country, any papoose knows that much. Stick out a foot."

Capturing one of Jonathan's swollen and lacerated feet, he peeled off the scrap of sock and began smearing on the thick paste he had concocted.

"What's that?" gasped Jonathan.

Jim smiled a little. He knew the marvelous numbness that was creeping through the abused flesh. "Oks-pi-poku. Sticky root. Hold still."

Jonathan held still. Tears of relief sprang into his eyes and his thick lashes dropped down hastily to cover them. Jim softened in spite of himself. After all, they were bone tired and hungry and half sick with worry, and they didn't trust him— yet. Why should they? Nine years and two thousand miles couldn't be wiped out in an hour.

As he secured the last strip of blanket bandage comfortably around Jonathan's ankle, the black eyes opened to meet his own. For a moment their minds met, in a wordless truce. Then Jonnie grinned slowly, and tried out a ragged voice. "Much obliged. I think I'll get there now."

Jim nodded. Then he straightened swiftly, and moving to the fire, began to hack off chunks of meat and pile them on bark slabs. "Let's eat," he said.

Chapter VI

It was Jim who roused first in the chilly, drizzling daybreak, two mornings later. He came instantly wide awake all over, as he always did, and from long habit glanced first at his rifle, then at his horse. Both were safe.

Then he looked toward the river. Today they would start through the gorge.

He got up and walked to the end of the wagon, stroking Buckskin's beautiful arched neck and gazing thoughtfully into the gorge. He'd traversed it once, last summer. In a good canoe. It was bad enough even then—fifty miles of the roughest, most treacherous river he'd ever laid eyes on, full of rapids and tearing currents, winding, bending, boiling, crammed with submerged obstacles, any one of which could rip your craft and you wide open. But the walls of the mountains that had crowded the mighty Columbia into this narrow space rose sheer and black from the water's depths, and for wagons there was no other possible entry into the valley, between here and California.

His eyes moved from the river to the heights above, toward which he and Dan'l would soon be starting with the animals. That would be a new trail to him. He and Tom had crossed south of Mount Hood, and if this was anything like that—

Two nights ago Rutledge and his son Ned had appeared

after supper, and the six of them had made what plans they could for a journey that was at best a wild gamble. They would build the raft large enough for both families, but what about the animals? Hire these Injuns around here to drive them over the mountain and you turned up missing a few head —say about half! But you couldn't take critters on a raft.

"I'll take 'em over," Jim had spoken up.

They'd all looked at him with a mixture of hope and doubt. "That trail," Rutledge said, "I've heerd it ain't wuth the name. It's winter up yonder, boy."

"I reckon I kin get 'em through. I'll take Dan'l to help out. That'll leave you and Jonnie and Ned to pole the raft."

It was the only way out, and they had decided on it. The raft was built and ready now. They'd worked all day yesterday cutting small trees and lashing them together. The remaining problem was food.

Jim turned away from the river and moved silently to his pack. The prime pelt he had captured and rough dressed last week on Powder River had sunned on its willow hoop all the way to the Dalles, and now lay folded with the others among his possibles. Shielding it with his body from the light rain, he shook it out and examined it carefully for signs of dampness, almost surprised that it looked so fresh. It seemed years since that morning he had said good-by to Tom. He wrapped it in a piece of old buffalo robe and tucked it under his arm. It galled him to spend good beaver just for food, but his meat was gone now and there was no time to hunt. Winter was already breathing down their necks.

Summoning Moki with a soft guttural, he started for the Indian lodges that fringed the settlement. These Chinooks up here must have something more sensible than potatoes.

When he returned half an hour later, Jonathan was up, padding awkwardly about the feeble remnants of last night's fire in Jim's other moccasins, which since yesterday had replaced

65

the blanket bandages. Jim watched him and shook his head. Jonnie had a good deal to learn about walking in moccasins.

And about staying alive, thought Jim as he came closer and closer, unnoticed. When he was almost on top of his brother, he let out a piercing war whoop, then grinned at Jonathan's dash toward the wagon and his rifle.

"It's only me," he drawled.

Jonnie whirled, then sagged against the wagon's tailpiece. "Lord a'mighty! Your idee of a joke—!"

"By gor, it wouldn't've been much of a joke fer you, if I'd been a Cayuse," Jim retorted. "I could've tuck yer hair twict over. You better learn to keep yer eyes skinned." As Jonnie shrugged and started back to the fire, he added, "Say, why you walkin' that-a-way?"

Jonathan turned a face like a thundercloud. "These moccasins! Troublesomest things I ever had on."

Jim relented. "Ain't you ever taken no notice of Injun's footprints, Jonnie?"

"Footprints? No."

"It might come in handy right now if you was to notice mine."

He walked across a stretch of thin mud to make it easy, but Jonathan only stared blankly at the tracks until Jim made him put a row of his own right beside them. "By golly!" Jonnie said then. "Yours are pigeon toed!"

"And yours ain't. Now do you git it?"

"You talk like I was half witted! I reckon you mean I should start toein' in."

"You reckon right."

"By golly, the things a feller's got to do to get along in this country!"

Jim grinned and stooping beside his sack, took out his knife to loosen the thongs that sewed the top of the parfleche together.

66

"What's that?" inquired Jonathan.

"Pemmican."

"That's a new one on me."

"You've eat jerky, ain't you?"

"You mean that dried buffalo meat? Lord, yes, we lived on that, once we left the Plains."

"Well, this here's jerky, only they pound it all up fine and pack it in a parfleche and pour melted fat over. This stuff's got body to it. Sticks to yer ribs."

"Well I'll swear. How d'you cook it?"

Jim shrugged. "Any old way you want. Fry it, roast it, boil it—or jest dig out a hunk and start chewin'."

"That'll likely be it! If this rain keeps up we can't make no fire. Think that bagful'll last us through the gorge?"

Again Jim shrugged. "You gotta make it last. Weather'll hold, all right enough, or else git worse."

Sally and Dan'l appeared a moment later, and with only one doubtful sniff at the contents of the bag, Sally produced her skillet and started following directions without protest. Maybe she'd been thinking things over. Jim smiled to himself as he remembered her reactions of last night, when they'd been eating the last of the haunch. He'd remarked, with enjoyment, that panther meat knocked the hindsights off of every other kind, even buffalo. Sally's eyes had flown wide open; the bite halfway to her mouth ended up in the fire. "Panther! Is *that* what this is? Why, I'd as soon eat cat! Or *dog!*"

And when Jim had inquired what was wrong with dog, she'd acted as if he'd said something revolting. Jonnie'd taken it as a huge joke, but to a mountain man it wasn't funny. "Meat's meat," Jim had told them flatly. "You'll find out if you ever git hungry enough."

It wasn't unlikely they'd find it out before they reached Fort Vancouver, he thought now as he walked down to where his animals were tethered. At Sally's summons to breakfast he merely grunted, "I've eat a'ready." No sense using any more of that pemmican than necessary, before they even started. Hunger was nothing new in his life, and he was in far better shape than the others to begin with. He could live off short rations and his reserve strength for a good long while; and off the parfleche soles of his moccasins after that, if need be. He'd done it before. He wondered, with a flicker of amusement, what Sally would think of boiled moccasin for dinner.

By the time he'd divided his pack into two loads, one for Buckskin and one for the mule, the others had finished eating. As he started back around the wagon they were standing there together, Jonnie kicking dirt over the fire, Sally scrubbing at the skillet with a bunch of leaves and talking in a low, emphatic voice, Dan'l looking from one face to the other.

". . . just *wish* there was some other way!" Sally was saying. "I don't see how I can get on that old raft and just go off and leave him— Oh Jonnie, can't we find some other way?"

"Sis, I don't see how. Don't think I ain't racked my brain! I feel the same as you. But it'll take Mr. Rutledge and Ned and me, all three to manage that raft, and the cattle's no one-man job—"

"Aw, shucks!" Dan'l's voice sounded disgusted. "You talk like I was a baby! Jim'll be with me, anyhow!"

"That's half what I'm worryin' about!" snapped Sally. She dropped the skillet and grabbed the boy by the shoulders. "Don't you listen to that Injun talk of his, you hear me? Don't you—" She broke off, gave her head a quick little shake, and suddenly pulled Dan'l to her and hugged him with all her might.

"Sis," said Jonathan. He turned her gently and put the skillet in her hands, giving her an awkward pat. "Go on now and finish stowin' things away. Ain't no good to think too much." As she started for the wagon, wiping her eyes fiercely on a corner of her apron, he turned back to the little boy. "We ain't thinkin' you're a baby. It's just— Crimeny, be careful, Dan'l! Will you?"

"Aw, cracky, Jonnie! There ain't nothin' to— Why this ain't—" The swagger drained out of Dan'l. In a small voice he finished, "Yeah, sure, Jonnie. I'll—be careful."

"All right." Jonnie straightened, wiping his palms on his thighs. "You'll be fine. Safe as a church, prob'ly. Go on and help sis pack." He turned away swiftly and kicked a last covering of dirt over the coals, while Jim watched grimly. Easy to see how much they trusted him! When he stepped at last out of the shelter of the wagon, Jonnie snapped almost angrily. "Come on, let's get this wagon to the river."

The next couple of hours were furiously busy. At the river bank they were joined by Bob Rutledge and his son Ned, a lanky, freckled-faced boy with big hands and his father's warm smile. Together the four dismantled both wagons and loaded them onto the raft, along with a mountain of household goods. Jim wondered what anybody could want with all that fooforaw. Crowds of other emigrants up and down the river's edge were loading up too, and every few minutes one of the clumsy craft would push off into the water, to start its long and perilous journey through the gorge.

The weather grew steadily worse, huge slushy snowflakes alternating with the chilling rain. Mr. Rutledge glared up at the sky as the last boxes were made fast. "Crimeny! Maybe we better hold off for a day or two. Wait for better weather."

"Wait fer better weather and you'll be here till spring," Jim said bluntly.

Rutledge sighed and nodded, and sent Ned to the post after his wife, his twin daughters, and Sally. Jim eyed the twins curiously as they scrambled down the rocky bank in the wake of the large, comfortable, breathless woman with pink cheeks who must be Mrs. Rutledge. They were sturdily built fourteen-year-olds with their father's red hair; Bess neat and timid,

Maggie mussed and talkative. Under cover of her chatter, Jonnie turned anxiously to Dan'l. "Now keep wrapped up good, you hear?" As Sally rushed over to hug the boy once more, Jonnie faced Jim with a look that was like a threat. But all he said was, "Take care of that young 'un."

"You mind the raft!" Jim flung at him. "I'll handle my end."

"Yeah," said Jonnie slowly. A grin flicked over his face and was gone. "Guess we'll both have our hands full. We'll meet you at the Cascades."

He turned abruptly and leaped aboard the raft. Weighted down with people and possessions, it was already awash, but Rutledge settled the womenfolk in the crude shelter formed by baggage and wagon top, and shouted to Ned and Jonathan to look sharp. All three grasped their poles and braced themselves, and with Jim and Dan'l shoving and straining on the bank, the unwieldy craft began to shudder free.

"Oh, Dan'l, good-by Dan'l, good-by honey!" cried Sally. "Oh, Jonnie, what are we doin'! We *can't* leave him here."

But at that moment the roaring current caught the raft at last and swung it free. Immediately it was bobbing and twisting down the dark river, and a moment later had careened around a rocky point and vanished.

"Cracky!" gulped Dan'l, and Jim, glancing down at him, saw near panic on his face. "They—they went awful fast, didn't they? One minute they was here, right with us, and the next—" He broke off, his lower lip shaking uncontrollably.

"We ain't hangin' around neither," Jim said. "Come on."

"But what if I never see 'em again? What if we don't *get there?*"

Jim grabbed the boy by the shoulders, hard. For a moment the desperate loneliness of the small figure in its bunchy wraps filled him with pity. But he kept his voice rough. "I'll git you there, understand? I'll git you there!"

He waited only until the panic had faded from the boy's face, then turned him firmly away from the raging waters and toward the campsite, where Buckskin and the mule waited among the milling stock. One strong swing and Dan'l was on Bad Medicine's back atop the divided pack, before the beast had time to get temperamental. Calling Moki to stand guard beside the mule, Jim set about convincing the indignant Buckskin that she was going to carry the other half of the pack and him too, whether she liked it or not. Eventually the new order of things was accepted by both animals, and they were starting up the slope toward the snowy heights two thousand feet above the gorge. Ahead of them wandered four skinny oxen, two cows and a heifer, Rutledge's saddle horse, and a furiously busy Moki.

"Jim, d'you think they'll make it through the rapids on that big old raft?" came Dan'l's small voice. "D'you think they'll get there, Jim? I—gee, I never even said good-by to sis."

"You'll be sayin' hello to her afore too long. Shut up, now, we got a mountain to climb."

Dan'l said no more, and presently both were too occupied with the problems of bewildered cattle, steep and slippery footings, and their own discomfort, to talk had they wanted to. Before noon it was snowing in earnest. The afternoon was a steady climb through a world they could not see for the swirling flakes. The wind howled constantly at their backs. The cattle, bawling their protests, kept floundering off the incredibly rough trail.

"Say, you reckon we *can* get these critters through here?" shouted Dan'l at one point, after they had struggled half an hour to free one of the oxen from a drift.

"Stop jawin' and pull," grunted Jim. He tightened his knees about Buckskin's shivering sides and hauled again on the oxen's lead rope, putting all the rawhide strength of his shoulders and back into the pull. This time, with Bad Medicine and Dan'l straining on another rope, the beast scrambled free.

"There, you ornery, moth-eaten old piece of cussedness, you!" panted Jim, yanking the ropes loose. "Git off the trail onct more and I'll leave you to freeze solid!"

He pulled the hood of the grizzly cloak up over his head and fastened it with fingers stiff from cold, narrowing his eyes to slits as he faced once more into the wind. Freezing solid would be no trick at all in this weather.

It snowed steadily for five days of struggle.

By noon of the sixth the storm let up enough for them to see the treetops, and an hour or so later the snow stopped entirely. But the skies did not clear.

They made camp that night in the dubious shelter of an overhanging rock ledge, wrapping themselves cocoonlike in buffalo robes and huddling close to the animals and each other. Jim gave Dan'l a portion of the pemmican he had kept out of the bigger sack, but contented himself with a few handfuls of snow, as he had done every second night so far. There was no way of telling, yet, how long the crossing would take, and how much colder it would get. Better make this food stretch as far as possible.

He tightened his belt and thrust his hands into the warmth of his armpits. It was a bleak enough scene framed by the rock ledge—trees weighted with snow, the dark shapes of the cattle huddling with their backs to the wind, a little stream running black and wickedly cold through a white world.

"Jim?"

"Uh?"

"Kin I ask you somethin'?"

With an effort Jim got his mind off a fire and a hot meal. "Yeah, sure."

"Well—" Dan'l clenched his teeth to stop their chattering, and spoke jerkily through them. "That grizzly you killed that time when you was only my age. How'd you kill him, Jim?"

"Oh, that. Why, I strangled 'im."

"Cracky!" Dan'l shot upright, jaw agape.

"With my bare hands," Jim added.

Slowly a grin spread over Dan'l's wind-chapped face. "You're foxin' me. What happened, honest?"

"Put a little lead in his brain, that's all."

"Was it a big 'un?"

Jim indicated the silver-tipped cloak with a bob of his head. "That big."

"Cracky. Wasn't nobody there to help you?"

"I'll say there warn't! I was the only one fool enough to light out upwind."

Dan'l pondered this a minute, then stirred and sighed. "What d'you wear that feather for, Jim?"

" 'Cause I risked my neck gettin' it. Means I've counted coup."

"How d'you count coup?"

"Oh, they's quite a few ways. You hit a enemy with a quirt or yer coupstick afore you've hurt him—while he's still armed to the teeth. Or you touch the first one kilt in a battle. Or steal a horse some risky way."

All at once the old life was all around him, blotting out this world of snow and darkening skies. Involuntarily his fingers crept up underneath his cloak to touch the necklace lying warm against his throat.

"Are you a Injun now, Jim?" Dan'l's voice came softly out of the gloom. "Sally says you are."

The necklace seemed to lose its warmth. Jim stirred impatiently. He wasn't going to fret about what Sally and Jonnie thought!

"Jim," said Dan'l dreamily. "I don't care if you are a Injun. I wisht I'd killed a grizzly. I wisht I was just like you."

"*Wagh!* You don't know what you're talkin' about."

73

"Yes I do."

Jim turned. The boy was watching him solemnly, his eyes clear and earnest in his shadowed face. A deep comfort stole over Jim. "Jonnie wouldn't like that," he said softly. "Now shut up and go to sleep."

But for a long time after Dan'l's breathing was quiet and steady, Jim lay there wakeful, thinking of the vicious river far below him, of the raft and its occupants. And when he awoke in the gray dawn Jonnie was still on his mind.

In the same dawn, miles away, Jonathan uncurled his stiff muscles and sat up, peering about him through the dim light. Sally was still sleeping there at the other end of the wagon bed on her lumpy arrangement of boxes and soggy bedclothes, looking as uncomfortable as he felt. Through the arch of the wagon top he could see Rutledge moving about outside.

"Wake up, sis," he muttered. "Time to get started."

He edged his way out of the cramped interior of the wagon, feeling weary, dirty, and as cold as death. It was raining again —of course. It had rained every minute it was not snowing, this whole six days. And each day the river seemed to grow more treacherous, the beating wind stronger, their progress slower, and their condition more desperate. Sally's feet were so swollen she could no longer wear her sodden shoes. Ned Rutledge's boots had disintegrated altogether from the constant soakings, as had his father's and Maggie's; they stumbled about in wrappings of old rags. Bess, the other twin, had been ill.

Fifty miles of this! thought Jonathan. Wonder how many of 'em we've covered by now? Not many, with that wind allus beatin' us back. Lord, how I wish we was through with this blasted gorge.

He stepped down reluctantly over the wagon's tailpiece

into the two inches of water that covered the logs of the raft. It would be awash ankle-deep as soon as they cast off and pushed into the current, he knew. Only the trick of resting the wagon boxes on top of the dismantled wheels had kept their beds from being flooded instead of merely sodden.

Flexing his sore shoulders he waded toward Rutledge. "How do we know this ain't yesterday?" he inquired. "Or the day before, or the day before that? Same rain and wind, same nasty-lookin' rapids up ahead, same fine, level campsite—" He jerked his head toward the tumbled black boulders that constituted the bank, around one of which strained their anchoring rope.

"Well, I got muscles I didn't know about yesterday," grunted Rutledge. "Seems like the same old ordinary ones I been usin' all my life ain't enough for this here Columbia. I been breakin' out a new set ever' mornin'."

Jonathan returned his sour grin. Then as Sally appeared, shivering, at the opening of the wagon, he sloshed back to get the bag of pemmican and dole out breakfast.

"I wish Dan'l was here with us, 'stead of up in that snow somewheres," murmured Sally. "Oh, Jonnie, I can't feel easy about James. He's so *Injun*—"

"Funny thing is," said Jonathan carefully, "we still look alike, him and me, same as when we was little fellers. Remember that picture?"

"Why, Jonnie Keath! James don't any more look like that picture—or like you—than—than—"

"I know, I know, he wears braids and he's—well, he's changed, all right." Jonathan thought of the lean, wild grace of Jim's body, the eagle feather aslant above his scar-licked face. "Still and all, Mr. Rutledge said he suspicioned who Jim was, minute he pulled that letter out, 'cause he—we resembled."

"Well, I can't see it!" declared Sally. "And I don't want to see it, what's more. He's a savage! Eats dogmeat, wipes his knife on his shirt, can't even read—"

"Lots of folks can't read, sis." Jonathan got up wearily, pulling the thongs tight over the remaining pemmican. What made him defend Jim? Everything she said was true, more than true. The way he threw that knife! And then there was the matter of that heathen little buckskin bundle Jonnie'd spotted tied to Jim's braid the first night he'd come. Jonnie knew what it was. He hoped Sally didn't, she'd disown Jim completely. But then she didn't remember the Jim he'd known when they were children together, hadn't been lonesome for him all these years, and wanting him back . . . He shook off the mood irritably. "Best we worry about Jim later. Right now we got plenty on our hands just stayin' alive."

Before the murky dawn had given way to bleak daylight, they were casting off. The wind seemed to be falling off a little—of course, thought Jonathan grimly, since we got rapids ahead. Half their fight had been against that wind, which seemed obstinately set on keeping them in the same place; one day they'd made scarcely a mile in eight long hours. But let the water grow white with hidden obstacles, let rapids and whirlpools loom up in their path, and the wind was sure to vanish, leaving them to race headlong over the swift current, fighting to control the raft's progress by thrusting with their poles at the rocks that jutted out of the swirling water like bared fangs. With the next smooth stretch, back would come the wind and they'd be fighting just as hard to keep moving at all.

Since the first day, all of them had ceased to think of the river as a mere body of water, rushing through natural causes to the sea. It was a monster, intent on their destruction, roaring with fury at their presence in his black-walled gorge, call-

76

ing the rain to drench them and the snow to blind them and the wind to madden them and the rapids to drown them. Every mile negotiated, every obstacle dodged, was a cheating of the giant.

Along toward noon Ned Rutledge, stationed at the foremost corner as the raft swung around a bend, let out a shout of alarm. "Watch it, Pa! This side, this side—!"

Through the veil of rain Jonathan saw Rutledge splash across the pitching logs, sending up fans of water with every step. At the same moment he glimpsed on his own side a dark shape looming under the surface just ahead. As the raft jarred against whatever obstacle Ned had sighted, both Rutledges thrust hard, causing the whole clumsy craft to swing in a semicircle.

"Take it easy!" yelled Jonathan. He aimed his pole toward the looming shape ahead and braced himself. An instant later there was a grinding jolt that seemed to tear his arm from its socket. The logs under his feet tilted perilously, then bounded free, drenching him with icy spray. Before he had time to do more than catch his breath, the raft was careening forward again, leaping like a live thing, smacking down on the black, running current with bone-jarring force.

From the Rutledge's wagon top, under which the four women huddled through the long, chilling hours, he heard the familiar sound of Maggie's cheering. In spite of his throbbing arm he grinned.

You didn't get us that time! he told the giant.

"Hungry?" Sally shouted in his ear a few moments later.

He nodded without turning, as the raft skimmed dangerously close to a jumble of wagon bows, soaked canvas, and logs, ruined goods—the wreckage of just such a craft as their own. "Lord a'mighty!" he grated, feeling his flesh crawl as they swept past. "There's one didn't make it."

77

"There was another near where we tied up last night," Sally said. "Well, that's only two so far. Think how many there was startin' off from the Dalles!"

He felt her steady herself against his shoulder as she shoved pemmican into his mouth. "Wonder why we don't see none of the others?" he mumbled. They had sighted only three other emigrant rafts in the whole six days.

"Well, some's ahead of us, and the rest's behind. We'll crowd up again at the Cascades, I reckon." Suddenly her determined cheerfulness deserted her. "Oh Jonnie, I wonder if Dan'l— It must be powerful cold up yonder."

"Yeah." Jonathan raised his eyes to the snow-swept heights, then looked away fast. "They'll get through. They *got* to get through. By golly, if Jim don't get Dan'l back safe, I'll—"

"Hush," said Sally fiercely. "Open your mouth."

Jonathan obeyed, getting almost as much rain in it as he did pemmican, and choking as a result. At the same moment he heard a hoarse shout from Rutledge and the raft lifted as if it meant to fly, then gave a heavy lurch and came down with a crash. Through the sheet of spray that shot out from under it, Jonathan caught a glimpse of Sally's white and desperate face as she fell headlong on the pitching logs, still clinging tight to the bag of pemmican. With an exclamation of pity he bent to help her.

"Crimeny, sis! Any bones broke?"

"No. No. Get back to your polin', Jonnie, I'm all right." She got up, one hand pressed to her side. "Dratted old river! Here, Jonnie, the bag got wet, but—"

"I'll eat tonight. Go on in the shelter, you ain't safe here."

It ain't fair, it's too rough for her, he thought incoherently. She had come mighty near to going overboard.

But there was no time to nurse his fright and no time to worry. The river was still tossing them about with malicious force, and fresh rapids boiled up ahead. Jonathan thrust hard

78

and harder with the pole, his thoughts veering again to those white-drifted slopes above, and the two who were up there somewhere in the snow and wind. The raft edged past a rocky little beach late that afternoon, and his heart leaped at sight of a group of scrawny cattle, coats roughened with cold, hunched miserably in the wind. But there was no sign of a mule or a beautiful wild mare—or a small boy. It was some other emigrant's cattle; Jonnie spotted the burly drover just as the whole scene vanished around a twist of the river. What were they doing down here at the water's level? Was the high trail impassable after all?

Oh, crimeny, why did I ever let Dan'l out of my sight! he thought. I never should've, I never should've.

Then even his fear faded in the weary confusion of rocks and drenching spray. The whole world narrowed itself finally to the ache in his shoulders, the wet, the cold, the next rock.

Chapter VII

A couple of days later Jim and Dan'l scrambled down the steep embankment to the same rocky little beach, driving before them the skinny cattle, who lowed dispiritedly as they faced the churning river. They could be driven no farther on this side; the mountains were impassable.

An emigrant raft appeared around a bend, the men fighting wind, rocks, and hidden obstacles like demons. Had Jonnie's raft passed yet? Both Jim and Dan'l shouted questions as the vessel whirled by, but the wind tore their words to shreds.

"What'll we do?" yelled Dan'l finally over the thunder of the water. "Stock can't ford this!"

Jim shook his head. Nothing could ford this, certainly not these half-starved animals. They would have to ferry the beasts across somehow or other, and it would cost them days of delay. The pemmican was already ominously low.

"Jim?"

He looked down into Dan'l's anxious face. "I'll git you there," he repeated stubbornly. "Go git the hatchet out'n my possibles. We're gonna build another raft."

It was three days before the last terrified animal was across the river. Mud coated and exhausted, Jim and Dan'l slept among tumbled boulders, and next morning strained upward again, into the teeth of fresh snow. The trail on this side was rougher, steeper, more strewn with pitfalls than the one they had already come over, if that were possible. Only the dwindling food supply enabled Jim to distinguish one day from the next, as they struggled through a white and swirling world where they could see ahead only a few feet at a time, where the gusty wind drove the snowflakes into their sleeves and down their necks, stung tears into their eyes, and then froze them on their lashes. Every branch, every twig was laden and bent with snow, and the stumbling animals wore inch-thick caps and cloaks of white.

But what worried Jim was the increasing weakness of himself and the boy. He had dared take no more than a few mouthfuls of food for several days now, and had cut even Dan'l's rations by half. Surely they would reach the Cascades tomorrow, or the next day! How long could fifty miles be? But still the trail led on, still the snow fell from the dirty sky.

At last one evening as they halted for the night in a rough little clearing, Jim dug into his pouch to find only one small morsel of the pemmican left. His eyes went to Rutledge's half-starved little heifer, then away again. It outraged his pride to have to kill for food one of the very animals he had contracted to deliver safely.

Automatically he set about making camp, but there was a slow drowsiness about his motions. The air was deathly still this evening, and so cold his nostrils stuck together when he breathed. His fingers felt like wood, his feet like stumps. Clumsily he dug a rude cave out of the side of a snowbank, and motioned Dan'l into it. The boy was groggy with fatigue and hunger. Well, from now on it would have to be the moccasin soles, or that scrawny heifer—or nothing.

As Jim turned to pull Dan'l's buffalo robe from his pack, the landscape seemed to lurch as he staggered, and the boy's voice, murmuring something about roast buffalo ribs, faded to a great distance. By gor! thought Jim. Maybe I best start on them moccasins tonight. But he leaned against Bad Medicine's bony side for a moment, swallowing hard, and the light-headedness passed. He tugged the robe free and flung it to Dan'l, then tossed the last chunk of pemmican on top of it— a chunk no bigger than his thumb.

"Ain't you eatin'?" asked Dan'l sharply.

"Not tonight."

"Didn't eat last night, neither," Dan'l said.

"Don't matter. I'm used to goin' empty."

"For two and three days in a row? You're lyin'."

"Shut up and eat your own," Jim growled. It was a momentous task to drag his own robe off Buckskin, to loosen her pack, to make his fingers move, to lift his arms.

Dan'l had become very still. "Jim," he faltered. "Are we runnin' out of food?"

"We got plenty."

"You're lyin', Jim Keath!" Dan'l's voice rose weak but shrill. "It's gettin' low and you been starvin' yourself so's you can give it to me."

Jim turned on him. "Fergit that and eat! I said I'd git you there, didn't I?"

An expression of stubbornness settled over Dan'l's snub-nosed face. "Not gonna eat unless you do."

"By gor, you eat that or I'll lay into you!"

"Go ahead. I still won't." Dan'l lay back, his fist tight about the scrap of pemmican, tears of weakness and protest spilling over.

Panic touched Jim. He dropped to his knees beside the boy. "Why won't you?"

"I just won't. I can't! Cracky, Jim, *you* wouldn't! We— We're *brothers!*"

Slowly Jim sank back onto his heels. "Yeah, brothers," he murmured.

After a long, still moment he reached for Dan'i's chunk of pemmican and meticulously divided it into equal parts.

It was then that Moki struggled into view through breast-deep snow. From his mouth dangled the limp carcass of some small animal.

"Wait, Dan'l! Don't eat yet!" Jim pushed both scraps of pemmican into the boy's hand. "'Moki! Here!"

The dog growled deep in his throat.

"*Moki!*" snarled Jim. The sight of the fresh dark blood on the snow turned him savage with hunger. He rose slowly, letting the robe fall, and stepped past the wide-eyed Dan'l.

Moki retreated, his growls unmistakably hostile, his lifted lip revealing a row of wolfish, sharp white teeth.

Jim forced himself to halt. The dog stopped too. Slowly Jim dragged his eyes away from the meat and turned aside. It took all his will. He stood there fighting to keep his head, waiting until he felt Moki's tenseness relax, and heard the growls die away. At the soft sound of slavering, he looked around. The dog's attention was now on the meat, which he was tearing as he held it with a forepaw. It stained the snow around it vivid red.

Jim gathered his tired muscles. Soundlessly, with infinite caution, he began to approach. One foot was lifted with slow, elaborate care, put down soundlessly; after a long, tense wait, the other. His jaws ached from clenching, and craving blurred his vision until the coveted meat seemed to dance crazily. But each step brought him nearer, and Moki did not know yet. When he was still three paces from the dog, he got a whiff of blood. It sent saliva flooding into his mouth, cracked his patience. He sprang.

He heard Moki's yelp, felt a bright flash of pain as he seized the meat; the dog's jaws had closed on his hand. Under him the hairy steel-muscled body thrashed and clawed as they struggled together, filling the air with snow. Moki's savage snarls mingled with his own no less savage Crow cursing. Gradually he became aware that he was doing all he could, and it was not enough, the dog was stronger than he. For lack of the smallest margin of strength he would have to watch his own dog eat while he starved. Fury sent strength to him from somewhere, that last spurt needed to force aside those flailing paws and sink his own teeth into Moki's ear. Hair filled his mouth; he bit down with all his strength, at the same time twisting his captured hand until the dog's head was forced into an unendurable angle. At last the traplike jaws snapped open, freeing him and the meat he still clutched. He rolled clear and staggered to his feet, sending Moki sprawling with a cuff as he did so.

As the dog tumbled away, yelping, Jim grabbed for the branch of a low pine and clung there. He was crusted with snow, his knees sagged under him, his lungs ached. The struggle had all but finished him. But it was strength itself he held now in his torn hand. Meat.

"Jim, you're bleedin'," quavered Dan'l.

Jim lifted his hand. The wound was a nasty one.

"It don't—matter. Don't—be scared, Dan'l. I'll fix it."

He stumbled back through the trampled snow to the dugout, pausing to gasp a last insulting "Squaw!" over his shoulder at Moki. Then he fell down beside Dan'l to examine his prize. It was far from choice; a small and considerably chewed-up mink, its wet fur already freezing into stiff little points. But it was meat.

He skinned it raggedly, his knife made unskilled by the trembling of his hands. Returning the two morsels of pemmican to his pouch, he gave Dan'l a haunch of the mink and hacked off the other for himself. Chewing it ravenously, he felt warmth and life flow back into him. They'd get there now, heifer and all, with any luck.

84

By the time he had cracked the cleaned bone and sucked out the marrow, the scenery had stopped dancing and blurring before his eyes. Trees and snow-capped rocks were firmly anchored to the ground again, their outlines distinct, their shapes normal. He felt a surge of triumph as he began to bandage his throbbing hand with matted buffalo hair and a strip of buckskin. Jim Keath hadn't gone under yet, not by a long chalk.

Turning at the sound of a soft whine, he watched Moki slink closer, his plumed tail raising little clouds of snow as it thumped in apology.

"Thought you'd keep it all for yourself, by gor!" Jim muttered. He glared at the dog a moment, then reached out to ruffle his ears and push his nose into the snow, finally tossing him the scrawny remainder of the mink.

"Jim," said a small tense voice at his side. He looked around to see Dan'l still holding his piece of meat.

"What's wrong? Eat!"

Dan'l swallowed. "I—I'm goin' to."

Jim softened. Poor kid, he thought, it's rough doin's fer your first winter in the mountains, anyway you lay your sights. Rough and small and lonesome.

But all he said was, "We best save the pemmican. You guessed it. It's the last we got."

Dan'l's eyes met his for a moment. Then suddenly he stuffed the haunch into his mouth. He tore off a bite and chewed fast, his breath hard and uneven but his young face stern. At last he swallowed.

"How was it?" said Jim.

For answer Dan'l took another bite. Around it he muttered, "Meat's meat."

Jim grinned for the first time in days. "By gor," he said, "I'll make a mountain man out'n you yet!"

There was a long silence in which the darkness crept down

85

over their still white world. Moki slipped through the dusk like a shadow and dropped down against Jim, who buried his fingers in the dog's ice-stiff hair. Scratching gently, he sat listening to the soft, desperate sounds of crunching and tearing as the cattle tried to make a meal off twigs and bark.

"They say," finally came Dan'l's small, yearning voice at his side, "they say that valley's same as paradise, where we're headin'. Hardly ever snows there, nor freezes, nor nothin'. They say it's like spring all year 'round, with berries and nuts growin' wild all over the place, and game a-plenty—" He drew a deep breath, and tossed away the mink bone, picked clean. "I'm mighty anxious to get to that valley, Jim."

Jim only grunted. He was anxious to get to that valley too. He was more anxious than he cared to admit, just to get to the Cascades and find out if Jonathan and Sally were all right. They must be there by now, if they'd made it at all—they must have been waiting for days. Maybe, he thought, they'll be gladder to see me this time, if I git Dan'l there safe.

"Jim," Dan'l said, "Jonnie don't think you mean to stay with us, once we get settled. I heard him tell sis. He thinks you're just gonna claim the land and then go off again, and live like you been livin'. But you ain't gonna do that, are you?"

And Jim found himself answering slowly, "No. I'm gonna stay."

Dan'l heaved a relieved sigh and snuggled against him. Brothers, Jim thought. He hesitated, then put his arms around the shivering child. After a while his shoulder grew stiff, and one of his legs went to sleep. But he never moved throughout the long night.

Two days later they reached the Cascades. It was none too soon. The cattle were skin and bones; years ago—could it have been only yesterday?—the brothers had eaten the tiny lump of pemmican, and since then there had been nothing.

Jim's eyes had not focused properly for hours; he swayed with Buckskin's every stumble, barely able to cling to her emaciated back. Dan'l lay stretched along Bad Medicine's neck, strapped on with a length of rawhide; he had not yet reached the state of total weakness, thanks to the extra rations earlier on the journey, but it had been a task almost beyond Jim's strength to hoist him up that morning, and he knew they dared not risk a fall. Well, it was over now. The trail was descending, and he could hear the roar of the Cascades.

Emerging from timber halfway down the last rock-strewn slope, he halted involuntarily at the chaotic sight below. Here at the brink of those falls no vessel could navigate, the rafts had landed, the scattered emigrants gathered once more for the portage ahead. Over a jumble of rafts, wagon parts, baggage, milling people, and animals, Jim could see a few sway-backed canvas tops already jolting over the hub-deep ruts that led westward through the mud. Where was the Keaths' wagon? The Rutledges'? How to find them in this shifting confusion?

All the disasters he had pictured during the long two weeks flashed through his mind once more. Then Dan'l pointed.

"There's sis!" he croaked. "There's our wagon!"

There it was, with the big triangular stain on its canvas, beside it the blue splash of Sally's dress. Mud, cold, hunger ceased to matter. Dan'l turned—a shapeless small bundle of bedraggled wrappings, incredibly dirty, but with the ghost of his old grin curving his cracked lips.

"Let's surprise 'em!" he said.

He urged his mule down past the straggling cattle, Jim following. It was no trick to hurry unnoticed through the jumble of wagons below and halt their tired mounts beside their own.

Sally's back was to them. She was bent over a box, listlessly pulling out sodden garments and hanging them over the great wheel. Her rag-bound feet were caked with mud, her hair spilled untended over her drooping shoulders; every move she made was heavy with fatigue.

"Sis—" quavered Dan'l.

She whirled. For an instant she stood transfixed, her face twisting with such blinding, painful joy that Jim turned away his eyes. She gave one wild scream—"*Jonnie, come quick!*" then stumbled forward, laughing, sobbing, flinging herself against Bad Medicine's side to seize as much of Dan'l as she could reach. She pressed her cheek against his dirt-encrusted thigh. "Oh, Dan'l you're here, you're safe, you ain't dead. *Jonnie!* He's come, he's come—!"

At that minute Jonnie hurtled, white faced, around the end of the wagon, a hammer in one hand and a wagon tire in the other. At sight of Dan'l he dropped both and lunged forward. Eager hands tore at the thongs that lashed the boy to the mule; he was pulled down and hugged again and clung to. His voice rose shrill with weakness and excitement.

"Cracky, sis, you still got pemmican? I'm most cavin' in— you oughta seen us, we ate raw mink meat! Moki hunted it and Jim fought him for it—fought Moki—and we ate it, and I'm a real *hivernant* now 'cause I wintered out, but we ain't had *nothin'* for a couple days, and—"

Jim, unnoticed, stood silent beside Buckskin. Then Jonnie turned. "Couple of days! Good crimeny! Looks like Jim ain't eat for a month!"

"Fought Moki?" Sally cried. "My stars above, look at that filthy bandage! Jonnie, run quick and borry some chewin' tobacco from Mr. Rutledge and I'll make a poultice."

Jim was ashamed of the warmth that swept through him. *Wagh!* Look at him standing there waiting and hoping for their attention, like any squaw! Had it shown on his face?

It was the impassive son of Scalp Necklace who followed them to the wagon, and food.

Later, when Jim had eaten, been doctored, slept, and was sitting beside the tall wagon wheel, eating again, he heard Jonnie's footsteps, hard and eager, coming up behind him.

"Jim. Dan'l says you told him you meant to stay on with us, after we get the claim. Is that right?"

Jim answered guardedly. "Oh, I reckon."

"Crimeny! You mean it?"

"Sure. Got to winter somewheres."

There was a pause before Jonathan said, "Oh."

At the tone of his voice Jim looked up, then rose quickly. "Wait, Jonnie. I figger to stay longer than just a winter. If I'm wanted."

"Wanted? Why, blast it, of course you're wanted."

Sally, folding and repacking the soggy garments, was listening tensely to every word. It would suit her better, Jim knew, if he'd just sign that claim and then get out. Well, he wasn't trying to suit her. "All right, I'm stayin', then," he told Jonnie.

He turned away and began to yank tight the drawstring on the bag of pemmican. Jonnie strode off to finish mending his tire, murmuring, "We'll leave at daybreak. By golly, we're almost there!"

There remained only five miles of portage before they were through with the gorge.

Five miles. The worst miles of the two thousand that stretched back to Missouri. From sunrise next day until well after dark they waded knee deep in snow and mud and water while the heavens continuously pelted them with more. Everyone was afoot now, and half of them barefooted.

Dan'l and Ned Rutledge walked first, driving the animals; the women followed, Maggie and her mother half carrying Bess, who appeared to be near collapse. Sally stumbled beside them until she was hysterical with the pain of her tired and frozen feet. Jim swung her atop Bad Medicine, who wavered a moment and then staggered on. The reassembled wagons brought up the rear of the procession, Jonathan and Mr. Rutledge grimly forcing their oxen over an incredible trail in which the mud lay so deep that no one dared look behind for fear of seeing the wagons overturned and lost forever.

Yet other wagons had got through somehow. There was a top-heavy shape, only half glimpsed through the curtain of rain, rocking and swaying ahead of them right now, and more were following. The trick was to keep moving, not think or feel or hope or count the hours, but only keep moving.

And at last it was finished, the portage was made, the five miles were behind them. Soaked through and almost dead with cold, the two families crowded into their battered wagons and somehow fell into exhausted slumber. It was more than a day later when they could gather strength to build the raft that would take them the last lap. But this time there was no fear in the parting as Dan'l and Jim, onshore, shoved the raft free into the current. It was easy poling now, on into the valley, and the animals would find food in the descending hills. The gorge was licked.

As they took the trail once more, Jim turned for a moment toward that vicious cleft which had so nearly succeeded in keeping them forever. Behind it, like a world infinitely far away, lay Powder River and Absaroka, the Plains and Taos, and Tom—all his old, familiar haunts and his free-roaming life. He was cut off from all that now, every mile of that snowbound trail rose a separate barrier. What was ahead?

Uneasily he fingered the medicine bundle tied to his braid. A glimpse of Dan'l's bright head moving along the boulder-strewn trail reassured him a little, but before Jim followed he fished a small bag of kinnikinnick and a scrap of red cloth from his pouch, and hung them on a low branch as an offering to his helpers. Then he nudged Buckskin with his heels, and headed west.

West, to another reunion with Jonnie and the others at Fort Vancouver, where man and beast could rest a day or two, where the trail-weary emigrants replenished supplies on credit, had horses shod and wheels mended, or merely wandered about the huge stockade basking in the pale sunshine that was like heaven after the gorge and staring at the bustling, well-fed people—blacksmiths, coopers, Hudson's Bay clerks in black cloth coats, Indians, traders, gaily dressed voyageurs.

West, then south—along the broad, silver-gray Willamette, into a new land; a rain-misted valley lush with promise, each rise crested with timber, every hollow deep with grass.

Good country, reflected Jim, as he held Buckskin to a walk beside the squealing wagon. A man could find food and clothing here year in and year out, though he'd have to cross the mountains for buffalo if he wanted the best lodge skins. Oregon. Oyer-un-gun, Place of Plenty, the Shoshones called it.

Clyde Burke, a spare, middle-aged man from the next wagon back, spurred alongside Jonnie to shout enthusiastic prophecies. Had Jonnie noticed how rank the ferns grew, how many creeks there were? No droughts in this country, no sir! They'd all grow rich from wheat and lumber—just wait a few years, more and more people would come, there'd be sawmills, flour mills, villages, towns, great cities.

Jim rode forward out of earshot and out of sight, consulting meanwhile that portion of his brain which was an accurate map of every peak, forest, canyon, watercourse, and ridge within a thousand square miles. Another river should open out from this one not far ahead, and westward along its banks a couple of miles was a place he and Tom had camped one night last summer.

He was back in an hour or so, wheeling Buckskin in a flurry of tail and hoofs beside the lumbering wagon. "Place over west'ard a piece might do you," he told Jonnie.

"Where? How far?" Sally called down eagerly from the tall wagon seat.

"How's the water?" added Jonathan.

"It ain't fur. They's a creek and two springs, I think. And it's on a little river. I fergit the name."

"On a river! Is there much timber to clear?"

"No more'n anywheres else around here."

Jim could sense Jonathan's excitement, and see him firmly control it. "How about—does it lay pretty level?"

"Rolls a little, is all. They's camus and blackberry on the glades, and fish in the river."

Sally drew a long, tremulous breath. "Sounds mighty good."

"Come on, then."

An hour later the wagon creaked into a little clearing lighted by the pale rays of sunshine now breaking through the clouds. The wheels slowed, made their final squealing revolution, and came to a halt under a towering oak tree. The oxen reached eagerly for the grass.

For a moment no one moved or spoke. There was the river, willow edged and tranquil, filling the silence with low music. There were the dark firs rising yonder, just where one might build a cabin, and emerald grass sweeping down from them. Beyond lay gently rolling glades, a tangle of blackberry and hazel, a wooded hillside—a whole, peaceful, untouched little valley drowsing there in the late afternoon sun, just waiting for the Keaths. Certainty, and a deep content, stole over Jonnie. Five long months of journeying were done.

"Sally," he said. He looked up at her, sitting tense and straight beside Dan'l under the weather-beaten arch of the old wagon top. Quite suddenly his eyes were brimming with tears. "Sally, come on and get down. We're home."

"You're sure, Jonnie?"

"Well, ain't you?"

Sally drew a long, deep breath and came to her feet, pointing. "I want to build the house right there, in front of them big trees. And I want to plant them rose slips I brought yonder by the front door. And mother's lilac. We can have a real table to eat off of again, and real chairs, and a fireplace—"

"Cracky!" yelled Dan'l suddenly. "Lookit that fish jump! I bet that river's crawlin' with 'em! I'm gonna cut me a pole, by cracky, I'm gonna—"

He scrambled to the ground, talking faster and faster, and Sally followed. The clearing rang now with their excitement, and weariness fell away like a discarded garment.

"It'll be just one room at first," Jonathan was saying. "But we'll add on. And look! Yonder's a good space for the garden, soon's I get it cleared some. Let's walk over that ridge and down to the glades, Jim says they's two springs and a creek. I bet this soil'd grow *anything!*"

Jim watched them hurry across the clearing, skirt the timber and vanish over the ridge, then reappear a few moments later in the sunlit glades beyond. Dan'l clambered up the slope from the river, yelling incoherently about ten-foot trout, and dashed after them.

An impatient tug on the bridle aroused Jim. Buckskin was reaching for the lush grass. He slid off and let her have it. For a moment he stood still, breathing the clean, moist air and watching the breeze dance in the fir trees. Then he walked slowly down to the water's edge. *Still waters, green pastures . . .*

Easing down on his haunches, he watched the minnows darting about in the clear brown shallows; noted a longer, darker shadow that might be a trout lurking there where the trailing branches of a willow stirred lazily in the current. Yonder up the bank was a trampled place where deer had sometimes come to drink, and there was a scarred tree—old beaver sign.

Yes, it was a good place. They'd ruin it now, of course. They'd ruin the whole valley, Jonnie and Rutledge and all those others. Cut down the forests and scare away the game and spread fields and houses and cattle and sheds and wagons and clotheslines over the whole face of this wild and beautiful country—tame it and plow it and fill it with people.

He listened to the soft, running whisper of the river and remembered its whispering Indian name—the Tualatin. Then he rose abruptly, walked back up the bank, and began to unload his mule.

Chapter VIII

Jim slapped a big chunk of elk meat onto the spread-out hide and hacked off a slice with his knife. He cut this into strips about an inch thick, scored them crisscross, and carried them over to the high willow-sapling rack he had built near the big oak tree.

Squaw's work, he thought grumpily, as he added the elk strips to the venison already spread out on the rack. Meat making was not his favorite occupation. He'd done plenty of it, during the years with Tom, when there was no squaw handy to do it for them. But he'd never quite got over the feeling that he was demeaning himself. A man hunted the meat and made his kills; later he ate all the jerky he wanted. But the chore that took place between times was none of his affair.

Still, he reflected as he poked damp fir branches into the slow, smoky fire burning under the rack, it wasn't as bad as the sort of thing Jonnie had been busy with ever since they found the claim a week ago. Swamping brush, cleaning stray saplings out of the clearing, digging up the stumps afterward. What did they want so much open space for? The cabin wasn't going to take all that room.

Jim saw no sense in bothering with a cabin anyway—

counting the new hides, they'd soon have enough to make a good snug tepee, and that forest was full of lodge poles. But Jonnie and Sally wouldn't think much of that idea. He grinned fleetingly at the notion of Sally keeping house in a Crow lodge. No, it had to be a cabin. There was already a growing stack of logs yonder by the fir trees, and he could hear the clear *whack—whack!* of Jonnie's ax back in the woods, trimming another. From the direction of the river came the sound of vigorous splashing and slapping and singing as Sally scrubbed the last grime of the trail out of jeans and petticoats.

Jim turned from the fire as Dan'l emerged from the woods —Moki, almost invisible beneath a load of firewood, stalking sulkily at his side.

Jim laughed aloud at the expression on the dog's face. That morning, to Dan'l's fascinated delight, he had rigged a travois —two poles harnessed to the dog's shoulders and lashed together at the far ends to trail the ground, forming a crude sled —and it was on this the wood was piled. Moki hadn't suffered this indignity since he'd carried Red Deer's wood in Absaroka, and there was lugubrious self-pity in every line of his body.

Jim leaned against the meat rack, shaking with mirth. "*Wagh!* Ain't you mistreated!"

Moki whined piteously, making a terrific show of effort as he staggered forward, straining at his load. Jim only laughed harder, but Dan'l looked worried.

"Honest, Jim, I'm scared I piled too much on him. I know you said he could pull a lot, but, gee, lookit the way he's walkin'! You reckon I've hurt him?"

"He'll live," drawled Jim. He reached out and took a piece of elk off the meat rack, dropping it to the ground. The effect on Moki was instantaneous. He trotted forward as springily as if the pile of branches was so many feathers, sank to the grass between his shafts, and began gnawing the tidbit.

"Well lookit that!" exclaimed Dan'l in disgust. "Here I been feelin' so sorry for him—!"

"He ain't nothin' but a old faker," Jim chuckled, leaning over to loosen the dog's harness and drag the travois aside. "Him and that cussed mule, they don't take to work no more'n I do."

He turned ruefully to the spot sheltered by the spreading branches of the big oak, where he had a couple of hides pegged out on the ground. More squaw's work! But they were good hides, and he didn't trust these sloppy Multonomah Indians around here to do a decent job of tanning them.

"Want a chore?" he asked Dan'l.

"If it's *your* kind of chore!"

Jim grinned at him and pointed to the graining tool lying on the ground nearby—a curved bone in which an iron blade had been seated. "See how that fits yer fist."

He walked to the oak tree and squatted by the nearest hide, looking it over critically. Then he pegged out the new elk skin beside it, hair side down, and set Dan'l to work, happily scraping off all the flesh and sinew.

As Jim went back to his meat making he was again conscious of the sounds of bourgeway activity from all directions. There was a muffled crash from the woods that meant another tree was down. From the water's edge rose the sound of splashing paddles, and voices shouting greetings. The Rutledges, to the twins' and Sally's mutual delight, had settled directly across the river, and a day seldom passed without the scrape of a canoe prow or the bump of a log raft against one bank or the other as the two families shuttled back and forth on neighborly errands. Jim's knife slashed irritably into the elk carcass. All this banging and whacking and chattering and coming and going—a man couldn't hear himself think.

But Sally and Jonnie thrived on this life. Both of them worked every day from sunrise to dark and never seemed to mind. They were bursting with plans. Any free minute Jonnie had, he spent striding about the glades and along the creek, planning the cattle shed here, the first wheat field there. In the evenings he sprawled beside the supper fire ciphering in the dirt with a stick to find out how many bushels to the acre he'd have to get to pay their debt at the Hudson's Bay post in Willamette Falls.

Sally was the same. Chattering vigorously, to anyone who would listen, of a future cozy with rose bushes, kitchen curtains, and quilted counterpanes, she dealt just as vigorously meanwhile with the drudgeries of the present—scrubbing and mending, making candles and soap out of the by-products of Jim's hunting, airing blankets and patching shirts. Jim marveled at her. Nothing daunted her; she'd put up with any hardship or tackle any chore, so long as it had to do with making a home. And she still found energy for determined little attacks on the more uncivilized of Jim's ways—his erratic notions of when it was time to eat, his habit of cleaning his knife on his shirt front, his persistence in wearing at his belt that little horn of castoreum, which she declared made him smell like a whole passel of wild animals. She reminded Jim of a hummingbird—tiny, beautiful, and fierce.

He was just finishing with the elk when she appeared on the steep path from the river, lugging the big basket of wrung-out clothes. Even Jim, unaccustomed as he was to taking thought for any squaw, could see that it was too heavy for her. Somewhat sheepishly he walked down and hoisted it to his shoulder, carrying it up to the oak whose spreading branches she used for clothesline.

"Well, thanks," she said in surprise. Then she flapped out a shirt and tossed it over the branch. "Dan'l honey, did you catch any fish this mornin'?"

"Too busy totin' wood," the boy answered, pointing to the travois.

98

"Then we'll eat the rest of the deer haunch. Run fetch it out of the wagon while I finish hangin' these things, then call Jonnie in. It's most noon. My stars, don't the days fly."

Half an hour later, as the four of them sat together finishing the last of the cold haunch, Jim frowned and looked around to the east. In a moment he got up and walked to the edge of the clearing to stare downriver.

"What's wrong?" Jonnie asked him.

"Somebody comin'."

"Why, I don't hear nothin'."

"Use yer eyes, Jonnie! That mule stopped chewin' five minutes ago."

Every head turned to Bad Medicine, who had been grazing up near the fir trees. He was standing motionless, his ears upright and every muscle quivering.

"Well, shucks!" said Jonnie. "Who sets around watchin' a mule chew, anyhow?" He walked over to stand beside Jim, adding, "You ain't serious?"

"Sure, I'm serious." Jim saw the mule's ears go down. "White man," he told Jonnie. And as he noticed birds spurting out of a thicket downstream, and heard a distant chattering of squirrels, "Probably a wagon, too. No more'n half a mile away."

Dan'l dashed up to them. "Say, lookit how Moki's actin'! I think he heard something too!"

"Did he describe it?" inquired Jonathan drily. "Accordin' to the mule, it's a white man with a wagon."

Even Jim had to grin, but he went back to his eating unperturbed by Sally's giggled "I'll believe all that when I see it!"

Ten minutes later a tall gray horse cantered into the clearing, bearing a big, tow-headed, square-shouldered boy with a sack of corn meal under his arm and an air of holiday making.

"Fetch out that banjo, Jonnie!" he yelled. "You're about to have a passel of company!"

Jonnie let out a whoop and ran toward him, Sally and Dan'l right behind. "Sam Mullins, by all that's holy! Ain't seen you since The Dalles—how's your mother? Where's your claim at?"

"Company, Sam? My stars, what company?"

"Ever'body you know! They's a wagonload right behind me—Dan'l, how's the boy? Miss Sally, I got a little present for you. Just some ol' meal, but it'll fill these folks up. Don't you worry, they're bringin' their own grub . . ."

Everybody talked at once as they pulled Sam off his tall gray and towed him across the grass. Jonnie's face was flushed with delight, his long arms swept this way and that as he showed off his property. Sam admired, and commented, and complained about Oregon rain and his own poverty, lugubriously pulling his pockets inside out while Jonnie flung back his dark head and roared with laughter.

"Man, you ain't the only one! Sis, here, she's got patchin' down to a fine art. Sam, you gotta meet my brother. Jim, hey Jim! Shake hands with the best doggone coyote shooter and cattle doctor ever come out of Kentucky! Dan'l, run fast and yell for the Rutledges to hustle on over here. Sis, you and me better hunt up somethin' for all them folks to set on."

Jim shook hands, hearing the squeal of wagon wheels even as he did so. He liked Sam's looks and self-conscious grin, but found himself tongue tied. Sam was too, suddenly; he shifted his feet and darted glances at Jim's necklace, and a few moments later loped off hastily as his trail-widowed mother arrived with the Millses.

Behind the Millses came the Howards, the Burkes, the young Selways—all the others of the wagon train who had settled within a twenty-mile radius of the Kearhs. To Jim, it seemed that the whole world was suddenly converging on the clearing. But Jonnie and Sally were in their element, pumping hands and shouting delighted greetings, dragging out crates and boxes and blankets in lieu of chairs. The glades became cluttered with wagons and saddle horses. Shouts rang from the river as canoes were beached, and children tumbled out of them to run whooping and chasing through the fir grove and over the glades. Men slapped each other on the back and reminisced about the Plains and the Snake crossing, talked crops and plans and bushels to the acre; women swapped bread recipes and croup remedies and rose slips until Jim was ready to cut loose and run. Jonnie kept pulling him forward to shake hands with somebody, then turning to welcome somebody else, leaving Jim surrounded by stares. Jim stood it about half an hour, then disappeared.

Rutledge discovered him a little later, lurking on the farthest outskirts of the crowd, prowling nervously between woods and river and keeping a sharp eye on Moki, who was as jumpy as he was.

"Why, son, I was wonderin' where you'd got to," said the man kindly. "No need to be shy of these folks, you know."

"Make too thunderin' much racket!" mumbled Jim.

Rutledge laughed. "They're a mite noisy, I'll give you that. But it's the first time we've all been together since The Dalles, and they's a lot to catch up on. A lot to celebrate, too, by golly! Besides, there ain't no danger around here, these valley Injuns are friendly. Folks are safe when they's this many of 'em together."

"Safe. *Wagh!* I feel safer when they ain't a bourgeway within twenty mile! Look there—what's Jonnie fixin' to do now?"

"Why, he's gonna give us a tune or two!" Rutledge spoke reminiscently. "Dunno how we'd've got acrost them prairies

101

without that youngster and his banjo. We had some mighty fine times around the fire at night, with the wagons drawn around close."

He ambled away a moment later, but Jim didn't notice. He was too busy watching Jonnie, perched on the tailpiece of a wagon with one knee cocked up and the banjo slanted across his tough, lean body. He was laughing, and the curly black lock that always fell over his forehead jiggled in time to the melody he was plucking from the strings.

Jim caught only a few notes through the fresh wave of merriment that rose as Ned Rutledge drew Sally to her feet, called out something to the crowd that was gathering in a laughing, clapping circle around him. In an instant three more couples were in the center of the circle and a dance had started —the gayest, most rollicking dance Jim had ever seen.

The heavy-booted men suddenly found a lusty grace, stamping and pivoting and swinging their partners in response to the orders Jonnie was chanting as he strummed out the music. The watchers clapped and roared encouragement, the dancers circled and spun, crossed and recrossed and wove in and out, the women's skirts swirling like opened flowers, the patterns of movement flashing swift and intricate but always coming out just right.

Jim had forgotten all about watching for danger; his rifle trailed useless from his hand and his ears were full of the banjo. Jonnie's medicine was powerful indeed, for it could make folks forget the miles ahead and the miles behind, forget trouble and a strange land and loneliness at least for a while.

With a final whirl the dance broke up into a flurry of laughter and panting people. New squares formed, and Jim, absorbed in the rhythms of a different tune, did not see Sally detach herself from a chattering group and start in his direction. She was within a few yards of him before he noticed her. Her cheeks were flushed and her eyes bright.

"James—come dance with us!"

"Me?" He took an involuntary step backward. "No. I— I— No."

"It's fun, I'll teach you. I will, James." She hesitated, then moved toward him tentatively and stretched out one hand— her first gesture across that invisible line. "You're just standin' here all alone—"

He longed to grasp the slim hand held out to him, let it draw him into that charmed circle where the others lived. Could he—? Then a fresh burst of merriment from the dancers brought all his shyness back. He turned and fled through the trees, plunging deeper and deeper into the tangle of oak and wild plum and hazel until both music and laughter had faded and there came to his ears only the small, secret noises he knew and trusted—the whir of a wing, a crow's call, the wind.

Let them go on and dance, he wasn't going to go back there and be stared at. Let them all crowd around Jonnie—

He stayed away, prowling aimlessly among the trees or hurling pebbles into the dark, clear river, until the night dropped down and he knew the last wagon would be gone. And the next morning, spotting the Rutledge twins paddling across bursting to talk it all over with Sally, he abruptly went off hunting.

Jim spent much of his time hunting, those first few weeks. But even as he rode through virgin forest and along the banks of wild little streams he could hear the ring of axes, the distant shouts of men to their oxen, from the other claims round about.

In spite of himself, he grew more and more curious about the bourgeways and their ideas, their hard-bitten, good-humored faces and their ceaseless labors. Why did they want to fight this good country so? Why did they insist on growing wheat and raising potatoes, when they could fill their stew pots every day in the year from woods and streams? Why must they mark off a tiny space of ground and chain themselves to it, when they could have a thousand square miles to wander in?

He could not quite put down the queer fascination he felt for these peoples' clothes and belongings. He would lurk in the trees surrounding a new-built cabin, watching a man sharpening a plow or uncrating a massive sideboard, or a sunbonneted woman unpacking cups and plates and pewter spoons. Then he would ride slowly on to his deer tracking.

One day it was a smell that stirred him. He had made his kill—a good young buck—and was riding home at his leisure, eating a chunk of warm raw liver off the point of his knife, with Moki trotting alongside and the laden mule clopping behind. He had just splashed across the stream that bordered the Mills' claim when an enticing, oddly familiar odor drifted to his nostrils. What was that? Something from long ago.

He left the animals in a thicket and crept forward. Through the trees he could see the Mills' half-finished cabin, and the cook fire that smoldered near a battered wagon. He watched a woman take a steaming skillet from the ashes; then, unbearably attracted by that half-remembered fragrance, he left the trees and moved across the clearing, still chewing the last of the liver. He had no thought of sneaking up on her, but his moccasins made no sound, and when she turned she found a feathered Indian at her elbow, his face, hands, and carelessly held knife smeared with blood.

She dropped the skillet and let out a screech that frightened Jim fully as much as he had frightened her.

"What the Sam Hill—" gasped Mr. Mills, stumbling around

the corner of the cabin. He stiffened at sight of Jim, then suddenly relaxed. "Oh, lordy, it's Jonnie Keath's brother. What d'you want, son? It's all right, Martha, will you hush? Nobody's gonna scalp you."

Jim spoke warily. "What's that in the skillet thar?"

"In the skillet? Why, it's hoecake. Good jumpin' jiminy, boy, lookit the blood on you! What you been doin'?"

"Just eatin'."

Mills' wife edged rapidly toward the cabin, motioning back her children, who had appeared from all directions.

"For the land sakes, Ben, give him some hoecake, if that's what he wants. Give him anything!"

Jim rode homeward wondering angrily if they thought he'd been eating bourgeway babies. "Jonnie Keath's brother!" He'd never yet walked into the post at Willamette Falls without hearing that phrase, without feeling curious or doubtful or suspicious eyes follow him down the room.

"Don't worry about it, Jim," Jonnie always advised when he complained about it. "They don't trust you because they don't know you yet. And they've heard a lot of tales—about you keep wolves for pets, and held up the trader at The Dalles with a knife at his throat, and—" Jonnie's white grin would flash. "I do my best to squash all that fool talk, but the truth is, I don't know you very well myself . . ."

Would they ever get to know each other, Jim wondered. He often caught Jonnie studying him as they sat around the supper fire at night, staring at his necklace or his braids or his scars as if trying to penetrate the barrier of those nine years by sheer will power. And Jim did his share of watching and puzzling too, wishing he knew how to make medicine like Jonnie made it—with a warm smile, a banjo, a pair of candid, steady black eyes. Jonnie didn't know how to trap or steal horses or even read sign, but there was never a man who didn't like and trust him on sight.

When Jim reached home with the tale of his bloody hands and Mrs. Mills' reactions, Jonathan laughed until he shook. But then he grew thoughtful. "That'll go the rounds," he said. "Why'n't you steer clear of the other folks for a while, Jim? I can sure use you here." He jerked a thumb toward the meat rack, now dark with much smoking, and the fresh-killed buck and the numerous pegged hides. "Ain't you about through with that job by now?"

"Them hides? No, they got to be sunned some more and then twisted—"

"I mean the huntin'."

Jim looked at him in surprise. "Why, thunder, Jonnie, you don't never git through with huntin', no more'n you git through with eatin'."

"Well, sure. But we got enough meat to last a good while, and we can always get squirrels or fish to fill in. Seems to me the important thing right now is to get our cabin up. With you and me both loggin' . . ."

"You mean you want me to start choppin' trees too?"

"Yeah. Anything wrong with that?"

"No," admitted Jim glumly. "But lookee here. S'pos'n we chop all them trees and sweat a couple weeks more to git this cabin built, and then we want to move on. We can't fold up no cabin and take it with us."

"Move *on*? Good lord a'mighty, who wants to do any more movin'? I had a bellyful of that last summer!" He came around the fire and dropped down on the grass beside Jim. "Why, this is *home*. It's what we come all this way to get. Now we got it we can take root like one of them old fir trees! Don't you get that feelin', Jim? Look yonder at the glades. We'll have them knee-deep in grain by summertime, and a kitchen garden by the woods there, and smoke comin' from our own chimney. This place is *ours*, Jim, soon's the surveyor's been around and you sign that claim. Six hundred and forty acres of it, debt free! Man, I ain't doin' no movin', I'll tell you that! We're stayin' put!"

Jim listened dubiously, envying the glow in his brother's dark face. "I'll help you, Jonnie," he said finally. "I'll start loggin' tomorrow."

Chapter IX

But the next day the surveyor made his appearance, and tree chopping was halted on both Keath and Rutledge claims while the official staking out began. This was entirely all right with Jim. He enjoyed his reprieve until he realized that Jonnie had something on his mind, and the nearer the day drew for signing the papers, the larger that something seemed to grow.

Jim didn't find out what it was until the final day of the surveyor's activities. Everyone gathered at Rutledges' for the noon meal, and Jonnie, Rutledge, and the surveyor left immediately afterward for the measuring and staking of Rutledge's last few acres. Jim hung around restlessly awhile, listening to the girls chatter, then called Moki and started off through the woods that covered half the claim. A few minutes later he heard the men's voices and the clank of the chain, swerved away from them—and suddenly caught the sound of his own name. He stopped, halting Moki. Then, soundless as a shadow, he drifted closer.

". . . ain't had the chance to keep in practice," Jonnie was saying stiffly. "Like he says, there wasn't no books where he was. But it's him got to sign them papers, so I wondered . . ."

"I see. No, he don't have to sign in actual writing," the surveyor answered. "He can make his mark, and the clerk can witness. It'll be just as legal."

"Sure it will, sure it will!" That was Rutledge's voice, deep and reassuring. "Now don't be frettin' about that, Jonnie."

The quiet tones faded, along with the sound of the chain. After a moment Jim wheeled and went his way.

So Jonnie was ashamed of him because he couldn't read and write. Because he hadn't stuck around that farm and worried his head with Pa's figures and ABCs every night long after sensible people had eaten their buffalo ribs and gone to sleep. Well, by gor, there was plenty of learning that couldn't be found in bourgeway books! How to stalk a panther or steal a horse, how to keep the man smell off a trap and throw a knife and know what kind of Injuns were coming before they got there, how to live well and comfortable for years in a country where bourgeways starved or froze or lost their hair to the first 'Rappahoe—!

But suddenly it was unendurable not to be able to write his name too. Maybe he could print it? *Wagh!* A man wouldn't forget a simple thing like that, even if he hadn't tried it for years.

Would he?

Scowling to keep away a prickle of uncertainty, Jim stopped in his tracks and ripped a piece of bark off a nearby tree. Then he drew out his knife and without allowing himself to wonder if it would come out right, he scratched a big "J."

He looked at it belligerently. There. He hadn't forgotten at all. Jonnie Keath's brother could do anything a bourgeway could do.

Now what came next, if you wanted to write "Jim"? Must be *m* from the way the word sounded. But it seemed like there ought to be something in the middle, just "Jm" was too short, wasn't it? He puzzled over it awhile, then decided uneasily that "Jm" were likely enough letters for a name that only took one grunt to say. Now for Keath. K—K—K— *Wagh!* How did you write that sound?

Ten minutes later he flung the much scratched bark against a tree trunk, sheathed his knife, and set off furiously for the river. With a few quick, practiced motions he made a little raft of branches, and stripping, piled his clothes on it. Then he plunged into the cold-running current, the raft trailing from a piece of vine clamped in his teeth and Moki swimming by his side.

But the thing was still nagging at him when he and the dripping dog climbed the bank on the Keath side. He dressed, fished a lump of charcoal out of the dead fire and sat for half an hour making scratchings on the back of a piece of old buffalo hide. Finally he flung the hide away and stalked down through the willows and caught trout in brooding silence until the others poled back across the river late in the afternoon.

"Well I'll swear!" exploded Jonathan when Jim appeared suddenly wading toward them through the shallows. "How'd you get over *here?* Where'd you go? We looked, and called—"

"What'd you do that fer?" Jim grabbed the towline of the raft and beached it with a jolt, hitching the rope around the nearest tree.

"Well, how'd *we* know where you was?" demanded Sally. "You might've told somebody—!"

"I ain't used to tellin' nobody where I go or what I do. Don't reckon to git used to it, neither!"

Jonathan and Sally headed up the slope to the clearing. But Dan'l hung back. "Hey, Jim, your hair's all wet. Didja swim that river?"

"Sure."

"Cracky! I bet I could do it too, you know it? But sis'd never let me go swimmin' in winter."

"*Wagh!* What's winter got to do with it? In Absaroka, warn't a week went by all year that the boys warn't called out."

"Called out?"

Jim nodded. "They was rivers thar, too. Fast ones. Cold ones. Somebody'd stick his head in your tepee—it might be black night—and he'd say 'Follow.' "

The picture sprang, vivid, into his mind, and the sensations. Creeping out, shivering with fearful excitement, to join the gathering crowd of boys. No telling where the strong young man ahead was leading so silently, or what he would require of you. It would be Eye of the Bear, or Steals Horses, or maybe Hides His Face, who always wore a buckskin mask to conceal his battletorn jaws.

"He'd strip, at the edge of the woods, and so would we," Jim went on huskily. "Then he'd start runnin' and never stop till he done a flip-flop into the river and swim a mile upstream. And by gor, we better follow! Winter or not. We learnt to swim dodgin' ice floes."

"Ice! But why?"

"Makes you quick and tough. Besides," Jim added, "it's handy to know how. Sometimes when you git older you gotta dodge other things in rivers."

"Like what?"

"Like Sioux bullets."

"Cracky!" Dan'l glanced uncertainly at the water. "I wanta be quick and tough too. But it looks awful cold."

"Why, thunder, this weather ain't nothin'!" Jim started up the bank toward the clearing. "I've trapped beaver streams so cold yer leggins would freeze to the float stick if you warn't careful."

"Float stick? What's that?"

Jim halted. "Why—why the float stick! Ain't you never even seen a beaver trap?"

"No, you got one, Jim? Show me, will ya?"

The sun had sunk into a low bank of clouds, and the woods were dusky. It was just the right hour.

"Come on," Jim said suddenly. "We're gonna hunt up along that creek back yonder till we find beaver sign. Then we're gonna sink us a trap."

He found his traps where he had cached them, in the dry hollow of a stump near the big oak tree. As he crossed the clearing to head for the woods, Dan'l cavorting breathless with excitement at his heels, Jonathan looked up from the fire he was building.

"Dan'l! Where you off to?"

"Just up the creek. It's awright, I'm with Jim."

"But it's supper time!" protested Sally.

Jim frowned impatiently and kept walking. "It ain't supper time till you're hungry. I ain't hungry."

"But you will be, later!"

"Then I'll eat later!"

"Me too," chimed in Dan'l loftily. "I ain't hungry neither. Me and Jim, we got trappin' to tend to."

Jim plunged into the woods. Likely he ought to make the boy do like Sally wanted. *Wagh!* forgit it, he told himself. I hardly seen the boy lately.

He took his time moving up the creek, teaching Dan'l to watch for tooth marks on bark, for collections of twigs and mud, for any sign of a slide on the edge of a pool. He began the boy's training in walking silently, too, in the fine new moccasins—the gaudiest in Willamette Falls. Jim had paid a plew for them the other day over Sally's disapproving protests.

They were half a mile upcreek from the river when he spotted unmistakably fresh beaver sign. He stopped. This was not the half-demolished old dam or deserted lodge he'd expected to show Dan'l. That branch wedged between two rocks in midstream had been gnawed, not broken—and no earlier than yesterday. He moved on quickly, almost forget-ting the boy behind him, and found a track, and a moment later a slide entering a half-dammed pool. Dan'l was tugging at his sleeve now, pointing excitedly. Jim nodded approval; the boy's eye was quick. He beckoned and led the way into the stream, unslinging one of the traps. Beaver still left, in this valley trapped and retrapped for years by Hudson's Bay Frenchmen! He could hardly believe it.

He motioned the boy to watch while he sank the first trap, made it fast with the trap pole and attached a float stick. The pungent smell of castoreum rose on the air as he uncorked his horn and smeared the bait onto the bent twig. Splashing all the man scent into oblivion, he went on upstream to another likely spot, and this time handed the trap to Dan'l.

"Do it all by myself?" breathed the boy in a tense whisper. When Jim nodded he looked scared, then fell resolutely to work.

Jim grinned, wondering if a thing had ever been done more carefully. He helped Dan'l jam the trap pole firmly into the mud of the creek bottom, then smiled as the boy surrepti-tiously rubbed a little castoreum onto himself as he baited the twig. One person, at least, liked the way Jim Keath smelled!

When they had again splashed out their tracks and were a safe distance away downstream, Dan'l let out his breath in a tremulous sigh of excitement. "Did I do it right?" he asked anxiously.

"Yeah."

"Just *exactly* right? I didn't forget nothin'?"

"Nope."

Dan'l took another long breath. He sounded—and looked—as if he were about to explode. "I've learned a sight of things from you, Jim," he said, his voice solemn with pride. "I betcha I wouldn't'a learned half as much in a whole year of doin' arithmetic."

Jim walked awhile in silence, then slowed his steps to a loiter. "Pa teach you to do 'rithmetic?" he asked idly.

"Oh, cracky yes!" groaned Dan'l. "And then Jonnie, after Pa died. I bet I spent more good time workin' long division than anybody in the world."

"I don't reckon you're much good at writin', though."

"Say, I reckon I am too! That's lots easier'n figgers."

"It is, huh? Let's see you write yer name."

Jim found a loose strip of bark and tore it off, handing it to Dan'l with the lump of charcoal he'd dropped into his pouch earlier. Dan'l rose to the bait instantly, seizing the charcoal with a swagger and scrawling "Daniel Keath" in bold flourishes on the smooth underside of the bark.

"Not bad," admitted Jim. It was actual writing there before him instead of the block printing he had expected. As far as he was concerned, it might as well have been Chinese. Very casually, he added, "Let's see you write mine now."

He didn't breathe again until Dan'l had finished and the bark was in his own hands. "Reckon you'll grow up to be a jedge," he commented.

"Shucks," said Dan'l. "I'd ruther grow up to be a trapper, like you. You think I could, Jim?"

"Mebbe. You learn fast. Come on, we best get movin'."

The bark went into his pouch as soon as the boy's back was turned. It burned there like a hot coal all the time they were walking back to the clearing, all the time he was frying fish for their belated supper, all the time they were eating. He barely heard Sally's fuming about Dan'l's being off in the woods after dark, or noticed Jonathan's thoughtful manner. He waited, outwardly calm, until they had all gone to bed, and until all sounds of restlessness from the wagon had quieted.

Then he moved to the fire, shoved in the logs until the blaze sprang up bright, and fetched the piece if buffalo hide he'd flung away in anger that afternoon. Rubbing off the scrawled markings, he took the bark and charcoal from his pouch, and set grimly to work. The first rays of dawn were in the sky before he unfolded his cramped legs and crept wearily under the grizzly robe.

The following afternoon when he stood with Jonathan in the crude log structure that served as recording office in Willamette Falls, he wondered if he'd been a fool. There were no beaver in the traps this morning, which was a poor omen. In spite of the medicine bundle tied securely to his braid, he wasn't sure he could carry this off.

He listened nervously to the clerk's questions, the agreements, heard the rustle of papers and the scratching of the quill as the forms were made out. But all he was aware of was Jonnie's labored pose of indifference, the clerk's curious eyes, and his own sweating stage fright.

The devil with it! I'll make the mark, he thought. Better to do that much right than make a mess of this other. What's the difference anyway? Don't matter to me what Jonnie thinks.

No use. It mattered.

He took the pen, felt his fingers close over it convulsively. If Jonnie would only quit watching—

Wagh! Yer a squaw! he told himself angrily. You've counted coup on 'Rappahoe and Sioux, you've killed a grizzly. You gonna run from a piece of paper?

Violently he plunged the quill into the ink and bent over those hateful papers. Next minute he had signed a bold, black "JIM KEATH" at the bottom of the page—in writing, with every one of Dan'l's flourishes preserved and embellished.

Jonnie's quick-drawn breath was the most beautiful music he had ever heard. He straightened to meet his brother's eyes. The look in them was worth every moment of that grim and sleepless night.

Jonnie flushed to the hairline suddenly and headed for the door. Outside, he turned a face split by a wide and sheepish grin. "They's times when I wish you didn't walk so quiet. I s'pose you was somewheres in the woods yesterday, hearin' ever' word I said."

"I heerd enough."

"And I s'pose—" Jonnie's smile twisted. "I s'pose you got your own private opinion of me for carin' how the blasted thing was signed?"

"Mebbe. But so long as you did care— Ain't no bourgeway gonna show me up at nothin'! What they kin do, I kin do."

For a moment Jonathan studied him as if he were a riddle without an answer. "Why *did* you do it, anyhow? This time yesterday you didn't know A from Z, and I didn't think you cared. And how did you do it?" As Jim only grinned, he nodded and started toward the horses, laughing. "All right, don't tell me. I'm plenty satisfied just the way things are. Plenty!" He swung himself onto Bad Medicine, catching Buckskin's halter as Jim started past. "Man, do you realize what you just done? That land is *ours* now—ever' tree and bush and stick and stone of it! A whole square mile—"

He dropped Jim's halter suddenly and grasped his own, giving the mule a kick that made him squeal indignantly. "Come on!" he yelled. "Good crimeny, let's get on home! We got a cabin to build!"

Jonnie's excitement was contagious. In a burst of high resolve Jim plunged vigorously into the tedious labor of felling trees, trimming and notching the logs, and dragging them by means of oxen to the cabin site. For a time he did well, and it all seemed worth while, if it earned Jonnie's approval.

But prolonged toil was a foreign thing to him, and since Jonnie did not praise him nor marvel each day at his unaccustomed efforts, but only took them cheerfully for granted, his enthusiasm soon began to wane. The log pile grew with disheartening slowness; meanwhile the river called him, and the unexplored places of the hills. Every time he caught sight of Dan'l he'd think of something else he could teach the boy—games and skills young Talks Alone had learned in Absaroka. He began to drift away from the job whenever a vagrant thought beckoned.

"Lookee there, Dan'l, see them birds shoot up out'n that thicket downstream? They don't act that way less'n they're scared. They's likely a bobcat somewheres close."

"Hey, Dan'l, come up the creek with me a minute. I want to show you a brown bear's track."

More and more he enjoyed the boy's eager companionship, and more and more it cut in on the work both of them were supposed to be doing. Dan'l would vanish upriver in response to Jim's hail, and Sally would have to tote baskets of wash or buckets of water by herself, panting under the load and fuming that a body could never find that boy these days when there was work to be done. Or Jim would drag a new log to the heaping pile and then let the oxen stand idle while he showed Dan'l a medicine root he had found, or sniffed a changing wind, or followed the free circling of a hawk far overhead.

One day he was lounging against the log pile aimlessly tossing a small white object in his hand, when Dan'l glanced up from his whittling.

"Hey, Jim, what is that little thing? C'n I see it?"

"Sure. It's a little magic bone."

"A what?" Dan'l dropped the trencher he was supposed to finish by noontime, and ran over for a closer look. "Why, it is a bone, ain't it? All carved and polished. What's it for?"

"To play a game with. You try to guess which hand I'm holdin' it in, and I try to keep you from knowin'. Here, I'll show you."

So Jim arranged sticks and pebbles for wagers, telling of the trappers he'd seen lose a whole season's catch in half an hour, or the Indians who'd gambled themselves horseless, penniless, and even wifeless, playing the hand game. But it could make you rich, too, just as quick. You might go back to your lodge piled with hides and beads and weapons. "All depends on how you make the magic," he confided, his voice dropping cautiously. "The spirits'll work fer you if you sing to 'em just so—"

Stretching his hands toward the boy, he worked them against each other, chanting softly. "Natinachabena, ni nananaechana! Ni nananaechana! Na—tinacha—ben—ahh!"

He flung his closed fists wide part, and Dan'l, who had been watching breathlessly to discover in which direction the agile brown fingers had maneuvered the bone, shouted "That one!" and pointed to the right fist.

Jim grinned and scooped in the "bet" with a moccasined toe, revealing the bone in his left hand. "Watch closer. I'll do it agin and then you kin try."

Jonnie found them still at it when he strode in from the woods half an hour later in search of the overdue oxen. Dan'l stood triumphant guard over a growing pile of sticks and pebbles, and from his lips came a crooning, guttural chant.

"For the lova creation, what's goin' on around here, anyhow?" Jonathan exploded. "Is that young'un talkin' Injun?"

Dan'l turned eagerly. "It's the hand-game song, Jonnie. See all my horses and war shields on the ground there? Jim's got to guess which hand I've got the bone in, see, and—"

"Yeah, I see, all right." Jonnie's black eyes moved from the little hoard of rubbish to Jim's face. "Teachin' the boy to gamble?"

"Why not?" Beneath his outward carelessness Jim was puzzled and a little worried. Jonnie was angry, but why? In Absaroka everybody played the hand game; ponies changed hands so often no boy rode the same one two days in a row. "What's wrong with a game, Jonnie?"

But Jonathan didn't answer him directly. He turned instead to the boy. "Listen to me, Dan'l," he said gently. "They's plenty of old-fashioned American ways to throw away your money without learnin' any Injun ones."

"But shucks, Jonnie—"

"Wait. I ain't through. Dan'l, remember the mornin' after Mother died? When you and me talked? Remember what I said we had to do?"

"Sure! You said we must take care of sis."

"What else?"

"Well, and get us all out here where Mama wanted us to be, and build us a house, and all, and—"

"Yeah." Jonnie was nodding gravely. "And we ain't done yet, are we? I'm still countin' on you. Now you pick up that clasp knife and trencher and start earnin' your keep!" His voice was stern, but he reached out to rumple the bright hair before he turned back to Jim. "I've had a log finished and waitin' back yonder for a good thirty minutes. Let's get them oxen back to work."

"*Wagh!* Let 'em rest for onct. What's the hurry? Come on upriver with me, we'll git us a squirrel or two fer supper."

Jonnie's palms rubbed slowly against his jeans. "Sorry. I got a cabin to build," he said briefly, and headed for the woods.

Jim followed, irritably aware of his own promise to help. But why did everything have to be done Jonnie's way? Promise or no promise, a fellow had to cut loose sometimes and just be himself!

At length the tedious chore was done, the last log dumped on the pile, the last shake split for shingling, innumerable pegs whittled to substitute for unobtainable nails. The Rutledges had not been idle either, and the two families planned to join forces in raising the cabins now all was ready. It took brawn and numbers to lift the heavy ridge poles into place and weight the loose-laid shakes of the roof with braced poles. One evening Ned Rutledge crossed the river to announce that they were all set.

"So're we," Jonnie told him triumphantly. "But they's more of you, so we'll start on yours first. We'll be over bright and early in the mornin'."

They were astir at daybreak. The delicate rose of the sky over the fir trees promised a clear day, the air was mild, and Jim found himself whistling softly as he gathered wood. The younger Keaths were bustling here and there, filled with the happy urgency of much to be done.

Then Dan'l, on his way back to the breakfast fire with a bucket of water, noticed Jim's bow hanging on a branch of the oak tree under which were spread the grizzly robe and pack.

"Hey, Jim!" yelled the boy, running up the slope waving the bow excitedly while water splashed in every direction. "Can you shoot this thing?"

"Shoot it? Sure, if I got arrers."

"You got any?"

"Yeah."

"Where? I never seen 'em. I never even seen this before! Where's it been all this time?"

"Slung underneath my possibles. I keep it wrapped up in a hide when I ain't usin' it, that's why you never seen it. They's arrers yonder, in that quiver. Here, have some jerky."

"In a minute. I want to go get them arrows."

Dan'l dropped the bucket and dashed off again, leaving the stout, gaily decorated bow on the ground between Jonnie and Sally. "What'd you carry that thing around for?" Jonathan demanded.

"I use it."

"Use a bow and arrow when you've got a rifle?"

Jim shrugged. "They's times when a bow's handier. You kin let fly a arrer while yer thinkin' about loadin' a rifle."

"Oh, shucks, it don't take so long to load a rifle. Besides, they got sights. You can aim 'em."

Something in Jonathan's tone provoked Jim to argument. "What makes you think you can't aim this? I got plenty nicks in me says different. Let's have that thing, Dan'l."

He slung the quiver to his back, picked up his bow, and rose, scanning the sky. Across the pink and gold of the dawn a crow was flapping. Jim reached over his shoulder. All in the same smooth motion he plucked a feathered shaft from the quiver, flipped it into place, and let fly. As the bowstring twanged, every head craned up. Next instant the crow gave a convulsive jerk and dropped like a stone.

"Cracky!" yelped Dan'l. "Nothin' wrong with that shot! Who says he can't aim it?" he jeered at Jonathan. "Why, Injuns get all the buffalo they want with just a bow and arrow. Injuns can—"

"We ain't Injuns!" snapped Jonathan. "And don't you forget it!"

He got up abruptly, walked with his quick, wading stride over to the wagon, and began gathering tools together. After a moment Jim flung quiver and bow to the ground and followed.

"What's so thunderin' bad about Injuns?" he demanded.

Jonnie's hands slowed, then stopped. Suddenly Jim's anger was gone. In its place was a breathless waiting, a terrible anxiety to hear what Jonathan would say.

The answer came without hedging.

"They're savages. They're murderin', heathen savages."

For a moment Jim was too stunned to say a word. So that's what they thought of the people who'd raised him—what they thought of *him!* But how could anybody think that? Sally was watching him with that same steady, grave regard. She believed it too. And Dan'l's small face was creased with confusion.

Suddenly everything in Jim rose in rebellion. He remembered the deep, quiet eyes of old Many Horses, the Wise One; the patient training of Scalp Necklace, the laughter of the young men around the feast fire. He could almost feel Red Deer's gentle brown hands changing the leaf poultice on his torn chest, see her seamed and smiling face.

He opened his mouth to protest, then stopped abruptly. All unbidden, other pictures flashed into his mind—those same wrinkled brown hands reaching indifferently for a stone to crush the skull of a wounded pet dog; one of those laughing young men brandishing bloody yellow hair on a coupstick; the grim necklace of scalps from which a proud and patient old chieftain had got his name.

He swung away, profoundly shaken. "They was good to me," he insisted. "Warn't fer them I'd be wolf's meat."

"They wasn't so good to some of the folks in our wagon train."

"Sioux, maybe!" Jim burst out. "Comanches! Not Crows!"

"Injuns," said Jonathan relentlessly.

Out of the painful confusion of Jim's thoughts one fact rose clear, and he had to say it. "They're my people, Jonnie. My people."

"No, Jim. *We're* your people. Sally and Dan'l and me. And all the others in this valley."

Jim's face became impassive. He was more Crow than Keath, and he knew it. Maybe he always would be.

Chapter X

Cabin building turned out to be even more confining than tree chopping. Jim went to the Rutledges every morning with the others, but his heart was not in it.

"Cussed lot of trouble to go to, just to have a place to git in out'n the rain!" he remarked to Jonnie one morning as they headed for the raft.

"Rain?" Jonnie gave a laugh. "That ain't quite the point, is it?"

"What is?"

Jonnie shot him an exasperated glance. "Jim, you tryin' to get my goat, or what?" He cast loose the towline with a yank, but when he turned back to Jim he was cheerful again. "You wait'll we get our own cabin built, and start livin' in it. You'll find out the point."

Jim grunted and gave a shove with the pole that sent them into midstream, where the half-finished house became visible through the trees ahead. Point or no point, the solidity of those log walls was beginning to make him acutely uneasy.

Why would folks want to box themselves in that way? The stretched hides of a tepee kept out the weather but not the small sounds you listened for; if danger came you could duck under a loosened flap in any direction and be out, or even slit a wall straight up with your knife and walk through it.

And the sky showed through the smoke hole in the top, and the sun slanted in, and you could dismantle the whole lodge in a few minutes, roll it up and be ready to roam whenever you felt restless.

He was restless enough these days. All work and no fighting, no playing, no chasing or being chased—he felt like a squaw. He would sit back on his heels sometimes on the top log of a wall and look out across the river to their own glades, where Buckskin and Bad Medicine grazed idle. And a cold little ripple of astonishment and uneasiness would run over him. What was he doing, anyway, letting his horse grow fat and tame, and his traps rusty, and his senses dull, while he spent his days building bourgeway cabins? It would outrage Scalp Necklace and the other Crows who had trained him, if they knew. And Tom Rivers—he could imagine Tom's slow, incredulous grin and the dry sort of remark he'd make— "By golly, hoss, so you've turned carpenter! Now that takes some believin'!"

One noon as he leaped down with the others to see what Mrs. Rutledge and the girls had concocted for lunch, he spotted Dan'l sitting by the wagon whittling pegs, and an idea struck him.

He walked past the fire and the sputtering skillets and the bustling womenfolk, loosening the thongs of his shirt as he went. He leaned over Dan'l and quietly spoke one word, "Follow." He waited only long enough to see comprehension dawn on the boy's face, then made for the willows. Dan'l was behind him now, his breath quick and audible as they pushed through the underbrush. Jim stripped to his breechclout and then sprinted for the water. A flat, skimming dive took him with a shock of cold into midstream; he heard a splash and a gasp behind him and smiled, knowing Dan'l had followed. Turning like a beaver, he headed into the current.

He had swum no more than a hundred yards upstream

before he knew his powerful, reaching stroke had carried him far beyond the boy. There he was, bobbing about more than halfway back to the anchored raft, his wet head gleaming in the sun. Beyond, at the landing, the womenfolk were milling about all talking at once. Jim got only snatches of it: ". . . catch their deaths! I declare to goodness . . ." ". . . ashore this minute, Dan'l Keath!" "Oh mercy, oh oh oh, that water's *freezin'* cold—" that was Bess, the timid Rutledge twin. And Maggie, the irrepressible, giggled, "Looks like fun, though!" Ned and his father stood silent, and grinning. Jonathan was nowhere to be seen.

Jim grinned too, and drifted lazily back. When he reached Dan'l he hooked a strong wrist under the boy's armpit and said, "How about it? Want to go ashore?"

Dan'l dangled happily, puffing and spitting. "Not till you're —tired—by cracky!"

"All right, then. You're gonna dodge bullets awhile."

Jim loosed him and sank beneath the surface, then with a quick lash of his body angled headfirst toward the river bottom. When he came up he was twenty feet away and had a handful of pebbles. He began throwing them at Dan'l with wicked precision, ignoring the fresh storm that broke out from the bank downstream, and noting with satisfaction that the boy was dodging almost all of them, tired as he was. He had the makings of a good wily swimmer.

Suddenly something struck him behind the ear with stinging force. He dived instinctively, came up in a different spot, and to his astonishment saw Jonathan swimming toward him from farther upstream, his bare shoulders white against the clear brown water. As soon as he spotted Jim's head, he hurled another pebble. He was grinning and his aim was deadly accurate. Jim's heart gave a leap of excitement as he dodged a third missile and submerged to snatch a handful of fresh ammunition. This was something like!

For five or ten minutes the action was fast and wild enough to suit even Jim. He needed all his skill to dodge Jonathan's "bullets" and yet have time to pepper both brothers as well. Dan'l was yelling with delight and sometimes with pain, Jonathan was laughing and all three were diving, weaving, darting, and thrashing until the water creamed white around them.

At last Jim swam to Dan'l's side, hoisted the puffing little boy to his back as Jonathan appeared beside them.

"Good game," Jonnie said. "Take you on again sometime. By golly, you're good at dodgin' them things."

"You ain't such a slouch yerself."

"How 'bout me?" panted Dan'l in his ear as they started for the shore. "Feel like I—been in a—hailstorm. But did I do—all right?"

"You done fine." Jim tumbled him onto the mossy bank and moved into the willows, shaking water from his braids.

Jonathan was there ahead of him, already thrusting damp legs into his jeans. "Ain't had so much fun in years," Jonnie remarked. "You and me'll have to . . ." The words trailed off.

Jim frowned, looked down at himself to see what Jonnie could be staring at. The scars? They were nothing new by this time. "What's up?" he muttered.

"Jim," said Jonnie thoughtfully, "that bear nigh ruint you, didn't he?"

"He give me a good stiff slap."

"Crimeny!" Jonnie wet his lips. "Someway it never dawned on me— Sure a good thing them Injuns found you."

"Yeah." Jim turned away self-consciously. Lot of fuss about a few scars. Were they all that bad? He'd seen lots worse, like the ones under the buckskin mask of Hides His Face.

Jim found his clothes among the underbrush and had begun

to put them on when Dan'l emerged from the bushes, his fair skin glowing all over from the icy water. Still aware of the scars, Jim reached hastily for his shirt. But Dan'l's grin held the usual dazzled reverence.

"Boy, them are the very *gaudiest* scars I ever seen in my life. Say, that kid Bobbie, at home, he oughta be here! Allus braggin' about his little old tangle with a wildcat! I wisht he could see *this* onct! What's that'n on your neck, Jim?"

"Just a arrer nick." Jim was laughing with relief. "You got a couple bullet holes yerself."

He smiled down at the boy, and Dan'l grinned happily, touching the red splotches that marked where Jim's pebbles had hit. "I'll dodge 'em all next time, you see if I don't. We're gonna do it again, ain't we? With Jonnie, too," he added thoughtfully. "It's fun, all three of us."

"Yeah, all three of us. Get into them jeans now, afore they eat up all the grub out yonder."

He yanked his shirt over his head and reached for his belt, wondering why Jonnie was taking so long about getting dressed. Might be better, he thought with amusement, if they all went out together to take their going over from Sally.

Jonathan was sitting motionless on a mossy rock, one moccasin on and the other dangling from his hand, staring at the river and seeing nothing but the cruel pale sweep of claw marks on a lithe brown body. And a new understanding of the young Absarokee, Talks Alone, was growing in his mind.

No wonder Jim won't hear nothin' against them Crows, he was thinking. If they'd been good to me when I was all tore up like that I'd've thought they was the best folks on earth. By golly, I can see how he feels.

Jonnie made a point, after that, of joining in Jim's and Dan'l's games whenever he got a chance. He shot Jim's bow, tried catching fish with his hands, learned to mend a moccasin

—all in a vain attempt to catch more glimpses of those years in Absaroka that were like a wall between them.

"If we could get Jim's point of view, it'd be half the battle," he told Sally when she asked him indignantly if he planned to turn Injun too.

"Get *his* point of view? He's got to get *ours!* You're just encouragin' him to run wild—and Dan'l too. Neither one of 'em is worth shucks any more at helpin' Mr. Rutledge. That boy's always at Jim's heels. Ain't you noticed?"

"I've noticed," said Jonnie gruffly. She had touched a sore spot. Always before, Dan'l had tagged at *his* heels, copying his walk, quoting his opinions, thinking everything he did was wonderful. He was too proud to admit how much he missed it, too honest to blame the boy. "Easy to see why, sis," he mumbled. "To a young 'un, I ain't a patch on Jim. Besides, all I do nowadays is make Dan'l work. And I can't change that."

"Of course not. We got to change Jim!" Sally's eyes filled suddenly. "We got to fight him, Jonnie, we got to civilize him! Or he'll wind up stealin' Dan'l clean away from us, just like Uncle stole Jim!"

"Sis! Don't talk crazy! Jim'll tame down, he's bound to. Wait'll we get our own cabin built, and he's livin' our way—"

"What makes you think he'll live our way? Maybe he'll never tame."

Jonnie chewed his lip. "If I could get to know how he feels about things—if he'd only talk to me—"

But it was too early for that—or perhaps too late. Jonnie's plan had got out of hand. Jim welcomed him into any and all of his skylarking with Dan'l, but refused to confine it to off hours. When Jonathan wouldn't quit work to go prowling the hills with him, he took the boy anyway. And when Jonnie put his foot down on that, Jim went alone.

Blast it, sis is right, Jonathan thought exasperatedly. The

amount of work he does these days you could put in your eye
—and it's likely my fault for encouragin' him!

He pitched in twice as hard himself, trying to make up for
it; he came back across the river every evening so tired he'd
fall asleep before the meat was cooked. But when at last the
Rutledge cabin was finished and work started on their own,
the situation only got worse. In the morning Jim might buckle
down and do a few hours solid work. By noon he was likely
as not gone.

Tales began to drift back from the settlers round about.
Jim and the old Chinook devil who ran the ferry were getting
thick as thieves, ran the reports. Jim had got in an argument
with a Willamette Falls trader and put a knife through his hat.
Moki had chased an old sow clean around Sam Mullins' claim
while Jim held his sides with laughing.

"Good crimeny, Mr. Rutledge, what'll I do about him?"
Jonnie fumed one day as they hailed Jim for some job and
found he had vanished again. "He'll get us all in trouble first
thing you know. I can keep Dan'l's nose to the grindstone
even if he sulks about it. But Jim's another matter. You can't
boss him and you can't argue with him—no more'n you could
with a loaded gun."

"Let 'im go, bide your time, Jonnie," Mr. Rutledge told
him. "Jim's restless and mixed up, he don't know what he
wants, right now. Just bide your time—you can't make a lone
wolf into a house dog overnight."

So Jonnie took what help he got from Jim, and bided his
time with as good grace as he could muster, while heavier
and heavier on his shoulders settled full responsibility for the
cabin. It was up to him, and him alone, he saw that now. Jim
just didn't care.

All right, he thought fiercely. I'll do it alone, then. I promised Mother and I'll do it if it takes me a year.

He himself loved every log and shingle of it, despite the

129

hundred small miscalculations and unforeseen difficulties that beset him every day. He could hardly wait for the hour he could walk in the door and look around him at four sturdy walls, and know he was home. Jim would care then, he couldn't help it! That was the hour, Jonnie felt it in his bones, that Jim would come home too.

And at last the time came; early one afternoon toward the end of December, the house was complete. They stood in a row, all four of them, and looked at it in silence. It was a rectangular log building, mud chinked and crude, small against its background of towering firs. But to Jonnie it was beautiful beyond compare.

His eyes went over it possessively, anxiously, lingering on the buffalo robe hung over the entrance, the rough stones of the doorstep, the logs whose every chink and ax mark he knew intimately. Have to build a real door soon, he thought. Couple windows, too, first chance I get, and put Sally down a puncheon floor. Gotta build shelves and a table and somethin' to set on, and that chimney ain't much more'n a hole in the roof.

No matter. Out of that hole a thread of smoke curled up triumphantly. The clearing had a home in it.

Sally's tanned face was radiant under its halo of blonde tendrils. "I can't hardly believe it!" she whispered. "But yonder it is. Jonnie, I know it don't have a stick of furniture in it, but let's sleep there tonight. We could cut fir branches—and with mother's feather bed . . ."

"You bet we will!" Jonnie was remembering her sleeping on boxes, on prairie grass, in spray-drenched blankets. "You just bet we will! It's early yet, I'll bring in what we got and you can fix it to suit yourself. Dan'l—"

"I'll get the branches," offered Dan'l eagerly. "Remember, me and Jim's gonna sleep in the loft!"

He dashed off toward the fir grove, Sally hurried into the

cabin, and Jonathan started for the wagon. But Jim still stood silent and tense, a curious expression in his tawny eyes—almost like fear.

"Jim, what's the matter?"

"Nothin'." Jim turned, the expression vanishing under his usual impassive mask. "What d'we do now, unload the wagon?"

"Yeah. There ain't much. We had to throw stuff out all along the trail, the oxen was gettin' so starved and played out. But we'll cart in what there is."

He led the way to the wagon. This was the time he'd been waiting for, and he was banking on it heavily.

Hoping with all his heart, he began to unload the wagon. One by one, the crates and barrels and bits of furniture that had jolted the long miles across the wilderness were carried into their new home. There was little enough, but Jonnie knew and felt affection for each piece—a stool or two, Sally's little rosewood lap desk, the feather bed, and a small chest of drawers, the big Bible, some kitchen things—and the clock.

"Oh, blast it, sis," Jonnie said as he lifted it carefully from its packings. "I think it's broke inside. Hear that rattle? We'll likely never get it to run."

"Never mind." Almost tenderly she picked away the last bits of straw adhering to it. "We'll put it on that shelf over the hearth just like Mother done at home. It don't matter whether it runs or not. It's so beautiful."

Jonathan nodded agreement. It was beautiful. It was the only really beautiful thing his mother had ever owned, and she had loved it dearly. It was tall as a man's knee, made of bronze. The stem of the fat brass pendulum was concealed by a wooden panel painted with shepherdesses and cupids in a woodland glade.

"There," Jonnie said, setting it carefully on the shelf. "Now where's that little leather box? Jim, did you—"

He stopped again. Jim's face had gone quite pale under its deep tan.

"Jonnie," Jim breathed. "I'd forgot about that clock."

They stared at him in dismay. How could he have forgotten the clock, in nine years or even ninety? The whole Keath household had centered about it. Pa's nightly winding of it had always been a solemn ritual, and so was Mother's careful daily dusting. The narrow space underneath it had been used from time immemorial as a sort of strongbox; the door key lived there, Pa's medal from the war of 1812, a letter Grandfather Keath had once received from General Washington, Mother's egg money. The Bible always rested on the shelf beside the clock, Pa's dreaded hickory switch leaned against it, and every Keath child had heard from infancy the tale of its long journey from France in Mother's great-grandmother's trunk.

If Jim had forgotten that clock he had forgotten everything that used to be, everything he himself once was. Jonnie thought of the scars, and realized how it could have happened. But he realized also, that the whole process was being reversed now. Memories were flooding back.

He seized the moment. With one step he was across the room and opening the leather box Sally had placed on the dresser. In it were the family treasures—the medal, the letter, and the rest—and two other things his mother had clung to until the day she died, for they were all she had of Jim. One was a yellowed baby cap, which Jonnie laid on the dresser without comment, but making sure Jim saw it. The other was the picture.

It was a faded but curiously lifelike drawing of two small boys in stiff collars and bunchy suits, one sitting, the other standing behind him.

Jonnie held the picture out to Jim. "Know who that is?"

Jim wet his lips and nodded. He turned abruptly and

moved to the doorway. Then he swung back. "Some folks say we still look alike," he burst out.

"Been a long time since you looked like Jonnie," Sally said evenly.

"Oh, I dunno," Jonathan said. "I think we still resemble. That is, we would if—" he stopped short, but the damage was done.

"Yes, *if!*" Sally was moving forward like a cat about to pounce. Her eyes were on Jim, but her mind, Jonnie knew, was on that treasured baby cap and a grave by the Sweetwater. Too late, he opened his mouth to stop her. She was already talking. "*If* you'd cut them braids off. *If* you'd throw away that heathen necklace and get rid of that feather!"

"Cut off my *braids?* Get rid of my *coup feather?*"

"Why not? What use is it 'cept to make folks think you're Injun when you ain't?"

"Sis, wait!" snapped Jonathan.

But now Jim's mouth was as rebellious as it had been in the old picture. "You don't get rid of Pa's medal, do you?"

"My stars, what's that got to do with it?"

Jonnie cut in sharply. "It's the same thing to Jim, sis. Can't you see? It's the same thing!"

"The same as Pa's medal?" cried Sally. Suspiciously, she added, "What'd he do to win it?"

Jim opened his mouth to answer, then all at once clamped it shut. "I counted coup," he said at last defiantly. "A heap of times, not just onct. I could wear a dozen feathers if I was a mind to."

"I just bet you could! And I bet I'd rather not know how you got 'em or what they mean!"

"They mean I ain't no coward, that's all."

"Neither's Jonnie!" Sally flung at him. "But he don't deck hisself out like a savage to prove it! James Keath, you listen to me! You ain't in Absaroka now, you're in a civilized valley with civilized folks, livin' in a house again the way you was meant to. You ain't a Injun, you're a Keath, like us! All these things, the clock and all, they're yours, as much as ours. Why won't you cut off them braids and quit lookin' like a heathen? If you ask me—"

"That'll do, Sally!" thundered Jonnie.

But Jim only said softly, "I ain't askin' you." Then he turned and vanished outside.

Jonathan dropped the picture back into the box and glared at Sally. "Now see what you done! You can't crowd Jim, sis! Ain't you found that out?"

"I don't care, I meant it, I— Oh, Jonnie, go fetch him back!"

Jonathan had already plunged out into the misty afternoon. Dan'l, headed for the cabin with a load of branches, was staring perplexed in the direction of the river.

"Where's Jim off to? I thought—"

"Nowhere. Go on in the cabin."

Jonnie ran for the willows. Fifty yards upstream he caught up with Jim and forced himself to speak casually.

"For the lord's sake, Jim, Sally spoke outa turn and she knows it. Come on back. We'll knock off work and just enjoy ourselves the rest of the day—and tonight we can sleep in our new beds. Jim, come home."

Slowly Jim turned, the fine mist glistening on his cheekbones and scarred forehead and rigid chin. "I'll stick to sleepin' outside."

"Outside?" Jonnie's voice hardened. "You mean you ain't gonna live with us in the cabin at all? Ain't we good enough for you? What's wrong with sleepin' under a roof for once?"

"I can't do it."

The finality of the words hung on the quiet air, turning Jonnie wild with disappointment. "You 'can't' do it!" he echoed savagely. Suddenly he was shaking all over. "By golly, you mean you *won't* do it! You won't even try, you won't face up to it, you run away! That's what you been doin' all your life, is run away! Let the goin' get a little tough and you're on your way, you're gone, you're runnin'! And where's it ever got you, that's what I want to know? Where's—"

He stopped, gulping for breath. Jim had vanished noiselessly into the woods.

Jim didn't even want the slight confinement of trapper's clothes. He stripped to his breechclout and moccasins before he fled, in silent haste, north through the woods and over the ridge toward the glades and Buckskin. With the sight of that clock the doors of memory had flown wide open, loosing images as vivid and powerful as when they were fresh, nine years ago. He could see Pa's hand reaching for that hickory stick, hear the harsh voice that had dominated his childhood and finally driven him out of the old home and across the plains after Uncle. And he could see his mother's eyes, as he had seen them everywhere he looked those first few weeks, silently tugging at him to come back. Rebellion, grief, and crushing guilt alternated in him as if the years had never been.

He flung himself on the startled mare and was off like an arrow. He must get the gates closed on the whole thing, it was all he could think of. Never mind what Jonnie said. What right had Jonnie to bring it all back? And Sally! Had she known what she was saying? Cut off his braids, throw away his feather of valor—in short, deny that he was a Crow and a warrior and so enrage his helpers that the medicine would never work for him again! Well, they couldn't do it, he wouldn't stand for it. They could take him as he was or not at all, and it was time they knew it.

Rebellion flared higher now than guilt, fury swept through him. He streaked up hills and down gullies and across meadows, the wind flowing past his naked body, Buckskin's smooth muscles swelling and rippling against his thighs and her white mane waving like a banner. He would show the whole valley who it was and what it was that they dared to tamper with! Jonnie Keath's brother, *wagh!* He would show them Talks Alone the son of Scalp Necklace.

That was the day the rumors began to spread from cabin to cabin all up and down the east side of the broad Willamette; the day that settlers from the outskirts kept riding in to the post at Willamette Falls on lathered ponies shouting warnings of an imminent Indian uprising. No, not these sleepy Chinooks or Multnomahs, but real wild Injuns. No telling what kind, they'd only got a glimpse of one of them and that was enough—riding naked, he was, on a horse swifter than an antelope, and yelling bloody murder and shooting in all directions and scaring the wits out of the stock.

Later reports revealed that the horse was ten feet tall and the Injun's face painted for war. Still others insisted it was blood that streaked his cheeks and chest, and children were snatched from play and herded to safety behind bolted doors. Horses began to vanish—three saddle ponies were discovered missing from a claim about five miles upriver and several others from cabins beyond that. Eventually all were found tied to a tree at the edge of the placid village of Multnomah Indians down Champoeg way, and feeling ran high until it was discovered that the Multnomahs themselves were in an uproar from a late afternoon visitation which they insisted must be supernatural—a lone warrior whose paint nobody recognized, with the golden eyes of a wolf and the scars of a demigod's battle, whose horse's mane was made of white flame and who was totally impervious to the hail of bullets that followed him out of the village.

About moonrise that night—for the clouds had pulled apart to show patches of stars and the white glow edging piled black thunderheads—Jim and Buckskin trailed slowly home. There was a foul taste in Jim's mouth, his throat ached from yelling, and he had a bullet furrow in the side of his neck. But the gates of memory were shut—for the moment.

He wondered bewilderedly why he was coming back at all. Because he'd left the mule and Moki there, he told himself. Because he couldn't bear to part from Dan'l. Because the medicine song was pulling him back against his will and his common sense to the still waters and green pastures, so that its painful, incomprehensible magic could be fulfilled in spite of him.

It wasn't because of anything Jonnie had said, by thunder, he knew that much.

He sighed deeply, stopped a mile or so down the Tualatin to wash the stripes of vermilion off his face and chest lest Sally see them—no, only because the dried paint was uncomfortable —and then rode slowly home. The cabin was ghostly in the moonlight, the fire was out, the clearing silent. Moki alone slipped out of the shadows to greet him.

Jim dug his fingers into the dog's coarse ruff, clinging fast to him. At last he roused himself enough to eat a fistful of jerky, then wrapped the grizzly robe about him and fell into exhausted sleep.

Chapter XI

In the morning Jim wondered if he could possibly have dreamed the whole thing. Jonathan and Sally greeted him exactly as usual, asked not one question as to where he had been or what he had done, and did their best to pretend the quarrel had never been. This went on for several days. Jim was not urged inside the cabin; where he slept or how he dressed was never mentioned. Even when yesterday's rumors concerning the mysterious Indian with the scars began to drift up the Tualatin, becoming less fanciful and more shrewdly speculative all the time, Jonnie held his peace. He merely advised Jim not to take off his shirt when there were other settlers around.

Jim began to wonder incredulously if he'd won his battle overnight. Then one morning Dan'l asked an innocent question.

"Hey, listen, Jim, how come you don't just go ahead and cut them braids off now? Sis says she's bound she'll make you do it sooner or later."

Jim froze. "A Crow wears his hair long, and I'm a Crow," he said stonily.

"And you ain't gonna live in the cabin?"

"No."

That very day he cut lodge poles in the forest and set them

up beside the big oak tree, lashing them securely at the top and spreading them at the bottom into a roomy circle. Over this framework he stretched his hides—elk, deer, buffalo, anything he had in his possibles, patched out with rabbitskins. He worked on it for several hours, making a back rest and a bed frame of willow and rawhide to furnish it, hanging more hides in a heavy circular curtain inside, stuffing dried grass snugly under the outer edges until it looked uncivilized and good and natural. He moved his pack and his few belongings into it that evening.

The first real break was made. From then on the gulf widened continually. Jim cooked his own food at his own times, eating whenever the mood took him. He lived, dressed, and even bathed in his own wild way—in a sweat lodge he built just upstream from the raft landing. He would disappear into it for long periods with a pile of heated stones, then dash out in a burst of steam to plunge into the icy river and swim till he was exhausted. He took no part in the whittling and pounding and creating with which the others were busy as the cabin slowly acquired benches and shelves and utensils and beds and cupboards. He ranged the hills on Buckskin or brooded on his grizzly robe while the rain drummed on the hides of his lodge, or prowled with Moki and Dan'l through the woods, taking refuge in the only companionship that offered him unqualified approval.

Jonnie, sick at heart, found himself involved in a desperate tug of war over Dan'l. The boy had lost interest in the cabin as soon as Jim did, begging to move out to the tepee too. Refused that in no uncertain terms, he compensated by being with Jim every minute he was not actually engaged in doing chores. There were chores aplenty, but even Jonnie's enthusiasm had dimmed; the work was a burden.

"Seems like we'll never get through with all this, so's I can start clearin' land," he growled irritably one day, more to himself than Dan'l, as the two worked together behind the cabin, Jonnie finishing the last of the bed frames, the boy gouging out the inside of a bowl. "I gotta have wheat planted this spring, or we can't pay off that debt. And a garden— Crimeny, we got to have a garden!"

"Aw, you and Sally, you're allus worryin' about somethin'. We got along just fine settin' on the ground and eatin' our fish and pemmican off of bark with our fingers." Dan'l waved a contemptuous hand at the pile of newly made wooden forks on the grass between them. "What's the good of botherin' with all this fooforaw? You're a regular bourgeway!"

"And you're a regular rubber stamp of Jim Keath!" exploded Jonathan. "By golly, if he says a thing of a mornin', I get it back from you before nightfall! Ain't you got a mind of your own no more?"

"I sure do!" Dan'l came back at him defiantly. "I got a mind to be just like Jim, and you ain't gonna stop me!"

Oh, lord, thought Jonathan, clawing back his tumbled hair wearily. I shouldn't've busted out at him like that, he'll turn clean against me! How do you go about raisin' a young 'un, anyhow? How do you handle 'em?

January slipped into February, with the quiet, constant rain shadowing the valley, and the tepee standing there always before Jonnie's eyes, like a symbol of the split in the family and his inability to mend it.

The cabin at last complete and livable, he turned to his land. The stumps and blackberry thickets began to disappear laboriously, one by one, from the western acres of the glades, where the first wheat field would come into being.

"Jonnie, you look plum beat," Rutledge said one evening as he walked slowly down to the raft landing with a borrowed candle mold. "Ain't Jim helpin' you at all, son?"

"I doubt Jim'll be around much longer, Mr. Rutledge,"

Jonnie said. "When the snows melt up yonder in them mountains he'll go back."

"Jonnie, I bet he don't. Jim's tamed down considerable since I first seen him that day in The Dalles."

"He ain't no more tame than Moki, Mr. Rutledge. Not underneath. Watch him sometime. Watch his eyes."

"I been watchin' him." Rutledge drew deep on his pipe and talked around the stem. "You know, Jonnie, I feel mighty sorry for Jim."

"*Sorry* for him?"

The big man nodded slowly, his eyes thoughtful. "He don't seem to belong nowheres. He ain't a Injun, but he ain't quite a white man neither. He's a kind of a homeless critter."

"That wouldn't bother Jim none," Jonathan said bitterly. "He don't need no home."

Rutledge thought that over, with his huge hand cupped around his pipe and the smoke wreathing his head. "Jonnie, you're wrong," he said at last. "Ain't ever a man born on this earth that don't need a home."

Jonnie tried to believe him, he wanted desperately to believe him, but deep in his heart he couldn't. Jim had stayed away too long. He was too much Injun. It was too late.

Jonnie and Sally were plagued these days by small articles mysteriously disappearing from the cabin and its environs, then reappearing just as mysteriously exactly where they had last been seen; Dan'l was harder than ever to find when there was water to be fetched or wood to be chopped. The more settled and civilized the life around Jim became, the more restless and caged he felt. What did you do with yourself with no enemies to outwit, or sign to read, or distances to gauge, or routes to find, or hazards to watch out for? What did you do when you neither fought nor escaped, were neither hunter nor hunted?

You chopped trees, thought Jim resentfully. You aired blankets and built cabins and tables, and fussed with oxen, and measured off a beaver's worth of land, and built fences around yourself, and turned farmer.

Oh, no, thought Jim. Not me, nobody's gonna build a fence around Talks Alone.

He could go kill a deer, but it seemed foolish. They had plenty of jerky. He could ride up to the falls and talk to the old one-eyed ferryman, Iakhka Tcikeakh—known to the settlers as Jake. The old man's skull was flattened to a point after the manner deemed stylish by his people, and in addition to Chinook jargon he spoke real Chinook—a guttural, clucking, sputtering language which ignored the use of the tongue entirely and had to be croaked out with the lower part of the throat. That had been hilariously amusing—at first. But now it had lost its flavor.

Well, then, he could go out to the new field and grub out stumps along with Jonnie.

And with a scowl Jim would be off up the Tualatin or into the woods, anywhere away from the clearing and everything in it. He was almost ready to buck the gorge again and get clear away, back to Absaroka and the stretching wilderness, or to the cottonwoods rustling along the banks of the quiet beaver streams.

You ran away from Absaroka, too, said a nagging voice inside him. The streams are trapped out now, remember?

But every time the thought of Absaroka drifted across his mind, his games with Dan'l grew a little more reckless. They were playing a new game now, a dangerously exciting one for Jim as well as Dan'l, for it stirred his memory like distant war drums.

It always started out the same way—with Jim leaning over Dan'l unnoticed by the others, and whispering "Follow." Then he would disappear into the oak woods or through the willows, Moki at his heels, and the boy would watch his chance and slip away after him.

"We lost three horses in that Sioux raid yesterday," Jim would say sternly when they came together some distance from the clearing. "And we need three in their place. More if you kin git 'em. I'll wait the count of two hundred afore I stampede their loose stock. Best be outa there afore the alarm spreads."

Eyes shining with excitement, Dan'l would slip stealthily back to the clearing, which in his mind and Jim's had now become a Sioux village. Of course to make everything proper he should be wearing a wolfskin, and a coating of the Absaroka mud that dried gray as a wolf's fur over arms and face. But Jim had reluctantly departed from tradition because the sight of a wolf, so usual as to go unnoticed by the Crow squaws he had outwitted in his own boyhood, would attract Jonathan's immediate and murderous attention. Among bourgeways the best disguise was no disguise at all.

Counting the agreed two hundred, he would drift toward the glades, and a sudden unexplainable disturbance would break out among the animals—the oxen, Buckskin, and the mule.

"Now what are them critters so excited about?" Sally would exclaim, stopping short on her way to the cabin with an armload of brush cuttings.

"Dunno, they keep actin' that-a-way lately." Jonathan would leave off sharpening his ax and frown toward the glades. "Must be some varmint around the woods there."

"Well, they're calmin' down now." Sally would vanish into the cabin, only to emerge a moment later, flushed and exasperated. "Now *where* did them rawhide strings get away to? I cut 'em just special to bind me a broom out of this stuff, and they was right here not five minutes ago!"

"I'll cut you some more, sis. Hey! Where's my knife? Why, it was stuck right in this stump—"

And by this time Dan'l would be off in the woods, proudly dumping in front of Jim the strings, knife, and the squirrel-tail duster Sally had not yet missed.

"Three horses. Good. Kin you count coup?"

"Yeah, Jim—honest, I can this time! I touched Jonnie on the back of his collar afore I took that knife—an' he never even knew I was there!"

Jim's stern mask would vanish before a grin. "All right. When you've counted twenty coups I'll take you to steal a real horse. Now hang around outa sight till the fuss dies down, then go put 'em all back."

But one day Ned Rutledge and his father were in the clearing, lingering on the way back from a trip to Willamette Falls, and Dan'l's "horses" included Ned's jews-harp, which the boy had long coveted. It led him to protest the familiar order to "put 'em all back."

"Shucks, Jim, why do I have to? *You* never used to put back stuff you practiced on!"

"Well, we allus just stole meat off'n the dryin' racks. That's why we wore the wolfskins, 'cause they was allus wolves around stealin' the jerky anyways. But you mustn't ever steal nothin' valuable."

Dan'l frowned up at him, bewildered. "Horses are valuable. Real horses, I mean."

"Oh, well, that's different. Ain't no other way to git a good horse."

Jim paused, frowning a little. Here in this valley, that remark didn't sound quite the simple statement of fact it would have in Absaroka. He thought a minute, then amended slowly, "What I mean is, you don't steal nothin' valuable from yer own people—just yer enemies. Now go take them things back."

But there were no enemies here, he thought after the boy was gone. It was a queer life without them, it was what made this valley so uneasy. You kept feeling there was something missing, that you'd neglected something; you kept listening but not hearing anything except the wind in the trees, or the river whispering to you, or the nagging, insistent sound of Jonnie's ax. Nothing ever happened!

He padded restlessly through the wet woods, feeling as though he'd give almost anything for the sight of a war bonnet and a painted face emerging from the bushes ahead of him, for the sudden spring and the yell splitting the silence, and the wild ferocity blazing up inside himself, with something right there to vent it on. The only enemies he had now were things you couldn't fight—a clock, a cabin, a bleakness in Jonnie's eyes.

He snarled suddenly and broke into a run, dodging between the dripping trees with Moki panting behind, in a spurt for the glades. If he couldn't fight, at least he could ride—fast and hard enough to forget all this for a while.

He broke cover at the top of the ridge behind the cabin and bounded across the open space between the woods and the fir grove, running along its edge until the ground dipped and then flattened out into the broad stretch of the glades. Buckskin was grazing yonder along with the oxen, Rutledge's bay horse, and his own mule. She took fright the moment he darted out of the underbrush toward her, and he raced to cut her off, everything in him responding to the joy of violent action.

Moki, equally delighted, flattened himself into a furry streak and dashed around Buckskin's other flank, yapping and snarling almost under her pounding hoofs. She brought up short in a rear, wheeled and found Jim directly in her path. As she reared again he leaped with her, clinging to the rawhide rope she wore for halter. In another instant he was half on her back, one leg flung over and a hand twisted in her mane, sticking like a burr and yelling with delight as she plunged and raced across the glades. Plastered to her off side, he screeched a war whoop and aimed imaginary arrows over her tossing neck at the oxen milling confusedly on the other side of the field. As the mare swerved at the other end of the glades and turned sharply back, he lashed upright and then down again under her other shoulder, feeling her mane whip his face and the wind tear past as he pressed his cheek against her smooth-rolling muscles.

He was halfway back to the fir grove, laughing at the turmoil he was causing among the rest of the animals, when he caught sight of Jonnie coming down the near side of the ridge. His excitement dimmed instantly.

He fought the overwrought mare into some semblance of control and pulled himself upright, catching the halter into a tight loop. A string of Crow gutturals, alternately cursing and comforting, steadied her to a jerky canter and he halted her with a final wheeling rear alongside his brother.

"What's up?" he demanded, as he slid to the ground.

"Nothin's up. I just come to fetch Mr. Rutledge's horse. I got to watchin' you." Jonnie's eyes met his. "You make a good sight to see, you and that mare."

The words were as direct and simple as the look, and they filled Jim with wonder. Why, it was a truce. Jonnie was tired of this silent war, as tired as he was himself.

Almost afraid to speak for fear of spoiling the moment, Jim muttered, "She's a good horse."

"Fast as light, ain't she?" Jonnie flashed a quick, hesitant smile, then actually laughed as the mare reared impatiently and he sprang out of range of the plunging hoofs. "Crimeny! She's a beauty. But mighty wild."

"I like her wild," Jim admitted. "I scared her a-purpose so's she'd kick up her heels and gimme a little fun. Why'n't *you* try her onct?" he added suddenly.

"What? Me ride that critter? Lord, she'd dump me the first half minute! Plow horses is about all I've ever rode."

"Try her anyhow!" Jim was grinning now, thoroughly pleased with his idea.

"Stand aside, then! No tellin' what'll happen."

Jonnie moved eagerly to the mare's side and was halted by a whoop from Jim. "Hey, hold on! Don't come at her from that side or she'll kick you into the middle of next week! This here's a Injun horse. Git on her from the right."

"The *right?* Feels all backwards." Jonathan circled obediently, then stood there scratching his head and laughing. "By golly, you make it tough enough! No saddle, no stirrups—"

"Grab her mane, she's used to me yankin' on it. Ho, there, Buckskin, take it easy, you skitterin' little squaw." Jim soothed her in the guttural tongue she knew and trusted, while Jonnie grasped a handful of mane and pulled himself astride her. Instantly her head tossed up, jerking the halter from Jim's hand and all but unseating Jonnie. But he only gave a shout of laughter and hung on, sticking with her as she whirled and made off for the far end of the glades. He managed to stay on through her abrupt, snagging turn, and through most of her deerlike flight back. But then Jim saw him tugging on the halter to stop her, and knew trouble was coming.

It came in short order—Buckskin didn't want to stop, she wanted to run. And as soon as Jonnie's tugging grew insistent, she decided she wanted to buck and pitch, too. Jonathan sailed over her head in a graceful curve, landed in a rolling scramble of legs and arms, and sat up, dazedly watching her receding heels.

Jim was laughing so hard he could barely hoist his brother

to his feet. "By gor, that was the prettiest sight I ever see! Any bones broken?"

Jonnie shook his head, after a gingerly investigation of his anatomy. "Darn fool thing to do anyhow," he said with a grin. "I knew I couldn't handle her."

"By gor, you oughta have one you kin! You oughta have *some* kinda horse! Yer allus needin' one."

"I know it, but that don't get me one." Jonnie combed his fingers through his hair. "By golly, I wisht I had one just like Buckskin! After a day of grubbin' stumps . . ."

"Ain't nobody makin' you grub stumps all day long."

Jonnie let it pass. He shrugged and tried to grin, but the barriers were up again between them. "Well, Mr. Rutledge'll be down here in a minute wonderin' if I fell in the creek. I better get his pony—"

He started for the corner to which Rutledge's horse had retreated. Jim watched him go. An idea that struck him as brilliant began to form in his mind. For weeks he'd been wishing he could do something to make Jonnie look at him again —just once—as he had that day in the recorder's office. Now he believed he'd found it.

He started on a run to catch Buckskin. When Jonnie topped the rise back of the cabin, Rutledge's horse in tow, Jim was beside him on the mare, panting a little with exercise and inward excitement, hoping he could get his rifle from the lodge and his medicine bundle from the hollow stump upriver where he'd hidden it safe from prying eyes—and be out of the clearing before anyone asked too many questions.

Chapter XII

But the moment they came in view of the cabin it was obvious that something unusual was afoot.

"Well, look at that!" exclaimed Jonathan, halting in surprise at sight of Sally, Dan'l, and all the Rutledges clustered about four men on horses. "Sam, and Ab Selway, and Mr. Mills, and Mr. Burke. They must've just come. Wonder what's up?"

He started hastily down the slope and Jim followed, frowning because all these visitors were likely to complicate his plan. Rutledge heard them, and turned to shout at Jonathan. "Ain't lost your oxen, have you? They still safe and sound?"

"Why, sure. Why?"

"Some cattle's been stole from up around— Say! Yonder's the fella to help you, folks! Jim, come along over here, will you, son?"

Reluctantly Jim turned Buckskin away from the direction of the lodge and joined Jonathan beside the others. Rutledge looked up at him. "I bet my hat you've had some experience follerin' tracks. Am I right?"

"Sure." Jim slid to the ground, keeping a fast hold on the mare's halter and signaling Moki to keep guard. "You aimin' to ketch a thief?"

"Well, locate him, anyways."

"Whose cattle's stole?" put in Jonathan.

"Mine," spoke up Ben Mills gloomily. He was a thick-set man with a round pink face and rounder blue eyes. "And a couple of Burke's here, and Sam's milk cow. Eight head, altogether. We think they headed north—"

"Injuns?"

"No, a white man, that's sure. They's a boot print in Burke's pasture and another'n just like it at Sam's."

"That's what makes it so touchy." Clyde Burke, a spare, gray-headed man in a battered coonskin cap, scratched his ear uneasily. "It's a white man, likely a settler like us. We gotta go easy, find out where he's at and who it is, then keep an eye on him till the law gets here."

"Who is the law around here anyway?" Sally put in.

"Sheriff. He's a good 'un, too, they say. We've sent for him. But he's away down in Yamhill County right now."

"Aw, shucks!" Dan'l's eyes sparkled suddenly. "Just forget that sheriff and turn Jim loose on the job. I bet he could get your critters back."

Jim brightened. Now that suggestion had some sense to it! He listened attentively as Mills told of discovering his loss shortly after noon, of thinking the cattle must have strayed, until he found the stranger's boot print. He had ridden over to Burke's then, found everybody in a turmoil there over a similar disappearance, and he and Burke had decided to check all the claims south to the Tualatin on their side of the Willamette. Young Selway's one cow was safe, but Sam's was gone, and both had joined the search. Now that they knew everything was all right on the Rutledge and Keath claims, they intended to head back north, feeling that was the most logical direction to pick up the thief's trail.

"How about it, Jim?" said Sam Mullins. "Reckon you could help us track this feller? We got nothin' to go on but a couple boot prints five mile apart."

Jim was inwardly amused. The place was probably full of sign, if you knew how to look for it—and if these bourgeways hadn't trampled it all out with their clumsy boots. "Sure, I'll go. You comin', Jonnie?"

"Blast it, I got no horse."

"I'll fetch Bad Medicine fer you."

When he came back again from the glades he found Rutledge preparing to go along too. Everything was arranged for Sally and Dan'l to spend the night across the river with Mrs. Rutledge and the girls, if the search should keep the men away that long. Ned was to look out for all of them.

"Keep Moki too," Jim offered. "He's worth a couple extra sentries all by hisself."

Sam looked surprised. "I thought you'd be takin' him to smell out the trail."

"I'll take keer of the trail. Less'n this thief of yours is a mountain man, he ain't gonna be hard to foller. And mountain men don't wear boots."

"Well, I dunno," said Clyde Burke dubiously. "I hope you can find more traces of this feller than we could. We can show you the two boot prints, anyways. Come on, let's head back for Sam's."

Half an hour later Jim was bending over the print in Sam Mullins' creek bottom, while the others, still mounted, waited with varying degrees of doubt and curiosity to see what he would make of it. It was none too fresh, Jim found; the muddy front edges were pocked from the rain that had fallen about noon, and most of the thin grass mashed by the heel had sprung upright again.

He straightened, searching the surrounding grass which had prevented more prints from showing. There was cattle sign all around, of course, but it meant nothing since Sam's cow grazed here regularly. And the hoofprints of the man's horse would not be visible with the creek right here handy as a passage in and out of the bottom.

Jim frowned, remembering suddenly it was a bourgeway they were after. Keeping to the creek would be second nature to a mountain man or an Indian, but it surprised him a little that a bourgeway would have thought of it. He moved northward along the creek for a short distance to look for further evidence, and found it in the form of dislodged pebbles shining through the clear water, a couple of freshly broken twigs on an overhanging branch. The thief had gone northward up the creek, that was certain.

He walked back to the print and looked at it again. It was unmistakably a bourgeway boot. For a minute he was baffled, trying to make the two facts fit logically. Then a thought struck him. He gave a grunt and began to circle the print, squinting at it from all angles.

"Well?" demanded Burke a little impatiently. "You know the color of his hair yet?"

"I might, at that," retorted Jim. "Let's take a look at that print at your place. This feller went up the creek, but ain't no need fer us to bother with that. We kin cut through the woods."

He mounted and led the way. It was too soon to be sure yet, but if the print at Burke's should be plainer—

It was much plainer, traced entirely in the thin mud beside a big boulder at the edge of Burke's pasture. The minute Jim saw it he was sure he was right—if only the print of the other foot had showed too, he could have been positive.

"Well, you figger like us, that he headed north?" Mills asked.

Jim shook his head. "West. They's some Cayuses winterin' in the hills over yonder, 'bout seven, eight miles west of here."

"Cayuses!" All six men stared at him blankly.

"Why, the Cayuses live up around Fort Walla Walla, clean on t'other side of the gorge!" Selway exclaimed.

"They's a few up in the hills west of here, all the same," Jim insisted. "I seen their camp."

Burke was frowning impatiently. "Lookee here, Keath, Cayuses is thievin' enough devils, I give you that. And mebbe they's some around here. But we ain't *after* Injuns, we're after a white man. That there's a *boot* print."

Jim grinned. "But they was a Injun inside of the boot."

"Pshaw! I never see a Injun yet that wore boots!" Ben Mills snorted. "I think the feller's a white settler from up north of here somewheres."

"That's what he aimed fer you to think," Jim said. "Ain't much need to track this feller. We kin just head fer that Cayuse camp and ketch 'em afore they move on."

"And have to come back here and start all over when we find out the cattle ain't there!" retorted Burke. "Nawsir, I don't think that's smart. They's all sorts of Injuns around about, if you're so dead set on havin' it a Injun. Multnomahs acrost the Willamette south a ways, Molalas east of them, Chinooks up around Fort Vancouver—"

"We best foller the tracks, that's sure," Mills agreed. "If this young feller really thinks he can do it." He looked dubiously at Jim. "Ain't nothin' about that print a-tall that says it's Injun."

Jim shrugged and mounted Buckskin, who as usual was in eager motion before he was seated. If these bourgeways wanted to waste time, and risk having their cattle get clean away from them, it was all right with him, he'd follow the trail. But no Indian in his right mind was going to hang around long, with white men's stolen cattle tied to his lodge. And he was sure it was Indians. Boot or no boot, that print *toed in*. The foot that made it was used to moccasins.

153

He kept the impatient Buckskin down to a jumpy trot, enjoying the familiar sensation of being on the prowl. The forest was dense and wet, full of small rustlings and the scent of hemlock and crushed fern. Jim headed northward through it, the other horses strung out in twos and singly behind him. Mills was still muttering dubiously to young Selway, and Jim heard Sam Mullins make some remark about Moki.

"I reckon we'll find out Jim's a pretty good tracker with or without Moki," Rutledge said. And Jonathan added loyally, "Jim knows what he's doin'."

Jim smiled. Anybody but a bourgeway would know what he was doing on this trail. He might wish for Moki's sharp nose later, but along here the sign was plain as daylight; a trampled bush, twigs broken all in one direction on the side of a dead pine, disturbed swirlings in the carpet of damp brown needles underfoot. You'd have to be blind to miss it. That Cayuse wasn't even trying, he felt so safe in his disguise.

Jonathan pressed up beside him, presently, on the mule. "Jim, tell me somethin'. How you figger we're after Injuns?"

"You oughta know that, after the trouble you had learnin' to walk in moccasins!"

"By golly! I'd never've thought of that!" Jonnie said. He was silent a moment. "That still don't prove it's Cayuses. Why not Multnomahs or Molalas?"

"*Wah!* Bunch of squaws. Them Injuns ain't wuth the name."

Jonnie studied his brother's profile speculatively. "You know what, Jim? I think you're just *hopin'* it's them Cayuses so's there'll be a good bang-up fight when we get there."

"Mebbe I am." Jim fingered his knife hilt and grinned. Jonnie had hit close to the truth. But he had other reasons for singling out the Cayuses. For one, not even Molalas and Multnomahs were stupid enough to steal animals on the opposite side of the river from their villages. For another, both

154

of these tribes were far too beat by poverty and the ravages of smallpox to risk trouble with the white man. Jim had reconnoitered their villages in his solitary wanderings on Buckskin, and felt nothing but disgust for their squalid, spiritless ways. Cayuses were quite a different kettle of fish. They were warriors well feared for their ferocity up around Fort Walla Walla on the other side of the Cascades, where they normally lived. What this small bunch was doing in the valley he didn't know, unless they were castoffs from their own people. He'd been curious about them since the day a couple of weeks ago when he'd run onto their horses grazing in a sheltered pocket of the hills, and discovered eight or ten lodges in the woods nearby.

He was thinking of those horses now, as he automatically followed the broad trail of crushed underbrush and horn marks on trees that led ever northward through the forest. The memory of their well-muscled flanks and curving necks was as interesting as the hopeful idea of a bit of good lively fighting.

"Lookee here, Jim," Jonnie said presently. "Nobody ever said nothin' about this junket includin' a battle."

"You want them cattle back, don't you?"

"Sure, we do. But we got law in this valley, and that's what we got it for. Sheriff's on his way, remember."

Jim flung him an impatient glance. "Think Injuns are gonna set around and wait while he gits here?"

"We'll have to keep a guard on 'em. 'Course we never figgered it *was* Injuns. I dunno—"

"I dunno either! Only guard you kin put on a Cayuse is a good strong piece of rope. A bullet's better. Here, hold back a minute, Jonnie."

The busy, automatic corner of his brain had been hesitating between a flattened clump of weeds up ahead and a scraped place on a tree trunk farther to the left. Jim tossed Buckskin's halter to Jonathan and slid down to approach the flattened weeds. Dropping to a low crouch, he put his nose close to the broken stalks and sniffed. Old sign. Probably some varmint had rolled around there scratching his back a couple of days ago. He was up again instantly with one of his lithe movements, swinging atop Buckskin and pulling her to the left.

Jonathan swerved to follow him. "What was it about that bunch of weeds that told you to come this-a-way?"

"Didn't smell right. Sap's all run out'n them stems a'ready. Yonder's the fresh sign." Jim pointed to the faint scar on the tree trunk. "Cow's horn scraped along there."

"How you know it wasn't a deer's horn?"

"Too low! By gor, Jonnie, use yer head!"

Jonathan's grin was half sheepish, half resentful. "You wait. One of these days I'll show you up at somethin'. Plowin', maybe!"

"Hey, up yonder!" called Ben Mills from several yards behind. "You sure you know what you're doin'?"

Jonathan turned the mule and started back toward the others. "He knows, all right. And you notice we're veerin' west now, like he said we would. If it is them Cayuses, we better lay some new plans, hadn't we? The sheriff—"

Jim frowned and let his mare out into a faster pace as the woods began to thin. For the life of him he couldn't see why they wanted to drag in a sheriff. The whole thing was a simple, clear-cut problem of stealing back what had been stolen. He wished Eye of the Bear or Many Feathers were behind him, instead of this bunch of bourgeways. Or Hides His Face, who had carried the pipe—been the leader—so often when Talks Alone was going on his first raids. His breath came faster, as the memories drifted back over him, and the sensations—lying prone on a ridge with the enemy lodges clustered below you and your companions hidden all around, silent and waiting. The sun would be gone and the dusk gathering; the squaws on the plain below—maybe Blackfoot, maybe Piute, maybe Rappahoe—would be hustling in the last of the firewood, cursing the dogs that pulled their travois, herding the children into the safety of the village. You could hear their voices floating out on the cooling air, feel the prickle of buffalo grass against your naked chest and thighs, smell the odors of sweat and sun-baked earth and the vermilion that smeared your face. And all the time your eyes and brain would be automatically noting the arrangement of the lodges, the position of the picketed horses; estimating the number of warriors in the village and the location of their sentries.

Then full night, at last, the whispered plans; and three or four of you would steal down the ridge and past the sentries to prowl among the lodges, melting into their looming shadows at the sound of a laugh or a footstep. You would pass up the first horse you found tied to a lodge, and the second, searching for the perfect mare, the finest stallion, then suddenly it would occur to you that time was slipping away, that any second the companions waiting on the ridge would dash down to stampede the loose stock and the alarm would be raised. Hastily, you would cut the next horse you saw, turn silent but swift in escape, cut another in passing, grow reckless and swerve back to get a tall roan you remembered—then would come the sudden shout, the sound of whinnies and beating hoofs and the crack of a rifle. The whole village would erupt into an uproar of yells and running feet and bobbing torches, with the bullets humming like great bees past your head as you flung yourself on the tall roan and streaked for open country, your three prizes pounding along behind you. The chase might last for miles; you would lose your companions but never all of your raging pursuers. Sooner or later you'd find yourself grappling with another sweaty body in grunting, deadly combat while the horse under you struggled and shoved against your enemy's. You wouldn't feel the tear

157

of his knife through your shoulder, only the swift plunge of your own, and the blaze of ferocity inside you and the rush of wind on your face as you tore loose to freedom.

"Jim, wait!"

At the sound of Jonathan's voice Jim gave such a start that Buckskin plunged and curvetted, momentarily out of control. Totally absorbed in his thoughts, he had unconsciously increased Buckskin's pace until she fairly flew. Now he heard hoofbeats behind him, and another shout. "Lord a'mighty, wait a minute!"

He mastered the nervous mare. "Wait fer *what?*" he growled.

"For the rest of us," put in Rutledge, riding up beside them. "If it's Cayuses we're after, we best do a little figgerin'. Gotta know what we're gonna do when we get there."

The others had caught up now, and Jim found himself surrounded by a ring of lathered horses and puffing men. "You still followin' a trail, at *this* rate?" panted young Selway, dragging a sleeve over his gleaming forehead. "You set a pace, I'll tell you—"

"I'm for easin' up a little," muttered Mills. He was eyeing Jim almost suspiciously. "Horses is gonna play out on us first thing you know. Besides, it's gettin' on toward sundown. I wanta know where I'm headin' and what I'm gonna run into. Seems to me this ain't nothin' but a wild-goose chase so far."

"Yeah, ain't seen them cattle yet—"

"Better use our heads a little. Can't bust into a camp of Cayuse devils without no evidence nor nothin'. I—"

"*Wagh!* I'll show you evidence when we git thar," burst out Jim. "I'll show you yer *cattle*. Sign's been plain as a wagon trail!"

He wheeled the mare and started on again, across an area of glades and into trees on the other side. The light was fading from the heavy sky and the ground had been steadily rising for some time now. He needed no trail to take him to that Cayuse camp. In fact he hadn't been following the sign lately for the very good reason that it had vanished. He'd known it would, sooner or later, and had spotted the beginning of the false trail at a wide, shallow brook back yonder a way. The thief had driven the cattle into the brook, ridden across it himself to trample the opposite side with hoof prints that apparently led north through a fir grove. Then of course he'd come back and driven the cattle up the brook. It was what Jim would have done himself in such a circumstance, and he had kept the brook in sight, knowing he could pick up the trail farther along when it took to dry land again. Even that was a waste of time, it would be shorter to cut right for the camp.

There! Those broken ferns. Now he could turn away from the brook and head through this thicket.

Then he saw something, and halted Buckskin so suddenly she reared. They still doubted they were after Injuns, did they? Well, he could prove it now. He shot a defiant glance over his shoulder as the others rode up, and jerked his head at a pile of clothing stuffed under a bush.

Burke swung down and ran over to it, pulling out a rusty old jacket, a pair of broken boots, and a crumpled hat. "White man's clothes!" he cried. "But why would he shed 'em?"

" 'Cause he's a Injun," Jim snapped. "Bourgeways allus wear too many clothes, sure—but they never take any of 'em off! This feller figgered he was safe now. He got tired of playin' white man, he's hurryin'. And if you ever want to see them cattle agin, we gotta hurry too. I'm gonna leave the trail and cut straight fer that camp. You comin'?"

They believed him, then. Burke leaped on his horse and they all surged after Jim, not talking any more. Thickets, sloping glades, patches of forest flew by, and Jim loaded his rifle as he rode, hearing the small clicks and cursings behind him as some of the others did the same. The war drums were pounding in his veins now, harder and faster every minute. As he topped the last ridge he smelled the smoke of the lodge fires. The Cayuses were eating before they broke camp—probably felt safe for another hour or two, in this valley full of bourgeways. Jim grinned as he flung himself off Buckskin and crept through the fringe of bushes that concealed the hollow. They didn't know they had an Absarokee named Talks Alone stalking them.

Rutledge's hand on his shoulder brought him to a halt. "We there, son?"

Jim nodded, jerking his head toward the tangled edge of the ridge. Rutledge moved cautiously forward at his side until they both crouched on the rim, peering down into the hollow where eight or ten horses, as well as the stolen cattle, grazed quietly in the dusk.

"By golly, there they are!" breathed Sam Mullins, behind them. "Burke! Mills! Lookee here, we—"

"Shut up!" hissed Jim. The whispers and crackling twigs as the others crowded closer seemed as loud as gunshots. Rutledge nudged him and jerked a thumb toward the rear, herding everybody back into the woods where they had left the horses. Jim followed impatiently. What now? He ought to be getting the lay of the land, the position of the sentries, in the few minutes before full dark.

Rutledge turned to him when the group was complete, a curious gravity in his face. "Jim, what's your plan?"

"Why, smell out the sentries, a-course. Get rid of 'em on the quiet when dark's come, sneak down and git the cattle moved out'n there while some of you keeps watch up here. When you git a good start I'll stampede them horses and start shootin'. While they chase me south you kin git away east—"

"All right," said Rutledge heavily. "Now I'll have my say. This here's a peaceful valley and I ain't gonna be a party to stirrin' up no Injun trouble for *anybody's* cattle. Kill one Cayuse and they's gonna be five or six white settlers picked off in their own cabin yards before a week's up, and then we'd fight back and then the Cayuses would get some other Injuns to join with 'em, and first thing you know we got a real uprisin' on our hands. We're gonna settle this without spillin' blood or we ain't gonna settle it. That's my stand."

There was a moment's silence. Then Burke said, "You're dead right, Bob.'

"By golly, you are," came Jonathan's voice.

There were murmurs of agreement; the whole temper of the group calmed and steadied. In the fast-falling darkness came the sounds of rifles being uncocked and tossed aside.

Jim stood with clenched jaw, feeling one pair of eyes after another turning to him speculatively, feeling a solid wall of resistance building up against everything he was craving to do.

He swung away, seething with frustration. Nobody could deny that those Cayuses yonder were enemies—friends didn't steal your cattle. And if you couldn't get a little excitement out of your enemies, where in thunder could you get it?

Rutledge's deep voice came again. "Got any other idees, Jim, or should we settle down to watch this place while we wait for the sheriff?"

"*Wagh!* The sheriff!" Jim snarled, ready to defy them all, cut away and do what he wanted to and let them scatter the best they could. Then he saw Rutledge's quiet, waiting face, the challenge in Jonnie's eyes, and knew he wouldn't.

He heaved an explosive sigh and got himself under control. "I'll git yer cattle fer you without no sheriff! And without spillin' no Cayuse blood neither. Will that do you?"

"That'll do fine," Mills said cautiously. "How you aim to go at it?"

"Jest steal 'em back, is all. They stole 'em from you, didn't they? Or have I got to ask pardon afore I do it?"

Burke began to chuckle softly. "I don't reckon that's necessary. You mean you can really pull it off?"

Jim grunted scornfully. He could pull it off, all right, but there wouldn't be any fun to it. "Set down and rest yerselves, we gotta wait till full dark."

He watched them ease down among the trees, relief in their shadowed faces, and curiosity, and something else—approval. By gor, had he done the right thing for once? He darted a glance at Rutledge and found the broad, kindly face alight with satisfaction. And Jonnie—

There was that look again, blazing at Jim just as it had in the recorder's office.

Jim turned hastily and moved through the underbrush back to the ridge, full of an altogether new excitement. He was thinking of the plan he'd had, earlier today, for mending the rift between him and his brother. He could still make it work —he could make it work better than ever. Here was opportunity playing right into his hands. By thunder, after tonight Jonnie wouldn't care about the old picture and the leather box and the cabin no Absarokee could stand to live in. He'd be so pleased he'd forget everything, and they could start fresh.

Jim's glance swept the hollow in an eager search, failed to find what he wanted, and moved anxiously to the lodges half-visible among the trees beyond. There! Was that it? The light was growing too dim to be sure. Impatiently he waited for night. Then, after a word of instruction to the quiet group behind him, he crept on foot out of the sheltering underbrush along the ridge, paused a moment to listen, and vanished into the darkness.

Not quite ten minutes later the call of a white owl drifted softly across the night air. The men on the ridge stiffened. At the second call they scrambled to their feet and ran as silently as they could toward their horses. A moment later, taking Buckskin with them, they were circling southeastward away from the ridge, every ear strained to catch sounds of disturbance behind them, shots or shouts or war whoops. The silence was broken only by the thudding of their own horses' hoofs. Then, from somewhere ahead and to the left, came the soft lowing of a cow.

"By the almighty, he's done it!" exclaimed Mills. "Over this-a-way, men."

The group swerved and a moment later entered a patch of woods well away from the ridge and the still-silent Cayuse camp. Jim, waiting in a little clearing deep in the trees, heard them coming and hastily finished binding a long, thin bundle of brush together with a length of vine. He was panting from his recent exertions and almost feverish with suspense. Everything had gone without a hitch and he could barely wait until they'd put a mile or so behind them and he could light his torch and show Jonnie—

"Keep goin', fan out around the cattle," he panted as the first horsemen appeared in the clearing. They surged past, Rutledge in the lead with Buckskin in tow. Jim caught the halter and swung atop her, but held back until all the others had gone on. Then he pulled his prize out of the concealment of a thicket and followed eagerly.

The men had gone a mile and a half before they stopped for a breather. They were talking freely now, laughing with elation and relief, shouting back to Jim to hurry and catch up, and tell them how he'd turned the trick.

Jim paused in the shelter of a little rise just long enough to find flint and steel in his pouch and light his makeshift torch. Then, triumphant, he rode slowly toward them, holding the torch high and leading the gift he had stolen for Jonnie at a risk far greater than his brother knew.

Their eyes riveted on it as he approached, and he swelled with pride. They ought to stare. It was a gift good enough to

163

buy a chieftain's daughter. It was the finest young mare he had ever seen, tamer than Buckskin but proud of eye and dainty of foot, her neck arched like a good bow. And she was pure cream in color, with a flowing white mane. He had found just what Jonnie wanted—a horse exactly like his own.

He sat there with his knees trembling against Buckskin's sides, watching his brother's face and waiting for it to light with joy. But Jonnie seemed dazed—almost stunned. Everybody seemed that way.

"She's yours, Jonnie!" he murmured. "Just like you wanted. She's gentle, too. She—"

"She's *mine?*" Jonathan's voice was hard. "She *ain't* mine! She ain't yours neither!"

"Why, sure she is! I pulled a coup as neat as any I ever—"

"Jim, you stole that horse! Crimeny, you can't *do* that, it ain't right! You're breakin' the law same as them Cayuses was! You can't go stealin' animals away, it's—"

"What're you talkin' about?" demanded Jim. "Ain't that just what we been doin' tonight, stealin' animals?"

"That's different! The cattle was ours already!"

"They warn't when they was down in that Cayuse holler!"

"Oh, yes they was, Jim!" put in Rutledge. His blue eyes were stern in the light of the torch. "They never stopped bein' ours, no matter who had 'em. We only took back our own, the quietest way we knew. But this is wrong. This is makin' thieves of all of us—"

"Mr. Rutledge, he don't understand," said Jonathan, in a tight, shamed voice. "He just don't understand yet."

"By golly, I'll say he don't!" exclaimed Burke exasperatedly. "All this trouble to get around rilin' them devils, then he swipes one of their own horses right out from under their nose! We're in a wuss fix than before!"

Jim heard them through a fog of pain and outrage. "You

164

ain't in no fix," he growled. "If Jonnie—don't want her, I'll go put her back. Right whar she come from."

Jonnie's voice grated when he spoke, and his palms were rubbing along his thighs in that old gesture. "I couldn't keep no stolen horse."

There was a small silence. Then abruptly Jim wheeled Buckskin and started back the way he had come, the beautiful, rejected mare trotting behind. Jonathan watched a moment, his face twisting, then galloped after him. "Hold on. I'm comin' with you!"

"I don't want nobody with me!"

"Don't be a fool, there's danger. They'll be huntin' that ridge now—"

"*Stay back!*" It was a wild yell. Jim glared over his shoulder, gesturing with the torch. "Go on back to that cabin!"

"Blast it, I won't! They might kill you!"

"*Let 'em,* by thunder!"

Jim's torch sailed over both horses and landed in a flaming mass just in front of Bad Medicine. The mule halted abruptly, and Jonnie sat there staring at the blazing twigs until they burned out to nothing and the thud of hoofbeats had died away into the forest. Then he turned, his jaw tight and his body rigid, and went back to the others.

In awkward silence the men turned their horses and headed east.

Chapter XIII

It took Jim about five minutes of blindly furious riding to reach the hidden clearing in the forest. He stopped there, cleared his head with an effort, and flung himself off Buckskin to prepare for what lay ahead of him. Jonnie was right about one thing—the Cayuses would be up in arms, prowling the ridge. They'd be in an ugly mood, too. Jim didn't care. There was a violence inside him no more to be controlled than a buffalo stampede, and he wasn't trying. The one thing he craved was to plunge headlong into the worst danger he could find.

He tore off his clothes with savage haste, fighting to stave off the memory of Jonnie's shamed apology for him. The faster he got to the ridge the sooner he'd lose that humiliation in the uproar of battle and escape; the more wounds he got the less he'd ache from the one Jonnie had dealt him.

He was stripped to his breechclout now, strapping the tight bundle of discarded clothes to the apishamore just behind where he would sit. There was a chunk of pemmican in his pouch; he chewed it ravenously while he checked his rifle's loading and primed the pan. Next he must tie the medicine bundle behind his braid; in spite of his defiant shout to Jonnie, he had no wish to part with his hair just yet. The bundle would turn Cayuse bullets as well as Sioux. He reached hurriedly into his pouch for it, frowned, searched again—and then remembered. It was back on the claim, cached in the hollow of the old stump beside the Tualatin.

For a moment he felt utterly forsaken. Nobody in his right mind would ride into danger without the protection of his helpers; it was more than reckless, it was foolhardy. The spirits grew angry at such arrogance; they might take away their power from your medicine, they might desert you forever.

Jim dropped to his knees, grim jawed, and drew a packet of vermilion from his pouch. Never mind the spirits, never mind anything. He had said he would take that mare back where she came from and he meant to do it. Obstinately he shoved away a wave of foreboding as he crouched there in the dark striping his cheeks, his forehead, the bridge of his nose with the paint of defiance. But a moment later when he pushed through the woods with his rejected gift in the direction of the ridge, his heart sank at the empty feel of his left braid against his shoulder. He was alone indeed.

It was not long before he had company of a perilous sort in his wary progress up the rise. To his left he could hear the thrashing of several horses through the underbrush, the angry grunts of their Cayuse riders. Ahead of him on the right another party was approaching with a lack of caution that surprised him. Didn't they know he could hear them perfectly, and as long as he did hear them, could stay out of their way? He guided Buckskin and the stolen mare into a thicket and stayed there, a hand clamped over the nostrils of each, while the second party passed so close he could hear the squeak of their saddles. He eluded a third group with the same ease a few minutes later and had almost gained the ridge before he realized that all the searchers were behind him, fanning out across the wooded slope but moving down it, toward the east.

He understood, then, why they were careless of the noise they made. He was in the one spot they wouldn't expect him to be—within a stone's throw of their own camp. He smiled wryly in the dark. Pure rashness had gained him a safety he'd never expected—and wasn't sure he wanted. But the night wasn't over; they must have left sentries at the camp. Things were bound to get lively yet.

He moved southward along the ridge, keeping well back from the edge. It was certain now that his escape, if he managed it, would not be to the east, into the arms of those searchers. The gully up which he'd driven the cattle would be a good place to take the mare down; he could leave Buckskin in the thick clump of pines at the head of it.

In another few minutes he was looping her bridle over a pine bough and cocking his ears for sounds of movement in the gully below. All was still—too still to suit him. It was one thing to steal into that hollow on your own silent moccasins, sure of a swift horse under you when you'd pulled off your coup and didn't mind making a racket. It was quite another to reverse the procedure—have a horse to encumber you in the beginning and only your own legs to outrun pursuit. He took time to muffle the stolen mare's hoofs with chunks of moss tied on with vines; then he looked at her one last time, glimmering there in the darkness like a phantom horse, proud and gentle and beautiful. Why, *why* couldn't Jonnie have taken her? What was wrong with her? Just the fact that he'd stolen her from a Cayuse? But the Cayuse had stolen her from somebody else; that was the way you got horses. Besides, the Cayuses had no rights under all those fancy bourgeway laws. They didn't even belong in this valley!

He couldn't understand it. All he knew was that he'd given the best gift he could imagine, and it still wasn't good enough.

168

He led the mare out of the trees and down into the gully.

He heard the faint mutter of voices when he was halfway down—they seemed to come from above, to his right. He crept on warily, crouching to get the ridge between him and the sky so he could locate the sentries. Yes, there they were, two of them, blacker shapes against the gloom. He hugged the right bank of the gully and moved on. Then the mare's foot struck a loose pebble; she stumbled, the pebble rolled and dislodged another. The clatter seemed to fill the world.

Jim was running before he took conscious thought; there was a thrashing overhead and two shots rang out, spattering on the loose rocks where he had crouched an instant before. He heard grunts, a shout, crackling underbrush; they were racing toward the gully, reloading as they came. He dived beneath the trailing branches of a tree projecting out of the side of the embankment, and dragged the mare in after him. Clamping a hand over her nose, he waited. Almost immediately a figure hurtled over the bank a few hundred feet behind him, and another followed. Too far away to aim on a night as dark as this.

Jim didn't wait for them to get any closer. He sprang out of his shelter and onto the mare, bringing his heels back against her sides with a force that sent her spurting down the gully in a spray of pebbles. Two more shots followed him but he was an uncertain target, dodging and zigzagging and hugging the mare's neck close. Excitement rose up in him. The only course remaining now was the boldest, and it suited his mood exactly. He swung south as soon as he emerged into the hollow, circling its outer edge as fast as the mare could run. Light-colored horses were the hardest to see at night, he had that in his favor. And the hullabaloo that had risen from the lodges covered the beat of the mare's hoofs. Now if they did what he thought they would—

The first Cayuses erupted at that moment from the edge of

the forest where the camp lay, and raced for the loose horses. Jim laughed exultantly under his breath as more streamed out into the hollow—squaws, young boys, and the few warriors who were not beating the far slope of the ridge looking for him. By the time half a dozen men were mounted he had dived into the woods behind the lodges they had emptied. Branches crashed against him, vines tangled the mare's feet as she plunged headlong through a maze of trees and thickets. In another instant he caught a whiff of smoke and swerved toward it, sliding down from her back to pick his way, warily now, toward the first lodge. In a moment he saw it through the trees, faintly luminous from the cook fire inside. Now was the time for caution.

He stole closer, eyes and ears straining, rounded the last tall clump of ferns and stood with pounding heart at the edge of the tiny open space where the lodge stood. To his right and left and ahead he glimpsed other luminous cones, but all the noise was coming from eastward in the hollow, and the mouth of the gully. Swiftly he crossed the open place and tied the mare exactly where he had found her, to the lodge itself.

There, by gor! he thought bitterly. I done what I said.

He started to turn away, then stopped. He had seen a shadow move across the faintly glowing hides of the lodge— someone was inside it. He leaped for the clump of ferns and felt himself suddenly outlined in yellow radiance as the lower flap of the lodge was yanked up and the firelight streamed out. At the same moment a screech split the silence, and someone scrambled under the flap, yelling in a dozen different keys. It was a squaw, from the pitch of her voice, but Jim didn't wait to find out. He was already dodging through the tangled woods, hearing an answering shout from the direction of the hollow and the thud of hoofbeats as the searchers in the gully turned back to race toward this new alarm.

He'd have to use his wits now, and fast. He couldn't get

to Buckskin without running head on into his pursuers or else ranging in a wide circle to avoid them. There simply wasn't time for circling; he couldn't outrun their horses. Instinctively he doubled back on his own tracks, heading straight for the lodge again. The hoofbeats were thunderous now; as he glimpsed the lodge he heard the first Cayuses break into the woods behind him. The squaw was still standing beside the tethered mare, chattering excitedly to two others who had appeared beside her; Jim gave them a wide berth, slipped through the perilously thin fringe of trees between them and the next fire-lit cone, melted into the black shadow behind the third, and paused to gasp for breath. He could hear a small child wailing on the other side of the stretched hides, not a foot away from him. The sound faded as he set off again, darting from lodge to lodge in a northeasterly direction. Behind him the sounds of pursuit were growing vaguer as the Cayuses thrashed through the forest he had just quitted. But it wouldn't last long.

He swerved abruptly due east, passed behind a last lodge, and broke out of the trees into the open hollow. He was almost across it, running like the wind, when a shout rang out from the edge of the forest. They'd spotted him. It was all up now, the gully looked a mile away. He had time to curse himself for his own obstinate insistence on tying the mare exactly where he had got her, instead of simply sending her down the gully with a spank, and getting out fast. And then he was in the gully, and the first bullets ricocheted off the side of it.

He flung himself onto the vines that trailed down the embankment and began scrambling up them. He had almost reached the top when the Cayuses burst into the lower end of the gully. He froze to immobility, his fingers and moccasins dug into the vines and crumbling dirt, his cheek smashed against the rough, twiggy stems. The smell of sweat and earth and vermilion was in his nostrils as he clung there fighting for breath. They could either spot him and pick him off as easily as shooting a blackbird off a limb—or they could fail to see him and race on up the gully.

They raced on up the gully, yelling vengeance.

In an instant Jim had gained the top of the bank and was streaking through the tangle of underbrush to the clump of pines where Buckskin—the spirits willing—was still waiting. Once he was on horseback the odds would be evened, he could fight like a warrior instead of dodging and hiding like a fox chased by dogs. He reached her just as the first Cayuse emerged from the top of the gully, yanked free her halter, and flung himself with wild elation on her back. A rear and a plunge and she was streaking south, and the world was transformed into a confusion of yells and whining bullets and wind streaming through his braids. He felt a blow on his right shoulder, and a ripping pain. Twisted on the apishamore with a screech of defiance, he leveled his own rifle. He could see nothing but moving dark blurs behind him, but he heard a fresh confusion following his shot and took advantage of it to swing eastward and then south again in a broad zigzag.

Their aim was bad now, and he was outdistancing most of them, for Buckskin was comparatively fresh and their horses jaded from the chase he had led them. But there was one he couldn't lose—there was always one you couldn't lose. He swerved in and out between scattered thickets and the patches of pine that dotted the long ridge, and the hoofbeats behind gained steadily. He fired at the sound as fast as he could load and reload, but they only thudded louder, while Cayuse bullets buzzed closer and closer to his own head.

The Indian ran out of ammunition at last, but the flame in Jim's shoulder was hampering his own movements, and he had time for only one more shot—which hit, he could hear the Cayuse grunt—before he felt the jarring impact of another horse against his own, and an arm like steel encircled him, striving to drag him from Buckskin's back. He clung hard with his knees, twisting and struggling, striking out savagely with the butt of his rifle, hearing the rasping breath of the two beasts and the Cayuse mingling with his own. A new flame from a knife wound ripped across his cheek and the smell of blood rose strong through the smell of sweat and horses; he found his own knife at last and grasped at slippery flesh and struck hard, twice. Coarse hair scraped his shoulder as the Cayuse sagged against him; he shoved at the weight, twisted violently, and tore loose at last from that suffocating embrace. Then he and Buckskin were in motion again, plunging across a shallow ravine and up on the other side and running, flying, south and eastward down through the hills—and this time no hoofbeats echoed behind them.

He never knew how much later it was that he slid down Buckskin's heaving side and dropped full length beside a stream. He groped toward the water, whose bell-like murmur he could hear in the darkness. The moss was cool and wet under his aching body, the water an icy shock when he plunged both arms into it. He drank deeply, then lay there dragging air into his lungs and feeling the pain dance along the side of his cheek like flames, and his shoulder burn like a coal. Gradually the tumult of the last few hours faded from his brain and the thudding of his heart began to sound like voices. *"You can't do that, it ain't right!"* *"By golly, all this trouble to get around rilin' them devils . . ."* *". . . makin' thieves of all of us . . ."* *"Trouble in the valley . . . kill one Cayuse . . . trouble in the valley . . ."*

He sat up painfully, staring into the velvety darkness. Would dawn find livestock slaughtered, a cabin in flames, a settler lying bloody and still in the mud of his own dooryard? Then he remembered the squaw and sagged all over with relief. She'd seen him clearly in that instant of discovery behind the tepee, when he'd stood flooded with yellow light. She'd be able to swear to his feather and paint, his naked body. No white man would ever be suspected of any part of this night's work.

He drew a long, ragged breath and ran his fingers through the tangled lock that hung over his forehead. It was sweat drenched, clotted with blood and paint. He felt that way all through, inside him. Bewildered, he tried to summon pride in his recent coups, gain some satisfaction from the hullabaloo of danger and violence and escape he had finally stirred up after craving it for weeks. But he could not forget Rutledge's stern eyes, which once, back at The Dalles, had looked at him so gently in the moment of his deep humiliation. He could not forget Jonnie's shamed excuses for him, or the faces of those men.

But why? Why couldn't he?

The question loomed up, grew, and spread until it filled his mind. He was totally unskilled at finding the answer, for he had never before asked such a thing of himself.

He sat probing and floundering, trying to understand. Gradually the outer world faded from his consciousness, as for the first time in his life, one part of Jim Keath stood off and scrutinized the other. It was a curious experience, a little frightening. He had a clear sensation of slipping out of himself, then turning back to look. And there he was, sitting alone in the dark with his head in his hands, aching and sore from a night of blundering mistakes—too stubborn to admit how wrong he'd been.

You fool, he thought. It ain't coups you care about, it's what them men think of you. It ain't enemies you want, it's friends!

Without knowing it he'd outgrown this sort of life. He'd changed. Slowly but inescapably the thought completed itself: No longer was he Talks Alone, the son of Scalp Necklace.

He was Jonnie Keath's brother, and a white man. It was time to act like one.

He sat a long time, thinking about it. At last he rose stiffly to his feet. With the first motion he was again vividly aware of the darkness, the bell-like rush of the stream, the chill breath of the night air against his sore flesh. He moved across moist and spongy moss into icy water and stood there knee-deep, splashing away the grime and paint and dried blood he could feel but not see, while that busy corner of his brain automatically analyzed the mingled smells of horseflesh, earth, and fir trees. He was not thinking now, not peering inward at himself in that unaccustomed way. But he didn't need to.

He waded to the bank, unstrapped his clothes from Buckskin's back and dressed himself, shivering. A short while afterward he was riding down out of the hills and into the broad and sleeping valley. The violence of the night seemed far behind as he looked out across the lowlands, dim and mist swirled with approaching dawn. *Green pastures, still waters*—Jonnie's valley.

My valley, he thought experimentally.

In spite of himself, his eyes moved eastward, where the mountains lay hidden and snow locked behind their banks of cloud. But it was south to the Tualatin he turned his mare.

Chapter XIV

Jim rode into the clearing just as the sun broke through to touch the tops of the fir trees. Jonnie sat huddled in the grizzly robe directly in front of the door flap of the lodge. He looked as if he'd been there all night.

His head snapped around at the sound of Buckskin's hoofs, and as Jim slid to the ground and came toward him, he rose slowly and stiffly, like someone in a dream. Then suddenly he was across the intervening space and clutching Jim by both arms, examining him all over.

"You're all right? You're—oh, crimeny, Jim! That cheek —your shoulder—"

"Aaa, never mind them."

"Never *mind* 'em?" After an inarticulate moment Jonnie whirled and yelled joyfully toward the cabin. "Sally! Dan'l! Come outa there, *Jim's back!*"

There was an explosion of voices from the cabin and a moment later Dan'l burst out, half clad, Sally at his heels. The boy took one look then streaked down the slope to fling himself on Jim.

"Oh, cracky, they said you was mebbe gone for good! They said they'd likely gone and drove you off so's you'd never wanta come back! But I *knew* you would."

Jim crushed the boy against him with his good arm and

looked over the tousled gold head to Sally, who stood small and tremulous just behind Dan'l. She was enveloped in a hastily snatched blanket and her eyes were brimming.

"Drove me off?" he said.

"That's the way we felt," she told him shakily. "Jonnie and me. Allus naggin' you about your braids and all—Jim, it don't matter, ain't none of that matters! We found that out last night."

"It was one mighty blasted long night," Jonnie mumbled. "I ain't never lived through a longer. Settin' there waitin'—and thinkin'."

Jim was staring at them, swallowing. They'd wanted him back, they'd worried about him. And Sally was saying the braids and feather didn't matter.

"You mean it?" he said cautiously. "That it don't matter if I—"

Jonnie cut in. "We mean it all right! Ain't nobody gonna say another word about how you live or when you eat or whether you wear your hair hangin' to your heels or shave it off to your skull! Just so you're safe back—that's all we care."

Jim began to grin. Instantly three tired and anxious faces lighted with answering smiles. Dan'l clutched his good arm eagerly.

"Jim, what happened? Tell us what happened?"

"Oh, not much." Jim glanced at Jonnie and added, "I tuck the mare back."

Jonnie flushed. "It's a wonder to me you ain't dead."

"Well, it was close fer a while there," Jim admitted. Hesitantly, with one eye on Sally, he began to describe the happenings of the night, gaining confidence as he saw they weren't going to criticize him for any of it. Before long he was thoroughly enjoying the recital, counting his coups as he used to at the council fire in Absaroka, swaggering and proud of them. He laughed aloud as he told how he'd baffled the Cayuse by vanishing into the side of the gully, and threw out his wounded arm in a gesture that ended in an involuntary grimace of pain. His face went blank instantly but Sally uttered a horrified exclamation and whirled toward the cabin.

"My stars! Keepin' you here talkin' while that shoulder gets worse and worse—Jonnie, take him into the lodge while I fetch bandages. Dan'l, honey, go see to Buckskin." She was already hurrying toward the cabin, the blanket flapping around her.

Dan'l only clung tighter to Jim. "I want to hear the rest! Go on, Jim—"

Jim shook his head. It was just as well to skip the rest. "That's about all. I found Buckskin and got away."

"But you got hurt?"

"They was a little shootin'. Get along with you now."

The boy went reluctantly, and Jonnie followed Jim to the lodge. As they ducked under the door flap, he jerked a thumb toward Jim's wound. "That bullet still in you?"

"Yeah."

"Crimeny! It'll be nasty, gettin' it out."

"Not so bad. Arrer heads are a sight worse."

Jonathan gave a short laugh. "Well, mebbe you're used to havin' 'em in you, but I sure ain't used to diggin' 'em out. Better I do it than Sally, though. Let's get at it before I lose my stomach for the job."

Jim peeled off the buckskin shirt, then flipped his knife from its sheath and held it out. He stopped at sight of the red-brown stains that dimmed the blade. Conscious of Jonnie's probing eyes, he cleaned the steel on a lock of his damp hair before handing it over.

"Sold that shoulder of yours dear," Jonathan said softly.

There was no more talk then, for a few grim moments. But at last Jonnie let out his breath with a thankful "Whooo!" and flung the bullet away as if it burned his hands. Sally stepped 'into the lodge at that moment, wearing the familiar blue dress and festooned with long clean strips of what looked like petticoat.

"My stars, it's still bleedin'!" she began, then took in the situation. "You shoulda waited," she told Jonnie. "I could prob'ly have done that gentler. Now set down there on that bed thing, Jim Keath, you're gonna be doctored proper for once."

A few moments later Jim's wound was bandaged, the gash in his face taped with court plaster, and his eyelids drooping with a drowsiness he could no longer stave off.

"You go to sleep," Sally ordered, rolling up the extra bandages. "And *stay* asleep till noon, you hear?"

Jim grinned and lay back on his willow bed frame. She flung the grizzily robe over him, then left the lodge. But Jonathan lingered, looking down at his brother as if he wanted mightily to say something but didn't know how. "I'm gonna paddle acrost and tell the Rutledges," he muttered. "They was mighty anxious too. Mr. Rutledge was over here half the night." He paused, slowly rubbing his palms on his thighs. Then he muttered, "Sleep good, Jim," and left the lodge abruptly.

Two minutes later Jim sank into oblivion as into a sea of feathers.

Jim came wide awake all over, at the touch of Moki's nose on his hand. He sat up, wincing a little, and rumpled the dog's ears, wondering what else it was that had aroused him. A noise? A footstep? He heard it now, Jonnie's bold, incautious one. An instant later his brother's head thrust through the flap.

"Oh. You're awake a'ready. Best come out, Jim. They's—somebody wants to see you."

Puzzled, Jim reached for his shirt as Jonnie disappeared, and struggled into it—clumsily, because of the bandages and his shoulder's dull throbbing. Stepping outside, he noticed automatically that it was nearly noon and that Jonnie stood nearby, his back and shoulders tense. Beyond him— Jim frowned and stood still. There was a man, a stranger, framed in the cabin door.

As Jim watched, the man turned and started down the slope. From that moment he dominated the clearing. Tall, black bearded, he moved with a careless, powerful grace that Jim identified at once. Surely he was a mountain man! Jim's eyes flicked over him—moccasins, fringed buckskin, squirrel-skin cap—then riveted on the huge brass star fastened to the bosom of his shirt.

It was the sheriff.

Had they found out that it was no Indian but a white man in that camp last night? *Kill one Cayuse* . . . What would happen now? There was a jail in Willamette Falls. He'd seen it, brand new and strong, a small, thick-walled structure built out over the river. It had one tiny window covered with bars, and massive locks on the door. An icy sweat broke out on Jim's body as he pictured the dark, enclosed space inside, the walls pushing in. Everything in him screamed *"Run!"* but he stood still.

The sheriff advanced to within a yard of him, his glance running from feather to moccasins with a casualness that did not deceive Jim for a moment. This man would be able to describe him minutely a year from now. The glance shifted to Jonnie. "I reckon you two'd be the Keath brothers," boomed the sheriff.

"That's right."

"Well, my name's Joe Meek."

The wind suddenly left Jim's lungs. *"Joe Meek!"* he exclaimed.

"Heard of me, have you?"

"By thunder, yes!"

180

Jim looked the man over with new eyes. There wasn t a trapper in a million square miles who didn't know Joe Meek, at first hand or by reputation. Tom Rivers and Adam Russell had both had inexhaustible stocks of stories about his exploits —the grizzlies he'd done in, the Indians he'd outsmarted, his nerve, his wit, the bottomless pit that was his stomach, the unending supply of high spirits and enormously tall tales that made him welcome at any campfire between the Missouri River and the Sierra Nevada. It was like coming face to face with a legend. So Joe Meek was the sheriff of the Oregon territory! Jim's respect for law and order took an abrupt turn upward. "You come here to see me," he said warily. "What d'ya want?"

"Jest dropped in to git acquainted. They tell me you done a mighty pretty job of smellin' out some missin' cattle yesterday. Now I've seen you, I ain't surprised! When did you leave the mountains, boy?"

"Jest afore snow flew, last fall." Jim was warier than ever. Meek had the easy confidence of a three-hundred-pound cougar.

"No longer'n that, eh? Say, how was the beaverin'?"

"Warn't none."

Meek shook his head and grinned. "We cleaned 'em out fer good, I reckon. Put in eleven year myself at the job, so it ain't no wonder." He squinted again at Jonnie. "Say, lookee here, boy. Ain't I seen you somewheres before?"

"I don't think so."

Jonnie sounded baffled. But Jim, though equally mystified by the amiable tone of the conversation thus far, did understand this last. "My brother look familiar?" he asked Meek.

"By golly, he does. 'Ceptin' fer the eyes—"

"He's the spit of our uncle, Adam Russell."

"That's it!" burst out the sheriff delightedly. "So Russell's your uncle! Was you with him when he lost his hair?"

"No. I was in Absaroka by then."

"Oh, it was Absaroka, was it? Good country! But hard to git out of with all yer belongin's." Meek grinned. "I must've left more'n half a dozen good horses there at one time or another, without exactly meanin' to. You been back lately?"

"Not fer a couple years. Me and Tom Rivers—"

"Rivers! Say, you know ever'body!" Meek burst into sudden laughter. "Last time I seen Tom Rivers he was high tailin' it out of a thicket with fifty Comanches on his heels. He was in kind of a hurry. Passed up three jack rabbits while I was watchin' him."

"Where was you?"

"Me? Oh, I was hidin' in a prairie dog hole about a mile further on. You know, them things are right roomy, onct you git inside."

Jim was beginning to enjoy himself. "Must've been quite a rumpus."

"Well, it warn't no time to set around. We'd got back some beaver them dratted Injuns had stole from us the day before, and a couple of them fast little Comanche ponies had follered us off when we was leavin'. Warn't our fault, but you know Comanches. Their feelin's was hurt. Listen, where's ole Tom now? Set down here and catch me up on things, boy!"

Without quite knowing how it had come about, Jim found himself hunkered down on the grass beside the sheriff, talking as if he'd known him all his life. Meek fired questions, thick and fast, about Rivers and a dozen others. And in-between times he managed to find out more about Jim Keath than anybody but Jim and his family knew. Jim was a little astonished at this but too busy swapping yarns and good trapper's talk to give it much thought. He did keep wondering when the subject of last night was going to come up, and could see by Jonnie's bemused face that he was wondering too. But nobody could worry too much while roaring at one of Joe Meek's tales, tall enough to begin with and adorned with those added flourishes that had won him a reputation as the best liar west of Washington, D.C.

Jim was drawn to him as he had seldom been to anyone. Meek talked loud, laughed loud, radiated good nature—but he was thoroughly dangerous. Jim liked that best of all.

By the time Sally came out to invite the sheriff to stay for the noon meal, the purpose of his visit, if there were a purpose, had been forgotten. Jim walked beside him into the cabin, thinking hard. Meek hadn't got beavering out of his blood, that much was plain from every word he said. Yet here he was, with a dozen years of it behind him, settled down cheerfully to the length and breadth of one valley. How had he done it?

They all enjoyed that lunch, Meek most of all. His appetite had not been exaggerated. He polished off half a deer's haunch and a pan of hoecake, washing the whole down with quarts of coffee. And he commented on everything he saw, from Jonnie's home-carpentered furniture to the old Keath clock. At last he drained his cup and leaned back with a sigh of satisfaction, his tough, vigorous body showing no more bulges than it had an hour before.

"Miss Sally," he said with a grin, "either I'm the hungriest man in this here valley or you're the best cook."

Won over, Sally insisted that he stay on for supper too, but he laughed and reached for the squirrel-skin cap. "Nope. That horse of mine'll be thinkin' I aim to retire him. Walk with me down to the glades, Jim, and gimme a send-off."

It was exactly what Jim had been planning to do—he wanted a word with Meek alone. He fell in beside him readily, steadying the wounded arm with his other hand as he matched the sheriff's swift and silent stride.

"Meek, how come you to end up in this here valley?" he asked bluntly as they topped the ridge.

183

"End up? Thunder, boy, I'm just startin'." Meek grinned and headed down the other slope. "You wait'll them plug-hatted coyotes back in Washington wake up and make this territory a state. Anything kin happen then."

"Like what?"

"Why, hallelujah, I dunno, man. But somethin' big."

As Jim only looked more puzzled, he jerked his head impatiently toward the east. "Ain't you watched them wagons comin' over the plains?"

"Bourgeways," grunted Jim. He couldn't make out what Meek was driving at.

"Yeah, bourgeways." The sheriff smiled, then grew serious. As they reached his black stallion, he loosened the tether with a practiced hand and swung into the saddle. "Having a tough time settlin' in, ain't you? I know. I done that too, at first. Moseyed around, one place to the other, couldn't figure out what to do with myself. Seemed like if I couldn't bust out and chase a Injun or somethin' pretty soon I'd jest blow off my scalp lock."

"What 'ja do?"

Meek laughed. "By gosh, I planted thirty acre of wheat. Can you beat that?" He shook his head as if he still couldn't believe it. "Me, Joe Meek. I plowed."

"Oh."

"I was hungry," Meek explained apologetically. "Can't say I ever really tuck to hard work. But I tell you, Jim, I got so I tuck to this valley." His voice had turned thoughtful. "Folks around here are tryin' to git somethin' done. Somethin' big. Like I said, I ain't much count at workin'—so they got me shootin' their wolves for 'em while they get on with it."

He paused and Jim felt that three-hundred-pound cougar stretch and unsheath its claws. So here it came, after all.

Meek said, "Jim, this ain't Absaroka. It ain't Pierre's Hole or the Yellowstone, neither. All the rules is different. Now they was trouble last night up to that Cayuse camp. I didn't like it. I didn't like some other things I've heard."

Jim was suddenly conscious of the tell-tale furrows on his chest, half revealed between bandage and loosened shirt. Meek had heard about the Indian with the scars, about Jonnie Keath's brother and his wild ways. He'd come to find out for himself whether this wolf needed shooting or only warning.

"It's a funny thing," mused the sheriff. "I had me a time finding out anything about this rumpus last night. Ask Mills, they told me down at the Falls. Ask Burke. Rutledge'll know. Well, I asked 'em. And you know, them fellers clammed up on me like Blackfeet at a council smoke. Oh, sure, they knew the Keaths, they says. Fine boys. If t'warn't fer Jonnie Keath's brother they'd never've got them cattle back." Meek paused, nodding. "I'll go along with that—so long's there's no more trouble. Trouble's my business. I reckon you didn't know that before, boy. But you do now."

He was smiling, but it was plain enough what he meant. *Bust out once more and you'll have Joe Meek to reckon with.* Jim absorbed this in silence, along with the astonishing fact that nobody had wanted to inform on him. For Jonnie's sake? Or because he'd won their approval by taking that mare back? Both, perhaps.

He took a long breath. "I got a notion," he told Joe Meek, "I'll be too busy fer trouble fer quite a spell now. Plantin' wheat."

Meek's smile broadened. "I had a notion you was gettin' that notion. Good luck with it, boy, and watch your float stick." He straightened in his saddle, wheeling the stallion. "If wheat and spuds and fences get too much fer you," he added casually, "hunt me up and we'll swap a yarn or two. Might even put you to work. Anybody as can foller a passel of cattle twenty mile from two boot prints would make a good wolf hunter."

He cantered off across the glades, leaving a glittering vision in Jim's mind—himself straight and stern on Buckskin, a fine brass badge on his chest and Meek just ahead on his impatient stallion, speeding west or north or south in pursuit of lawbreakers, being always in the thick of every excitement from the Siskiyous to the Columbia, living a life of danger, forays, shrewd wits, and bold doings, "hunting wolves."

Jim squashed the vision with a disgusted growl. What was he thinking of? As far as Meek was concerned, it was yet to be proved that Jonnie Keath's brother was not a wolf himself. And it would take a lot of proving to convince the other settlers. Maybe if he plowed and planted wheat—there must be a kind of medicine in it, if even Joe Meek had had to do it before he learned how to live here.

Jim pushed away the echo of pounding hoofbeats, the gleam of a big brass badge, and angled up the slope into the woods, heading for the spot upriver where the medicine bundle lay, too long neglected, in the hollow stump. His helpers had served him well, against heavy odds and at a distance. But for them he'd be rubbed out or locked up, lost and finished instead of welcomed back with a chance to start afresh.

But for them—and Jonnie.

He reached up to touch one of the heavy long braids, profoundly relieved that they need no longer be a problem. Not even for Jonnie could he give up the braids or the feather, since it would mean giving up his helpers as well; but no bourgeway would understand that, and he doubted he could have explained. Now he didn't have to try.

He found the medicine bundle in the hollow stump and fingered it respectfully. Wrapping it in a clean scrap of elkhide from his pouch, he replaced it in hiding and hung cloth and tobacco from a nearby limb as a present to his helpers. He thanked them silently, wishing it were as simple to show gratitude to humans as to spirits.

He walked slowly back to the clearing, thinking about it. What did Jonnie want, really want bad? Not cloth and tobacco, not gunpowder, not the finest Nez Perce bow. Even a horse hadn't been good enough. Then what?

The answer came and he tried to evade it, because it stabbed him with the old unreasoning panic. He was still frowning and undecided when he broke through the last willows into the clearing and saw Dan'l and Moki turn simultaneously and rush toward him.

"Cracky! Where you been? Me and Moki's been waitin'—" Dan'l lowered his voice excitedly. "Can we play the 'follow' game, Jim? They's plenty of time before supper, and I seen three of Sally's trenchers I could swipe just as easy, and count coup too, I betcha, 'cause—"

"Hold on," Jim broke in. He hunkered down beside the boy. "Dan'l, we—we ain't playin' that game no more."

"No more? Not *ever* any more? But why, Jim?"

"Well, I kinda been thinkin'. Jonnie wouldn't like that game."

"Why, don't matter none what Jonnie thinks, he's—"

"It does, Dan'l!" Jim stood up. "It *matters*."

It mattered so much that his mind was suddenly made up. Turning his back on the bewildered, snub-nosed face, he strode to his lodge and snatched up the grizzly robe, his weapons and his pack, then walked swiftly toward the cabin, where Jonathan was helping Sally ease a fresh log onto the fire. Jim stopped in the doorway, waiting until they turned, then took a long, resolute breath.

"Kinda lost my taste fer sleepin' outside," he said. "From now on I'm livin' in this cabin with the rest of you."

Chapter XV

Whack! went Jim's ax. Whack! Whack! *Crash!* Suddenly he flung the ax down and with a couple of highly colored remarks in Crow, waded into the blackberry tangle and seized the offending root. He put his whole weight against it, yanking and tugging until it gave way and sent him sprawling. He picked himself up. In thunderous silence he scrambled free of the clutching thorns and snatched up the ax again. Whack! it went. Crash! *Whack!*

Five minutes later he set the ax blade against the ground and leaned heavily on the helve. Puffing for breath, he dragged his sleeve across his streaming forehead. From the next thicket the even, monotonous rhythm of Jonnie's ax went on, unbroken. Chunk—chunk—chunk—chunk.

Jim glowered at his brother. There had been hardly a pause in that sound all morning long. How in ten thousand devils did he do it?

The breeze was soft, the April sky dazzling. But here was this cussed blackberry thicket, the hazel bushes yonder, stumps, and more brush—all to be cleared before a fellow could enjoy life.

Wham! the ax went, fiercer than ever. Whack! Whack! *Crash!*

Jonnie grinned into the clump of ground oak he was clearing. He listened a while to the furious activity from Jim's part of the field, then stopped work and leaned his crossed arms on his ax.

"Hey, Jim!" he called.

The noises ceased abruptly. Jonnie strolled across the slashed area. "I got to wonderin'. When you're trackin' somebody—like you follered them cattle thieves, you know—and they've got a couple days' head start on you, that makes it pretty tough, don't it? You got to run all the way."

"*Run?* Are you crazy?"

"Well, you got to pick up that distance somehow, not just foller two days behind."

"But thunder, Jonnie, you'd kill yer horse if you tried to pick it up *runnin'!* No, you do it gradual. Git started a hour earlier than they're likely to, keep goin' a hour later. Don't stop long to eat. Keep a even pace but kinda slow, so yer horse don't git wore out. Run! *Wagh!* Slow and steady, that's the—"

Jim stopped. Jonnie was smiling broadly. There was a silence in which a blue jay jeered raucously from the nearby hazel bushes. Jim gave his ax a toss, caught it, and began to laugh.

"All right, I'll slow down. But thunder, they's a lot of this here scrub to clear away!"

"We can't do it all at once. Look back yonder where we started from a couple weeks ago. We're gettin' on."

"Yeah," Jim admitted.

He thought about it as he went back to work—at a more temperate pace this time. Jonnie was right. He usually was. And it was just like him to go at explaining a thing that way —making you prove his point for him before you even knew what he was driving at. Tracking! Running all the way! Jim had to laugh. No flies on Jonnie when it came to brains.

And they were getting on, that was certain, with the brush slashing and in a lot of other ways besides. Everything had changed. The tepee was gone. Its hides hung now over the rough walls inside the cabin; the lodgepoles were firewood. Sally's bed had been hoisted to the loft—to Dan'l's loud disappointment. He'd wanted Jim up there instead. But Jim was better suited the way things were. His willow and rawhide frame stood across the room from Jonnie's bed, under the window and not two steps from the door. It hadn't been so bad, sleeping inside.

There was a shed behind the cabin now, too, and a heifer purchased on credit from Mr. Mills was inside the shed. Jonnie had said, "With you and me both workin', Jim, we'll have another ten acres cleared before time to plow. Shucks, we can pay off that Hudson's Bay debt and have the heifer too—and maybe even a new dress for you, sis!"

Yes, they were getting on.

The axes chunked all morning, flashing in the sun. Jim shed his shirt before long, and kept himself rigidly to Jonnie's even tempo. But in spite of that, by noon he had worked up a steaming sweat and a hunger that made him feel like one vast cavern. He flung down his ax with relief when he spotted Dan'l trudging across the glades with the basket of lunch.

It was shady and cool beside the brook, and the slabs of cold meat and hoecake tasted like a feast.

"Me and Moki found a bear's track this mornin'," Dan'l told Jim eagerly. "Little bitty one. I think it was a cub."

"What kind?"

"I dunno. Black, I think. Listen, Jim, couldn't you and me go find it after you get through eatin', and catch it, and raise it like a pet?"

"Moki'd worry it to death."

"No, he wouldn't, he'd like it! Gee, couldn't we, Jim?"

"You take a cub and pretty soon you got its mama on yer neck. Don't forget that."

190

"You could handle her! Listen, when you get through with eatin'—"

Jim shifted unhappily. "Dan'l, I can't be goin' off after bears and such. I got work to do." He'd said the same sort of thing so often lately that he almost dreaded to see Dan'l coming. He hated to keep putting the boy off and putting him off, but there was no help for it. "One of these days I'll git finished here, and then you and me'll go huntin'."

"Meantime, Dan'l," Jonnie put in, "I reckon sis can use some help with moldin' them candles. You best take the basket and run on."

"Gee!" said Dan'l. He picked up the basket and plodded off toward the cabin, every line of him eloquent with disappointment.

The food didn't taste good now. Jim finished his quickly and went back to work, more impatient than ever to get the job done and over with. It was a chore to keep his ax going slow and steady.

But at the end of the day there was a wider swath of slash behind him than ever before. He couldn't help feeling a grim satisfaction as he shouldered his ax. He might not have enjoyed it, but he'd done it; even Joe Meek could boast no more than that. And he was through with it till morning, by gor!

He welcomed each day's end for more reasons than one. There was something good about walking over the ridge beside your brother, the sky red or smoky purple beyond the woods, and a delicious languor spreading through your tired body. They always made for the willows and plunged briefly into the Tualatin's ice water, afterward chasing each other headlong up the slope toward the glowing yellow rectangle of the cabin doorway. Jim won these races without much trouble.

"Racin' with you is no job for an amateur!" Jonnie complained that night as he arrived, puffing from exertion and cold water, at the outside bench where Jim was already pulling on his clothes. "How the devil did you get so fast on your feet?"

"Chasin' butterflies," Jim said with a grin.

"Doin' *what?*"

But Jim suddenly felt a little self-conscious. "*Wagh!* I was jokin'. Hurry up there, I'm half froze fer somethin' to eat."

It was good to go inside, too, out of the chilly dusk, and find the fire blazing, the cabin warm and filled with the smell of meat—all roasted and waiting for you. Dan'l and Moki sprang up at once from their tussling on the buffalo robe that covered the earthen floor. Sally, her cheeks flushed in their halo of golden tendrils from the heat of the fire, flashed a welcoming smile, then scolded them for running around with wet heads.

"Set down now and stay out of my way. I'll have supper on in a minute. Dan'l, hop to it, get the trenchers laid out."

Jim ignored the stools and the one chair, as usual, and squatted down Indian fashion against the wall. There was always this moment, just after he stepped into the cabin, when he wanted to turn right around and go out again. He wondered why. It was a cheerful enough scene in the light of the fire blazing there on the big stone hearth. The light shimmered over the satiny hides on the walls and struck glints from the row of pewter mugs hanging along the bottom of a shelf. In the shadows at one end of the room stood Jonnie's bed, covered by a faded scarlet blanket; over it jutted the loft, a braced platform with a ladder leading up to it. At the other end were table and benches, cupboard and churn, a shelf holding coffee mill and candle mold. Dan'l moved about the table, clattering spoons and trenchers.

Nothing to dread about all this. But there on the split-log mantel stood that clock, like a ghost in the room.

Jim got up restlessly and walked to the hearth. Sally had a

pot of something bubbling on the black iron crane, and it smelled good. So did the haunch that hung from the mantel on twisted thongs, glistening and dripping into a pan below as it slowly revolved.

"Man, I'm hungry," Jonnie murmured suddenly from where he sprawled on Jim's bed. "Smell that, will you? I could eat it all."

"You'll get a chance to try." Sally slammed the cupboard door and hurried across the room, shoving Jim impatiently out of her way as she bent to drag the hoecake out of the coals. Jim grinned, the clock forgotten and the restless moment over for another night. Sally went at cooking the same way he'd gone at those bushes this morning. She grabbed a handful of her apron and swung the pot outward on its iron crane. "Now if somebody'll just lift down that haunch while I dish out the mush, we'll be ready to eat."

Sometimes, after supper was over, Jonnie would reach for his banjo and make that potent medicine he understood so well—singing soft and lonesome so that you thought of every prairie trail you'd ever followed, or snapping erect with his fingers flying and his white grin flashing, fetching Dan'l to his feet in a leaping dance and heightening the color in Sally's cheeks as she laughed and clapped out the rhythm.

But tonight Jonnie chose the other thing they did together. When the food was cleared away and the fire replenished, when Sally had settled herself by the table with her patching and Dan'l sprawled on the buffalo robe, his drowsy golden head against Moki's gray one—then Jonnie went to the mantel and took down the big Bible.

Jim was mending a moccasin, but he stopped, frowning uneasily, as Jonnie trimmed the candle and opened the book. This was medicine too, a different, troubling kind like the clock made. Jim's muscles were gathered for leaping up and heading for the door when Jonnie began to read—and then he was caught, held fast by the curious strength and music of the words, by the puzzle of their meaning.

"And the earth was without form, and void; and darkness was upon the face of the deep. And the spirit of God moved upon the face of the waters . . ."

It was like a strange language; almost, but never quite, comprehensible, yet queerly familiar to Jim. He wished he knew what it meant, what it had to do with himself. But he was afraid to ask.

He was half afraid of the book itself tonight. Jonnie turned pages at random, and read, "The Lord will smite thee with the botch of Egypt, and with the emerods, and with the scab, and with the itch, with madness, with blindness, and astonishment of heart . . ."

A trickle of cold went down Jim's spine at these unimaginable horrors. How could the others sit there so calmly, hearing all that and never even stirring? It sounded like the blackest of magic.

Jonnie turned more pages. ". . . He shall cover thee with his feathers . . . thou shalt not be afraid for the terror by night nor for the arrow that flieth by day. A thousand shall fall at thy side but it shall not come nigh thee . . ."

Arrows and night attacks—Jim knew those well. Here was something he could grasp. Clearly it was a medicine song of unheard-of power. But whose? He was afraid to ask that too. He sat frowning, fingering the smoke-dark moccasin and wishing Jonnie would close the book.

At last Sally rose, gave a shake to the last pair of new-patched jeans, and tossed them over the table. "There! I reckon they'll hold together a little longer now. My stars, if I never saw another patch as long as I live— Jonnie, it's bedtime. Here's that shirt, such as it is. Ain't nothin' *but* patches by now—"

Jonnie put the big book away and laughed quietly, jerking a thumb at the slumbering little boy on the floor. "Looks like Dan'l's left us. Hey, there, wake up long enough to go to bed!"

Dan'l roused and stumbled up the ladder, mumbling "G'night."

"Good night," yawned Sally, following him.

Jim stepped outside to breathe the cold night air and look up at the stars. They were hidden behind clouds now, and the breeze was full of the smell of rain. He walked up through the firs to the ridge, spotted Buckskin's pale shape next to the mule's dark one at the foot of the slope. A muffled thumping came occasionally from the shed where the heifer was kept.

Later, lying in bed in the shadowy room, with the banked fire spilling crimson over the hearth and Jonnie's breathing mingling with the soft drum of rain outside, Jim wondered why he still felt he had not come home.

So the days passed, one very like the other, as spring drifted up the valley. One morning Sally asked Jim to row across to the Rutledges and ask the loan of their big iron pot.

"Time I set about my soap makin'. I'm feared to keep them saved-up fats and meat scraps around much longer, with warm weather comin' on. Dan'l, fetch them two barrels from the shed and a couple of noggins, and get yourself busy makin' lye while I finish up inside. I'll be out to help you directly."

By the time Jim climbed back up the bank, lugging the big kettle, Dan'l had the two barrels set side by side on a bench by the shed, and was lining them with dried grasses. As Jim drew near, the boy placed a noggin under the hole in the bottom of the barrel with a resentful crash.

"Seems like all we ever do around here any more is work," he grumbled.

Sally, her faded but carefully patched blue dress swathed in an enormous apron, went past with a shovelful of wood ashes. "Since when," she asked Dan'l, "have we ever done anything else? You're pullin' your share these days, is the only difference. Just set that pot down yonder, Jim, we won't be boilin' the fats for a while yet. Lye's got to get strong enough to float an egg."

She dumped the ashes into the nearest barrel and hurried off for more, while Jim lowered the kettle to the ground.

"What's the matter, Dan'l, they keepin' yer nose too close to the grindstone?"

"I reckon you wouldn't much care if they did or not."

"Why, thunder, you ain't sore at *me* about it are you?"

Dan'l didn't answer, but picked up a bucket of water and poured it over the ashes in the barrel, his snub-nosed little profile remote.

"Dan'l, I don't have time to play with you no more. I'm workin' too."

"Yeah, I know." The boy gave a halfhearted smile. "Maybe later on, though? When the clearin's all done? You said someday you'd show me how to use your bow and arrow, and teach me to talk Crow."

Jim chewed his lip. He couldn't be teaching the boy things like that—now. "Yeah, we'll find somethin' to do," he murmured. "Later on."

But there was no let up in the work when you were turning a stretch of raw country into a farm. The day came when the last stump was uprooted, the last hazel thicket laid low. At sunup the next morning Jonnie dragged out his plow, hardly willing to finish breakfast in his eagerness to get down to his two waiting fields. Ten minutes later, with a "*Hup!*" to his oxen, he thrust the plow share deep into virgin soil, watching over his shoulder joyfully as the rich dark loam turned back in fertile stripes behind him.

Jim, hoe in hand, paused at the top of the ridge. The face of the valley was changing, as he had known it would. He had ridden to Willamette Falls the day before after meal and salt, and everywhere he had seen these fresh dark furrows striping the land like open wounds, and emptiness where groves of fir and oak had stood. Their own claim seemed naked yonder, with the scrub oak all gone and part of the woods itself, and only a pasture's worth of glades left alone for the animals' grazing.

He reached out to touch one of the huge old firs that towered all about him. Plenty of forest left up here, at least, plenty on the untouched acres to the west. But how long would that last?

Jonnie marched up and down in the sunshine, his taut body aslant against the oxen's pull. Beyond him spread a sea of tree-tops, a roll of hills, then the perfect, glistening cone of Mount Hood—so lofty it dwarfed the range it sprang from, seeming to rise alone from level plains. Plenty of forest up there, too, among the snows—and plenty on the other side, where un-fenced wilderness swept away to Absaroka.

Hastily Jim started on down the slope to follow after Jonnie and break up the clods with his hoe. But he had noticed that the snowy mantle which had covered the mountain all winter had shrunk to a gleaming cap. There were no barriers now; the gates of the valley were unlocked.

Jim, working shirtless one day in July in the garden plot at the foot of the ridge, looked up to see Dan'l wandering aim-lessly across the pasture in the direction of the creek.

The boy seemed forlorn, in spite of the stubborn tilt of the bright head and its proud refusal to turn in Jim's direction. That hoped-for "later on" had never come; they hadn't played a game in weeks.

Jonnie was busy at the other end of the garden. Jim straight-ened, dropping his trowel, vaulted the rail fence into the pas-ture, and strolled toward the boy.

"Dan'l! Hey, Dan'l. C'mere."

The boy hesitated the fraction of a moment, then walked to meet him.

"Take off your clothes. You won't want nothin' hamperin' you."

The remote, guarded look in the gray-green eyes changed to one of interest. "We gonna do somethin'?"

"You are. Git off them clothes."

All eagerness now, Dan'l stripped off shirt and jeans, kicked them away and stood waiting. Jim smiled. It was a strong young body there before him, clad only in the moccasins and brief drawers. Well, he would make it stronger.

"Now," he said. He pointed suddenly. "Catch me that butterfly. Quick!"

After a startled instant Dan'l was off like a flash, darting here and there over the pasture in erratic zigzags, his hands clutching at the flitting spot of yellow, his fair skin gleaming against the dark woods beyond. It was a frantic race, full of unexpected stumblings and miraculous recoveries, and one headlong spill. Jim felt his own muscles alternately tense and loosen as he stood there laughing, all else forgotten. And when Dan'l gave one last desperate spurt and pounced on his elusive prey, Jim let loose a whoop of victory.

"Bring it here, now! Bring it here!"

Breathless and flushed with triumph, Dan'l came running. "Got 'im—by cracky!" he puffed. "Whadda I—do now?"

"Now you make magic. Let me have him."

Carefully Jim took the little creature and showed Dan'l how to rub the yellow wing dust on his chest, teaching him the words in Crow: "Oh, butterfly, give me your strength and swiftness . . ."

"What's that mean?" demanded Dan'l eagerly.

"Means he's got to make you as fast as he was. Don't tell

nobody, just say it and make the magic, and you'll win ever' foot race in the valley."

Dan'l was already off after another butterfly by the time Jim realized that Jonnie was standing at his elbow.

"So that's how you got so fast on your feet!"

Jim laughed. "I told you."

"Yeah," mused Jonnie. "Chasin' butterflies. You wasn't jokin' after all." He watched Dan'l's darting and dashing a moment, and added, "I think them Injuns knew a thing or two. Anybody'd get feather footed if he done that very much."

"You had to be, in Absaroka. We run foot races all the time, us boys, and by gor, we'd ruther've busted our lungs than come in last! All them strong, big warriors standin' there in their coup feathers, watchin' us. We had butterfly dust on us from spring to fall."

"Rough on the butterfly population," commented Jonnie with a grin. He added casually, "It ain't the dust or the words that turns the trick, it's the chasin'. But a-course you know that."

Jim didn't know anything of the sort. Medicine was medicine. But he didn't say so, he only turned and led the way back to the garden, whistling tunelessly. When they reached the potato patch where his trowel lay, Jonnie stopped beside him.

"Gettin' homesick, Jim?" he asked abruptly.

"Naa. I'm fine." Jim picked up the trowel and fell to work.

It wasn't quite true. The old life tugged at him no matter how he resisted. Scalp Necklace and the others would be winding over the prairie this month to new buffalo grounds; a thin, brown line of horses and travois and baggage, of squaws and darting, black-haired children and stately chieftains and reckless, hard-riding young men on feather-bedecked horses racing each other on the outskirts. The whole scene rose before him, a picture drawn indelibly on his brain; and when he shook his

199

head, trying to forget it, another rose in its place: a beaver stream flowing between cottonwoods in a high meadow, the sky shadowy with dusk, and the smell of smoke in the air.

Wheat and spuds and fences were getting too much for him, rapidly. It was about time he went to see Joe Meek.

A couple of restless weeks later, on a sun-drenched, somnolent day in the middle of August, he dismounted in front of Meek's cabin in the Tualatin valley. He was halfway to the door when Meek's Nez Perce squaw padded around the corner of the house, a knife in one hand and a skinned rabbit in the other. The sheriff wasn't home, she informed him. He'd gone south three sleeps past to settle some kind of trouble among the Umpquas.

Jim walked away, sullen with disappointment. He'd waited too long. By now he was wild to talk to somebody of his own sort.

He dug his heels into Buckskin and spurted over the ridge with Moki streaking beside him, heading east for Willamette Falls—which everyone was now beginning to call Oregon City. He'd trade the pelt in his pouch for Galena lead and replenish his supply of bullets tonight, and tomorrow he'd go hunting. At least he could do that much. Stay two or three days, maybe a week—it wouldn't matter, the grain stood waist high and golden in Jonnie's fields now, there was little to do until harvest, which would come all too soon to chain him down again.

But Jim didn't go hunting on the morrow. He didn't even get his bullets made. Striding out of the trading post in Oregon City an hour later, he saw Moki stop short, ears erect and nose quivering, then dash headlong across the rutted street toward the rail where the mare was tied. Alarmed at once, Jim leaped past the startled group of farmers and tradesmen on the porch, and gained the road. There he halted.

A man in buckskin was bending over Moki, one hand holding the bridle of a familiar tall horse while the other tusseled with the ecstatic dog.

There could be only one such pair of faded scarlet leggings, one such spare frame and battered hat. Jim knew—even before he fully believed it, even before the man straightened and met his eyes, smiling a slow and well-remembered smile.

It was Tom Rivers.

With a yell that cracked in the middle, Jim was upon him.

Chapter XVI

"Yep, hoss," Tom said, leaning back on his elbow and stretching out a foot to shove a log farther into the fire, "I kinda figgered all along it was this valley that letter was talkin' about. So Jonnie warn't no sperrit after all?"

Jim grinned. "Not by a long chalk. He's mighty lively."

"When am I gonna git to see him?"

"Tomorrer. We'll go on down there tomorrer."

Tonight, though, there was still too much unsaid—they'd barely started. After the first joyous confusion of back thumping, hand shaking, and incoherent questions and answers, their sole thought had been to get away from the town and the staring onlookers, off alone where they could talk.

But conversation during the ride west into the hills had been curtailed by the reckless pace they set each other, and limited to cheerful insults and the discussion of campsites. Even later, making camp and seeing to the horses, they had exchanged only scraps of information about themselves, Jim parrying Tom's frequent questions for no reason he could think of except that there was such a vast amount to tell and he didn't know how to start.

They were lounging now beside their supper fire near the banks of a little stream, chewing the last of the buffalo jerky Tom had produced from his possibles. It was good beyond all belief to eat buffalo again, to sprawl like this watching the firelight dance over Tom's familiar, weather-beaten face. He looked thinner than Jim remembered him, but his blue eyes were shrewd as ever, his drawl as soft, and his grin as warm.

He'd run into Black Jaw Hervey down at Taos, and heard about the boy in the wagon train who looked like Adam Russell, and had told Hervey the letter reached its mark. "We figgered you two must've got together at The Dalles, and from there they ain't no place much to go, exceptin' west. That how it happened?"

"Yeah, that's it. Tom, how was Taos?"

"*Wagh!* Mighty slow. Warn't but half a dozen trappers in the hull town, and more Mexicans than Injuns. Why, you couldn't hardly git you up a hand game."

"Warn't Peliot there? Or Evart?"

Tom shook his head. "Gone back to the States. Ever'body's gone. Scattered, dead, quit the trade. Hervey was headin' east when I left fer Californy."

"How come you went to Californy?"

"Shucks, I dunno. It was the only place I hadn't been. It's quite a place, if you savvy Spanish. Mighty nice weather. And trees? Hoss, you ain't never rightly seen a tree till you've met up with one of them redwoods. They're a mile around." His smile faded. "Rest of the place is kinda bare, though—down south in Mission country it is. And it don't never git winter there." He shrugged. "I dunno. It ain't fer me."

"Any beaver?"

"Naaa."

There was unexpected bitterness in the syllable. Tom fished in his pouch a moment and drew out his pipe. In the silence Jim could hear the stream running along out there in the dark, and the night wind high in the branches, and the soft ripping noise the horses made as they cropped the grass. It sounded lonesome.

"Tom, I thought you was gonna go git yer squaw."

"I did git her." Rivers smiled crookedly, his long fingers stuffing kinnikinnick into his pipe—that familiar long-stemmed Indian pipe made of the red clay known only to the Plains tribes, the bowl marked in black and white with a Blackfoot symbol. "I did git her. But I reckon she figgered there warn't much future in a beaver man no more. 'Long about a month ago, when we warn't too fer from Nez Perce country, she up and packed her parfleche, and roped her hoss, and tuck off home—back to them relatives." Tom smiled again. "I couldn't blame her."

It was Tom who was lonesome. Mighty lonesome. "You aimin' to stay here?" Jim asked gently. "You'd be welcome."

"Oh, I'll hang around awhile. But, hoss, I doubt if I'd ever git to feelin' natural in a valley."

"You could try it out. You gotta do somethin'."

Tom pulled a blazing twig out of the fire and held it to his pipe before he answered. Then he said, very casually, "I hear they's still beaver in the Rockies. South Park."

Jim watched him closely as the little flame dimmed and flared, dimmed and flared, over the glowing tobacco. Was Tom feeling him out? Before he could decide, Rivers tossed away the twig and lay back on his elbow, his grin veiled by a cloud of thin blue smoke.

"Lookee here, hoss, I come up here jest mainly to find out how you was makin' it. Ain't you gonna tell me? By golly, the next time I'm fool enough to hike it over a mountain range to hunt up a no-good, knife-throwin', yaller-eyed coyote what won't even open his trap . . ." He dodged amiably as Jim's knife came sailing past his ear. "Ain't slowed down none, I see. Well, I ain't neither." He reached up without looking and yanked the knife out of the tree behind his head. "Go on, that don't change my mind none. Start talkin'."

Jim grinned and settled himself comfortably. "What d'ya want to hear?"

"Want to hear about all this plowin' you been doin'. Jim Keath a farmer! By golly, that takes some believin'!"

Jim's grin vanished. "I ain't no farmer."

"Why, you said you got twenty acre of wheat gittin' along fer harvest."

"Jonnie's wheat. Fer all I care, it could be sagebrush."

Rivers leaned forward. "What's the matter, hoss?" he asked softly. "Ain't that medicine of your'n workin'?"

"It ain't the medicine's fault. It ain't Jonnie's neither. And by gor it ain't mine!" Jim shifted irritably, picked up a leaf and began tearing it to pieces. "Farmin' jest ain't in me, Tom. I done the best I could fer four, five months now. Livin' in the cabin, workin' from sunup to evenin', holdin' in when I wanted to bust loose. And by thunder, I been wantin' to bust! Ever' time I look up and see them mountains yonder, with the snows gone and the way open, clean through—!"

He flung the leaf away and got up, wandering restlessly about the fire while Moki's yellow eyes watched every move. Tom lay very still, puffing quietly. Presently he murmured, "Four-five months. What about afore that?"

"Well—I reckon I warn't even tryin', afore that. Didn't know how. I kept doin' things Injun, like I was used to. My sister, she sure don't like Injuns. She—"

"You got a sister too?"

Jim smiled, thinking of the shining hair, the fierce little chin, and flying skirts. "Yeah. Sally. She's only fifteen. Prettiest little thing you ever saw."

"So you're the oldest. Why, hallelujah, Jim, you mean them three young 'uns come all the way from Missouri alone?"

"Not all the way." Jim came back and sat down. "Not all the way. My mother was with 'em when they started. Tom, if only we'd been on the Sweetwater som'ers instead of on the Powder, I could've seen her afore she died."

He began to tell it all, then, at first slowly and with pauses to gather his thoughts, then more rapidly, reliving the whole thing as he described the snowy passes above the gorge, Dan'l's mutiny and his own tearing hunger, the journey's end by the still waters of the Tualatin. It was hard to explain the first taste of hoecake, and how he felt about the clock, but he made a stab at it. And the lonely, defiant weeks he'd spent in the tepee, the games with Dan'l, the beautiful rejected mare —he didn't skip anything. Most of all he talked about Sally and his brothers, trying to make Tom feel what he had felt, know them as he now did.

Especially Jonnie. "My brother, he's a wonder, Tom. He knows how the stick's floatin' when I git to feelin' itchy footed and no-account. He'll say, 'Jim, you take off huntin' today, I don't needja. Blast it now, git goin'.' He's figgered out how it is with me, though he don't never feel that way hisself. Ain't that somethin', now?"

"Yeah," said Rivers softly. "It's somethin'."

The pipe lay forgotten in his cupped hand, and his expression was hard to fathom. Jim sat up and rumpled Moki's ears. "It don't git no easier, all the same, stayin' put. I reckon it ain't never goin' to, fer a Injun like me."

"You ain't no Injun, hoss. Not any more."

"Mebbe not!" Jim burst out. "But I ain't no farmer, neither! Tom—" He paused, searching the older man's eyes with sudden hunger. "You said you heard they was still beaver back in South Park . . ."

Rivers' face changed. He spoke in a different tone, low and flat and tired. "Hoss, there likely ain't a word of truth in it. Stick to yer cabin. That medicine of your'n was a powerful lot stronger than I give it credit fer."

Puzzled and somehow uneasy, Jim studied the familiar

rugged profile, darkly outlined against the flames but quite unreadable. What did Tom mean? That he'd rather trap alone? Then why had he come a thousand miles out of his way to hunt up an old companion?

He shrugged the matter out of his mind and lay down to sleep. But he was still awake long after the fire had burned to crimson embers and the familiar humped shape next to him lay deep in sleep. There was something changed about his friend since they'd parted, nearly a year ago, by the banks of the Powder. But try as he would, he couldn't put his finger on what it was.

It continued to plague and elude him over the next month and a half; Tom "hung around" until September was all but gone. For Jim it was a strange period, in which the now familiar life in the valley, his family, the neighbors, his work around the claim, all took on a curious unreality, as if he knew them in a dream. His mind was absorbed with Tom, and his days, like an iceberg, were lived four-fifths below the surface, in a dark region where crosscurrents of thought and feeling, none of which he understood, tugged and strained deep inside himself.

Only one of the young Keaths failed to welcome Jim's friend wholeheartedly. The first morning they met, Jonnie and Tom had sized each other up and shaken hands on it, each thoroughly approving. Sally, too, was taken with Rivers' slow grin and easy drawl. Before he had been camped two days under the big oak where the tepee used to stand, she was treating him like an old friend of the family. She alternately pampered and bullied him, stuffing him with hoecake and venison, scolding him for his thin ribs, in a way that captivated him entirely.

Dan'l alone was unresponsive. Tom tried his best to make friends with the boy, hauling out his gaudiest yarns of scalpings and escapes, presenting him with a knife that had once belonged to a Piegan chief. Dan'l accepted both tales and gift, torn between interest and hostility, but he remained aloof.

"Looks like I've lost my touch," Rivers remarked to Jim one day, not altogether humorously, as they watched the boy's uncompromising young back recede in the direction of the glades. "Fust thing you know Moki'll be growlin' at me. And when dogs and young 'uns turn agin a man, ain't much use wastin' the gunpowder to blow 'im to hallelujah."

"*Wagh!* You ain't that ornery yet! The boy's got some fool notion in his head, that's all."

"It's sartin he don't keer much fer the smell of my bait. Him and that squaw of mine." Rivers' grin twisted, as it so often did these days. "Mebbe they're both right."

Jim scoffed at him cheerfully, but the boy's attitude puzzled him, and he mentioned it to Jonathan, who had an answer for him immediately. "Why, blast it, Jim, you goin' blind? He's jealous, that's all. Scared Tom's gonna steal you away and take you back to trappin'." Jonnie hesitated. "You could set his mind at rest. I tried to, but it's been a long spell since I carried any weight with Dan'l. He don't believe me."

"*Wagh*, he'll git over it," murmured Jim vaguely. His gaze had wandered out over the fields and treetops to the haze-blued cone of Mount Hood. And he was no longer thinking about Dan'l.

Harvest time came and went without really breaking through his preoccupation. He took turns with Jonnie at wielding the great scythe, tied endless shocks of wheat, and swung the flail, without giving much attention to any of it except the surprising fact that Tom should be there too, working good-naturedly by his side. He did realize dimly as he stood at last beside his brother surveying the bulging sacks of grain, that it mattered to him after all, that this was wheat and not sagebrush. But he did not stop to examine the discovery, merely

208

noting that Jonnie's grin was good to see, and feeling somewhat repaid for all those weeks of tearing out stumps and scattering seed. Then he went to find Tom. With harvest done, there was nothing to prevent their roaming as they liked, searching the hills for game and the streams for beaver, racing Buckskin and Tucky hard and fast over the hills, and pretending there was nothing on their minds but the next meal.

They went to see Joe Meek. He was home this time—home and bursting to talk. The bellow of delight he let out when he glimpsed Tom was worth half a year's catch, as Tom said afterward; and the spate of food and drink and trapper's talk and roaring merriment that filled the afternoon and night was as good as a regular old-time rendezvous. But now again, almost against his will, Jim found himself watching Tom curiously, puzzling over what it was about him that had changed.

One evening at Rutledges', when all the neighbors round about had gathered to pool their suppers and celebrate the bountiful harvest, he almost put his finger on it, though not quite. It was a merry evening, redolent with the smells of venison and wood smoke, noisy with laughter and the shouts of children—the hubbub twined and woven through with the twinkling notes of Jonnie's banjo.

And after the feast a group of the men gathered, as they always did, to prop their worn boots on fence rail or wagon tongue, and smoke and talk. Rutledge was among them, and Mills and Burke and Sam Mullins and Jonnie and Ab Selway and Jim—and Tom. He stood leaning against the wagon wheel puffing his long red pipe—lithe and lean in a way no bourgeway ever achieved, his weather-beaten features half hidden by the veil of smoke. He seemed removed from the others, drawn apart, though he stood in their midst.

". . . thirty bushels to the acre," Mills was saying with satisfaction. "You wait. The folks back east ain't gonna stay there long with that kinda haul comin' in out here! I bet they's wagons crossin' the Blues this minute, rollin' down them long rocky stretches to The Dalles, comin' through the gorge—"

"Man, I'm glad it ain't me," somebody muttered.

"They was wagons down to Oregon City yestiddy," Ab Selway offered. "Folks from away back yonder—Pennsylvania and Connecticut. Said they was hund'erds of folks piled up at The Dalles, waitin' on boats to take 'em through, and the boats are sceerce and the prices turrible. Reg'lar robbery, it's turned into."

"Why'n't they build theirselves rafts, like we done?"

"Why, shucks, the place is about stripped of timber by this time. Feller in the fust wagon, he told me they was talk of findin' a overland route—takin' the wagons right over them mountains."

There was an outburst of disbelief. "Why, crimeny, ain't no way through them mountains, ever'body knows that."

"You mean they's folks tryin' it?"

"They's some feller tryin' to take a bunch through. Name of Barlow. Hull crew of 'em'll be lost, a-course . . ."

"Mebbe not," put in Rutledge's deep voice suddenly. As always when Rutledge spoke, the others fell quiet. They all respected the huge, slow-spoken thoughtful man. "If they ain't no other way to get here," he went on, "I reckon they'll make it."

"But lord a'mighty, Mr. Rutledge," Jonnie said. "They say them slopes is straight up and down. And with the snow and all—seems impossible."

"Remember Windlass Hill, Jonnie? We all come down that, and by jiminy, *that* seemed impossible! Wasn't no pleasure jaunt fordin' the Snake this side of Fort Hall, neither." Rutledge turned thoughtfully to Tom. "What's your idee on it, Rivers? Think they's a way through them Cascades?"

"Fer a mountain goat, they is," Rivers drawled, scratching his cheek with the end of his long pipe stem. "Fer men on hosses, they is. Jim and me done it onct, but then we cut our teeth on high country. I wouldn't say no bourgeway with a wagon could make it."

The faces around him changed a little; Jim could see the stubborn pride come awake in everyone. "Up till couple year ago folks said no wagon could get past Fort Hall," Mills reminded.

"Or acrost them deserts."

"Or through the gorge."

Rivers smiled and nodded. "Yeah, I know. But you ain't seen a certain hill just south of Mount Hood. Ain't nothin'll grow on it but a few little old laurels. Too steep. Ain't no wagon ever gonna make that, and they's no way around it."

The men heard him in silence, unable to contradict since they hadn't been there. But when the talk rose up again it was brisk and undismayed—about the new settlement called Portland, across from Fort Vancouver, where the Willamette joined the Columbia; about this year's crops and next year's plans; about the burgeoning new government and the possibility of statehood in the foreseeable future.

Rutledge talked quietly to Tom, asking questions and nodding courteously at the answers—but Jim wondered what was in the big man's mind, for his face was thoughtful as he studied Rivers. He *knew* what was in Tom's mind; it was all there to read. Tom was far away, riding along over some remembered wilderness. At that moment Jim came near to glimpsing what it was that troubled him about his friend; but Tom turned suddenly to laugh at something Rutledge said, and the impression vanished. Jim knew only that Tom Rivers was the loneliest man he had ever seen, and his knowledge grew until the hubbub around him faded and the gay crowds vanished, and there was nothing left in his mind but Tom and the old, good days, and his own fierce and overwhelming loyalty.

Three days later, when Tom Rivers rode quietly out of the clearing in the murky gray of dawn, Jim rode with him. His belongings were loaded in the old way on Bad Medicine's back, Moki raced alongside, and Buckskin's nose was pointed toward the high Cascades.

Chapter XVII

Jim and Tom moved into the heavy fir growth which cut off the last glimpse of the cabin. This was all so natural. It might have been last year, when they had made camp in that same clearing and left in a daybreak just like this to start for Sioux country and another season of trapping. Jim's mind was a corridor of closed doors, with only one flung open—the door to last year and the year before—the way back.

Sunrise was almost upon them when they reached the banks of the Willamette close by the falls. They found the old one-eyed Chinook ferryman, Iakhka Tcikeakh, lounging beside his hut with his arms folded and a look of sour disapproval on his usually stolid face.

"Come on, Jake, move them lazy moccasins and cast off," Jim told him. "We want to git acrost the river."

Jake's one eye rolled somberly in his direction, but he didn't stir. Patiently, Jim began to repeat his request in Chinook jargon, only to stop in the middle. Three canoes filled with Indians were making their way to the bank a couple of hundred yards below the falls. "Much people," he said in surprise.

Jake grunted. "Hyas tillicum," he agreed, then added, "Hyas masahchie!"

"Much evil? Who is this much bad people?"

"Umpqua."

"Oh." Jim's brow knotted impatiently; he understood now. Fort Vancouver had been full of Umpquas for a week, and so had Oregon City. It was their yearly trading expedition, which brought canoeload after canoeload of them down the Willamette from their villages far to the south. Evidently they were beginning to start homeward; small bunches of them would be portaging around the falls here all day and likely tomorrow, and Jake, who was a true Chinook and hated Umpquas, didn't like it. Jim, on the other hand, didn't like being delayed—not this close to the Tualatin, with the sun nearly up.

"*Wagh!* You scared they'll steal yer cabin while you ferry us?" he demanded of the old Indian. "Tom, you got anything to bribe him with? No sense wearin' the horses out swimmin' 'em when they's a boat right here."

"Hoss, I'm about as plum broke as a man kin git, but you might try 'im on these here beads. The Nez Perces like 'em."

Jim took the packet of blue beads and offered it to Jake, jabbering menacingly in Chinook jargon meanwhile, and making gestures of haste. Jake took the beads and after looking each one over separately, stowed them in his dirty sash. But they could not get him to budge until the three canoes were landed, hoisted to the heads of the paddlers, carried around the portage, and set afloat again above the falls. Then, at last, the old Chinook grunted and consented to man his ferry.

No more than half an hour had elapsed, in all, but the incident had marred Jim's dreamlike peace of mind. As they scrambled up the steep rise on the east side of the river and set off toward the mountains, he found himself hurrying Buckskin, turning out of his way to avoid passing familiar fields and the cabins of settlers he knew. The Umpquas were on his mind, too, touching him with vague uneasiness. They were a troublesome crew; Joe Meek's disciplinary sortie into their territory last month had been only one of many. And the faces Jim had observed as the straggling line passed by him on

214

the way around the portage had been harsh mouthed and sullen, with flat, blank eyes. He had heard the Umpquas kept slaves.

He shook himself free from his depression, irritably hustling Bad Medicine, who wanted mulishly to poke. Suppose they did keep slaves? Suppose they were ugly as Cayuses and mean as Apaches? They lived far away south and were going there as fast as they could. They'd bring no trouble to the cabin on the Tualatin.

"What the Sam Hill's eatin' you, hoss?" came Tom's amused complaint behind him. "That mare's going like her tail was afire. You in a hurry?"

Jim laughed and forced himself to a leisurely pace, trying to shut those troublesome doors tight again. He began reckoning their probable route ahead—four days, maybe five, across the Cascades just south of Mount Hood; over the Umatillas and along the Snake, south through Cache Valley and Brown's Hole.

They rode up, and up, and still up that day, through the thick forests and across the ever steepening ridges of the foothills. In the late afternoon they put Moki to work smelling out game for them, and roasted chunks of venison haunch over their campfire that night. It was more than a little chilly up here in the high country, and the fire glowed bright and comforting under the dark canopy of the firs; the meat was warm in Jim's belly and Tom's drawl was as slow and humorous as ever. Everything was the same, just as it used to be. But Jim was unaccountably restless; he got up so many times to check Buckskin's tether or relocate the mule or pad down to the nearby spring for a drink, that Moki, who sprang up each time to go with him, finally gave a little whining yawn of protest and flopped down rebelliously beside the fire.

Tom threw back his head and laughed until Jim had to grin. "By golly, hoss, I can't say's I blame the dog. You'll have him wore out afore mornin', if you keep this up. What's eatin' you, boy? Yer jumpy as a prairie dog in a anthill. Somethin' on yer mind?"

"Naaa. Just can't settle down. Gimme my rifle yonder, Tom, I'll give it a cleanin'."

"You cleaned it twict a'ready, hoss. Wanta borry my pipe? Nothin' like a pipe fer puttin' a man to sleep."

But Jim only shook his head and rolled himself in the grizzly robe to lie staring into the fire. It was a long time before he fell asleep.

There was no hurrying the next day, because they were climbing in earnest now; the earth tilted up beneath the horses' feet until their path perforce became a zigzag back and forth across the reaching slopes. They camped on a sidehill strewn with boulders and huckleberry bushes, and were off at first light, their robes still fast around them to ward off the bite in the air. Up, and up—across a perilous ridge and up again through thinning trees. They were not far from the lofty spine of the Cascade range now—Mount Hood loomed huge and near on their left hand, its craggy peak thrusting high out of a wreath of mist.

It was still early morning on this third day when Jim thought he heard a shout. He reined in, staring in disbelief around the wild deserted scrub thickets and rocky slopes that were their trail. It was wilderness complete; not even Indians frequented this high country. There could be no one here to shout. But even as he started on, it came again—far-off and garbled, but unmistakably a human voice.

Tom pushed up beside him. "Hoss, am I goin' crazy, or do you hear that too?"

"I hear it, all right. And lookit Moki!"

The dog was standing rigid a little distance ahead, one foot upraised and ears stiffly cocked. He gave a gruff little bark and bounded forward.

"Might as well find out what's up," Tom said. "Looks like it's right on our way, anyhow."

Curious but wary, they rode on through the scrub and into a stand of fir. More noises began to drift to them—distant bangings and a curious sort of screeching; and as they drew nearer, an occasional bawl that sounded for all the world like cattle or oxen.

"What the *devil?*" muttered Tom. They made good time as they emerged from the trees and pounded briefly across a rocky level, then plunged into another tilted grove. The noises were plainer now, dominated by men's voices shouting some sort of orders. Tom and Jim burst out of the grove and pulled up short, for the earth had opened before them into a vast declivity—a canyon so deep the timber at its bottom looked dwarfed. It stretched on either hand as far as they could see; pitching steep enough down their own side but on the other rising almost sheer. They both recognized that opposite slope —it was the hill where the laurels grew, the most formidable barrier between them and the summit of the range.

But it was not at Laurel Hill they stared. Incredulous, their eyes were riveted on the object at its top—a familiar, sway-back object teetering on the very brink of that perilous drop.

It was a trail-worn bourgeway wagon.

Immediately the talk at Rutledge's flashed into Jim's mind. "By gor, they *are* comin' overland! The thunderin' fools—!" His eye traced a curious zigzag mark down the face of the slope. Tom saw it too.

"Good sufferin' catfish, hoss, one of em's done it a'ready, or I can't read sign! Lookee there!" He pointed downward; there, far below, a stained canvas top crept across the timbered floor of the canyon like a stubby caterpillar crawling through grass.

"By gor!" Jim whispered. "By thunder—" He lapsed incoherently into Crow, feeling an excitement different from

217

any he had ever known. His eyes snapped upward to the wagon at the top. It had moved; the four oxen were already over the brink, struggling in a wide diagonal down the face of the drop. Jim stiffened with dread; it looked like suicide. But forward came the wagon, over the brink. It tilted crazily, swayed and lurched and bounced, but somehow stayed upright. As it drew away from the crest, the tiny figure of a man came slipping and sliding on the upward side of the oxen, leaning almost horizontal as he braced his weight against the animals' guide ropes; a huge tree had been chained to the rear axle to drag behind and act as brake.

What would have happened without the tree Jim could only guess. Even with it, there was no controlling that top-heavy vehicle once the hill claimed it. The oxen scrambled and slid and skidded faster and faster in a frantic effort to escape the weight which bore down on them relentlessly, banging and bumping and careening at their heels. By the time they were halfway down the slope their progress had turned into a headlong rush, raising clouds of dust so thick it almost obscured the scene, filling the air with a wild confusion of noises—oxen's bawling and men's hoarse yells, the piercing squeal of wagon wheels, and the crash of limbs as they were ripped off the dragged tree and flew spinning into the air.

It was an act of chaos and daring, of courage so reckless that it etched itself on Jim's mind never to be erased. He sat rigid on his fidgeting mare, as unconscious of his fingers knotting on the halter as he was of Tom's soft and constant swearing at his side.

Then suddenly it was over—the dust settled and there was the wagon motionless near the foot of the slope, where a great tree lay directly across its path. A faint cheer rose from the top of Laurel Hill, and looking up again, Jim saw a line of people at the brink—children, women, men. A bunch of cattle and horses were even now being prodded over the edge to start their scrambling way downward; another wagon loomed behind them, and he knew there were more behind it. These bourgeways! They fought the country—but they conquered it. Stubborn, brave, magnificent fools, who didn't know an impossibility when they saw one. Fools? They were heroes! They had a medicine so big nothing could withstand it.

Nothing could withstand it . . . Suddenly the scene before Jim's eyes was blotted out, and another rose. He saw the vast sweep of the Plains, with wagons like this everywhere— crawling in little clouds of dust over every corner of the continent, turning off south and north to halt on plateaus, to seek out valleys, to swarm among mountains—to penetrate even the wild fastnesses of Absaroka. And everywhere they stopped, cabins mushroomed, gardens sprouted, dark furrows laid their stripes across the earth. Indians were crowded backward, bunched and milling; buffalo herds were scattered and slain and gone, and the prairies were no longer empty but teeming with life; towns sprang up to obliterate lonely graves, cattle fed where once the coyote howled.

The vision was gone almost before he glimpsed it, but its effect was staggering. Breathing hard and blinking, feeling the little hairs rise on the back of his neck, Jim shook himself back to the present. He felt as if everything were suddenly different, himself changed in some way he could not fathom, the whole world new. Yet only an instant had passed; the cattle were still scrambling down the slope yonder, the dust still settling below.

Tom gave a sudden whoop of delight and pointed downward. The wagon which had just made the furious descent stood deserted, its tongue lolling, while the man slapped his oxen angrily into place beside the great tree that barred his way. He roped the beasts to it, every motion one of exasperation, and they dragged it laboriously out of the way. Hitched to the wagon once more, they lumbered the remaining fifty yards down the slope and pulled up short on level ground, halted by the weight of the tree still dragging behind their own load. Instantly the man was off the high seat and cutting the tree free. Serenely leaving it in exactly the same spot as the log which had so angered him, he resumed his seat and the wagon disappeared into the timber.

Tom threw back his head and roared. "I knowed it! You watch, hoss! The next 'un down'll do the same doggone thing! By golly, if that ain't human nature . . ."

Jim never knew how long it was they stayed there, watching. He didn't even notice when Bad Medicine lay down, pack and all, in the middle of the trail. But by the time they finally nudged and prodded and kicked him to his unwilling feet, and started their horses down the near side of the canyon, the first two wagons were straining up it. Three more squealed faintly far below, crossing the timbered floor.

As Jim and Tom moved down parallel to the second wagon, its owner spotted them and hailed. Riding ahead of Tom, Jim ordered Moki to keep the mule on his feet and cut across the incline at an angle, intercepting the wagon on a slanting shelf. The man ran forward eagerly.

"You comin' from west'ard?" he demanded.

"Yep."

"Willamette Valley?"

"Yep."

"By gollies! Is it fer, boy?"

Jim shook his head. "Four, five days, in a wagon. Mebbe less."

"Four days! Y'hear that Martha?" The man yelled jubilantly into the wagon. "Four, five days, we'll *be* there!" He swung back to Jim. "Say, boy, is it all they say 'tis? The land and all? Can a man make a livin'?"

There was nothing you'd ever notice about this man. He

was undersized and scrawny, with a face you'd never be able to pick out in a crowd. Farmer, bourgeway, nobody—he was just another man. Yet with his own eyes Jim had watched him beat his oxen over that drop, slip, and slide and curse his way down beside them, fight the very mountain itself, and do the impossible.

"You'll do a'right, mister," he said huskily. "You'll do fine. They's a good valley down yonder, best I ever see. And plenty folks just like you. By gor, it's wuth the trip!"

He wheeled his mare and plunged on down the slope, the upthrust treetops swimming suddenly in a watery blur as his mind filled with Jonnie's face and a cabin on the Tualatin.

He never remembered much about the next couple of hours. Somehow he and Tom scrambled up Laurel Hill, crossed the ridge beyond, and rode up and on through layers of swirling mist. Mount Hood, towering huge and close to the left of them, appeared and reappeared through the vapor like a gigantic phantom. Jim rode unseeing, his own thoughts swirling in a misty confusion of images and voices—the wagon careening down Laurel Hill, Sally's shining hair and fierce little profile, Dan'l's eager laughter, fields deep with grain where forests once stood; Rutledge's deep voice saying, "If there ain't no other way to get here, I reckon they'll make it . . ." and Meek's, "Why, hallelujah, I dunno what, boy, but somethin' *big*. Ain't you seen them wagons comin' over the plains?" So Meek had glimpsed that vision too! It was big, by gor, it was bigger than all outdoors! And Jonnie had seen it all along. Clear as sudden daybreak, Jim remembered his black eyes blaze with it, heard his voice saying, "Why, this is *home*. It's what we come all this way to get!"

And here was Jim Keath leaving it.

Suddenly the confusion was gone from his mind. He didn't know he'd halted his beasts until Tom came pushing back through the clouds of mist toward him.

"What's the matter, hoss? That cussed mule actin' up agin?"

Jim sat without moving or speaking. Then suddenly he said, "Tom, let's go back."

"Go back?" Tom nudged Tucky closer, peering intently into Jim's face. Slowly his own changed, and a slackness crept over his body. He looked down at his thumbnail, smiling a little. "I wondered when you was gonna find out," he said quietly.

"Find out what?"

"That you belonged right whar you was—back yonder."

"You knowed it?" Jim faltered.

"Why, sure I knowed it. Knowed it fust night I saw you, and heerd you talk about it—about yer brother and all. I even told you, hoss, if you'll just think back."

Jim thought, and remembered. "Tom, I didn't know what you meant. I thought mebbe you was sayin' you'd ruther trap alone."

Rivers gave a short, soft laugh. "I reckon that's why I climbed a couple mountain ranges to hunt you up! No, but onct I found you, I knowed how your stick was floatin'. You're dead right, Jim. Go back."

"By thunder, you'll come too!"

Tom smiled again, slowly shaking his head. There was complete finality in the gesture. "Nope, hoss, I tried it, but it ain't my trail. When a man's spent twenty year beaverin', I reckon he's ruint fer anything else."

Jim stared in silence at the lean, tough figure with its battered hat, dark against the rolling white vapor. "That's it, then?"

"That's it, hoss," Tom said easily.

A swirl of mist drifted between them, blurring the trapper's outlines until he seemed almost to dissolve like a ghost, lacking all solid substance. And a ghost he was, Jim realized slowly—a man whose day was past, whose way of life had

222

vanished, heading back to a world which no longer existed. He knew now what had bothered him so these last weeks—why Tom moved alone through the noisiest crowd.

A soft laugh broke into his thoughts. "Sho, boy, don't look like that. Climb off and we'll have us a farewell feed, and a smoke fer luck."

Jim obeyed, but he couldn't respond to the other's drawling banter; the jerky choked him, and the smoke Tom puffed to east and west and north and south melted eerily into the fog. Too soon they rose and mounted once more, and the moment had come.

"Now listen, hoss," Tom said. "It ain't forever. I'll likely wander out this way next summer, less'n some Blackfoot gits me fust."

"Ain't the Blackfoot lives that's fast enough to git you, Tom."

Rivers grinned and wheeled his horse. "It might take two of 'em," he drawled. He gathered his reins, his face suddenly bleak. "Good huntin', Jim. Take keer of that medicine. It's done a powerful big magic."

He raised a hand in farewell, and Jim returned the gesture without trusting his voice to speak. Tucky's hoofs rang on the mist-wet rock; man and horse moved away, and Jim watched until they vanished into the drifting layers of white. The faint jingling of traps floated back on a wisp of breeze; then even that faded. Jim stood alone in swirling emptiness.

Slowly he turned and started down the mountain. Tom would come back next summer, and the summer after, and the summer after—each time more ghostlike and remote; then the summer would come that failed to bring him. And it would be clear that at last some Blackfoot or Comanche—or maybe two—had been faster than Tom Rivers.

Slowly, out of his desolation, a certain quiet settled over Jim. Why struggle against what couldn't be changed? That was the life Tom wanted, the death he would choose. A man seldom got more, and many a man not half so much. As for himself, he was through looking backward. He and Tom had parted once more in high country, but this time each was sure of his trail—that was the difference.

He rode on, downward and downward now, through the thinning mists and into brilliant sunlight. Below him stretched a vast and slanting landscape, deep with timber, easing into the gentler slopes of foothills and finally leveling off into the valley he knew he loved as he had never loved a place before. And far off yonder flowed the still waters of the Tualatin, and in a cabin on its banks were three people who meant more to him than all his wild and lonely freedom.

My valley, he thought. My people. Home.

A dark and glorious music rose up inside him as he looked —like thunder, like rolling clouds, like rivers and drums and running horses, all of it shot through with the bright, quick notes of Jonnie's banjo. It filled him, spilled over into a shout of joy that echoed down through the forest; it brought his heels back against Buckskin's sides with a kick that sent her scrambling and sliding in a wild rush down the mountainside with the mule stumbling behind. The way would be swift, now that they were racing downward instead of toiling up —now that they were going home.

The music still echoed in his ears as he stood on the east bank of the Willamette just five mornings after he had quitted it, and shouted joyfully across the river to Jake. It rang all around him as he spurted off the ferry on the other side and plunged through the tangle of oaks and wild plum that bordered the Mills' claim. It drowned the thudding of the animals' hoofs and Moki's excited barking and the pounding of his own heart as he sped through the last familiar stretch of wood and into the clearing, sliding to the ground just as Sally emerged from the doorway of the cabin, Mrs. Rutledge and the twins behind her.

She stopped short, and he came toward her eagerly. "Sally, I'm back. I—"

Then he stopped too, and the music broke off in a crashing discord. Her eyes were red from weeping, her usually volatile little face dull and weary. She stood with shoulders sagging and hands limp at her sides.

"So you're back," she echoed. "Well, you're too late. He's gone."

"Gone? Who's gone?"

"Dan'l."

"Dan'l? Gone *where?* What in thunder—"

"Nobody knows where!" she burst out. Suddenly she began to cry. "If we knew, you think we'd waste time huntin' through ever' Injun camp this side of—"

"*Injun* camp? Blast it, tell me what you're talkin' about!"

"Dan'l's what I'm talkin' about!" she almost screamed at him. Her hands clenched with fury. "You just rode away and left him, Jim Keath, you went off without sayin' one word and it like to broke his heart! Day before yesterday we woke up and he was gone. They was only this—"

She thrust her fist out toward him and opened it; on the palm lay a crumpled piece of deerskin, covered with Dan'l's sprawling, flourishing writing.

"Yes, I'll read it to you," she flung at him, her scorn so like a lash that he went rigid under it. She spread the scrap of hide in hands that shook convulsively, as did her voice. " 'Dear Jonnie and Sis. Don't try to find me. I have gone away like Jim done—to be a Injun.' And Jonnie and the men huntin' ever' Injun town to Fort Vancouver for three days and nights and not a sign of him! They're up at Mullinses now gettin' food and fresh horses to hunt some more but they can't find him, oh they can't find him!" She buried her face in her hands suddenly, the words breaking into sobs. "See what you done, Jim Keath! I wish we'd never seen you!"

Slowly, painfully, Jim gathered the tattered remnants of his thoughts and forced them into some sort of coherence. "I—know whar he is," he muttered. Her head lifted, her eyes wildly questioning. He nodded. "He's got to be. Ain't no other way to—"

He broke off, moistening his dry lips, while he struggled to make plans.

"Go to Mullinses," he said hoarsely. "Go fast. I'll leave the mule. Tell Jonnie I've gone to git the boy back—south'ard along the river—they kin foller if they want."

He wheeled and ran for Buckskin, not waiting to see how she took it or what she did. Back he pounded through the woods he had ridden through so joyously a few moments before. But this time his hands were like ice and his mouth dry with fear, one terrible picture before his eyes—a line of sullen Indians with flat, blank eyes carrying their canoes around the portage.

The Umpquas—who kept slaves.

Chapter XVIII

It was the hour before dawn. The river lay faintly luminous in starlight, just pale enough to reveal the thin black shapes of five canoes drawn up half into the bushes on the shore. On the sands of the little hidden cove nearby, the Umpqua camp—a cluster of silent hutlike shelters ranged around a dying fire—slept peacefully, secure in its concealment and its sentries.

And fifty yards away, at the top of the embankment which ringed the cove, the young Crow warrior, Talks Alone, lay belly down among the weeds and darkness, watching those two blanket-wrapped figures as a panther watches his prey.

White Jim Keath had vanished during the past terrible thirty-six hours of riding and searching and riding once more, blind with hate and frantic with the too vivid pictures that filled his brain. There was nothing of Jim Keath left at all in the painted face and glaring eyes of this naked savage. He watched the sentries, and in his mind he saw them sprawling under a knife thrust, clawing helplessly at arrows in their throats.

How could he best kill them, both at once, and without a sound? One squatted near the fire, which was no more than a nest of rose-red embers; the other hunched, a shadow among shadows, in the lee of the largest makeshift hut. Neither had made a move during the span of time that Jim had watched them, yet he could not be sure they were both asleep.

A little flame leaped up from the pile of coals, glinted on the fish heads that littered the sands around it, flickered briefly over the hard jaw and beady black eye of the nearest sentry. That one was far from asleep. Well, no matter. He would sleep soon—and long.

Stealthily Jim rose, one quieting hand on Moki who trembled by his side. He had left his rifle back yonder in the trees where Buckskin waited, for he could use only silent weapons tonight. He reached for his bow, then allowed Moki to press forward with him to the edge of the embankment. It fell off steeply, for a distance of about his own height, then sloped to the floor of the cove and the dense blackness of two trees.

Gingerly, he lowered himself over the edge, and dropped. A gray wraith that was Moki leaped beside him; both scrambled soundlessly down the slide of soft dirt and melted into the blur of dark beneath the trees. At the farthest edge of that blur Jim dropped to one knee, flipping an arrow to his bow. Then he pointed to the sentry beside the fire.

"Kill, Moki!" he breathed.

His stiffened arm and the curve of the bow made a black frame against the fire's radiance; through it he watched the dog slink toward the nearer guard. Then his own eye snapped to the farther one, by the hut. Feathers brushed his cheek as he took careful aim, the bowstring taut against his thumb, every nerve end quivering as he waited for the flash of movement that would tell him Moki had sprung.

It came. His thumb snapped straight; the soft *whang* of the arrow seemed to fill the night. Before the sound had faded he was on his feet, running across the sand to the struggling figures beside the fire. A plunge of his knife and all was still; he wrenched Moki loose and half threw him toward the embankment with a guttural command. Waiting only until the dog

228

started obediently up the bank toward Buckskin, he bent swiftly, plucked a glowing brand from the fire and sprang toward the biggest hut.

The sentry outside it was dead, as Jim had gambled he would be; he slumped, head lolling, beside the door flap, a feathered shaft sprouting from his breast. The bigger gamble was that his presence here meant Dan'l was in this hut. Jim's jaw clamped, his fingers sought the medicine bundle tied to his braid before he raised the flap and stepped into the black interior.

In a fir grove some miles to the north, Jonnie sat numb with fatigue upon his borrowed horse, while for the hundredth time since sundown he watched Joe Meek slide down from his black stallion and go poking with a torch into the trees ahead.

Would they ever catch up, Jonnie wondered. Could Meek actually follow Jim's trail at night, no matter how plain the sign? Most doubtful of all, had Jim himself guessed right? Nobody could know—maybe Dan'l was a hundred miles away from here; across the Columbia, up into the Coast range, somewhere far to the east.

Feeling the knots of panic jerk tight again inside him, he rested an arm on his saddle horn and put his head down, forcing himself to relax. Jim knew, he must know; and Meek would find him. Nothing to do but trust both of them blindly.

Behind him he could hear the restless movements of the other horses, the faint squeak of leather and the rustle of underbrush, the low voices of the men—Mills, Burke, Rutledge, Ab Selway, Sam. His heart went out to them, suddenly and wholly. What would he have done without his friends these past four days!

His tired mind flitted anxiously to Sally, waiting alone and fearful back at the cabin. But no, she wasn't alone. Mrs. Rutledge wouldn't leave her for a minute, nor the others. He could count on that. It was Dan'l who was alone. The boy's image filled his mind—the curly head, the clear eyes wild with grief because Jim was gone. Why didn't I see it comin'! Jonnie thought for the thousandth time. Why didn't I say somethin', do somethin'! Why did I ever want to find Jim again in the first place . . . And he knew it was because of a heart-sick day nearly ten years past when he, like Dan'l, had awakened to find Jim gone. All those years it had hurt, he had wanted his brother back. Well, he'd had him, for a while, but the price was dear. He'd lost them both now.

He jerked up his head, dragging a hand across his eyes, realizing dimly that Rutledge's horse had pushed up beside him.

"Take it easy, Jonnie," the deep voice came out of the gloom. "Jim's doin' all he can to right the damage."

"I wonder if he even knows he done it."

"I reckon he knows plainer than you, by this time, son. I got a idee he's seein' ever'thing mighty turrible clear—watchin' Dan'l start in to muddle up his life same way he muddled up his own. Nothin' like that to open a feller's eyes. Be glad you ain't him, Jonnie. He's feelin' ever'thing you are, and a lot more besides."

Slowly the bitterness drained away, leaving only weariness. "If only we can find 'em," Jonnie muttered.

Meek came back, grim, as he had been since the instant Sally burst into the Mullins' cabin yesterday morning to gasp out Jim's message. Then, he'd exploded, "The Umpquas! By the almighty, why didn't I guess it! Let's go, men, hurry."

Now he said, "We're gainin'. No more'n a hour behind him. I got a notion now where they might be campin', them cussed fish-eatin' coyotes! I'll lodgepole ever' man jack of 'em."

He leaped to the saddle and started headlong through the

trees, his torch held high. Jonnie spurred after him, ignoring the aching soreness of every muscle, his ears full of the thud of hoofs behind him, following the bobbing flare in front.

The torch Jim held—the smoldering branch yanked from the fire—gave but a feeble light in the hut's black interior, which reeked of fish and unwashed bodies. He thrust it here and there over blanket-wrapped shapes, half frantic with the need to see and the equally urgent need for caution. Hatred for those sleeping figures rose up in him—a craving to kick and yank them out of his way, fling them aside like so many rags until he found the one small bundle he wanted.

Something glinted suddenly in a far corner. Jim thrust the torch out, caught the unmistakable gleam of golden hair. Next instant he was leaping over the shadowy figures toward it, cursing the sudden uncontrollable trembling of his legs that threatened to sprawl him straight on top of some sleeping Umpqua. Stooping, he lifted an edge of blanket from the glinting hair, then sank to his knees. It was Dan'l. Dan'l with smudged and tear-streaked face, sleeping tired and helpless with his bound wrists pillowing his cheek.

It was fury that gave Jim back his strength and conquered the trembling—fury at the thong that bound those wrists, at the whole treacherous crew that slept around him. Swiftly he stretched out a hand now cool and steady, clamped it over the boy's mouth. The gray-green eyes flew open, and their first glazed, wild look of terror nearly unmanned Jim again, it told so plainly what these last two days had been. But he held the torch close, and the look faded to bewilderment, then blazed again with incredulous joy. The boy's eyes brimmed with sudden tears, and Jim gently took away his hand.

His knife was out, slicing that thong as if it were a captor's throat. Then his wrists freed, Dan'l sat up and pointed to his ankles. They were bound too, but not for long. Jim chafed the swollen flesh, wondering if the boy would be able to walk.

Well, he had to. A huddled figure nearby stirred restlessly and turned over, uttering a sigh that stank of fish. Jim thought fast. How long had it been now, that he'd been prowling about this hut? Three minutes? Four?

He hoisted the boy to his feet and stood supporting him, holding his brand on a sudden impulse toward the pegged-down hides that formed the wall of the hut. Good! The raw-hide rope was plainly visible. He ground out the torch against the earthen floor and stooped once more; a flash of his knife and he was lifting the loosened skins and drawing the boy outside into the fragrant air of night. But with the first step Dan'l gave a sharp little moan of pain. It was quickly stifled, but Jim's anxiety redoubled. If the Umpquas were light sleepers . . . He felt Dan'l stumble and he tightened his grasp on his arm, worrying about those thong-numbed ankles. Then they were around the hut somehow, and running across the open toward the embankment and safety.

But Dan'l stumbled again, staggered, and half went down. Jim whirled and lifted him—and heard a cry of alarm from the hut they had just quitted.

"Oh, Jim, they've waked up—" gasped Dan'l.

Jim didn't wait to find out what would happen. As a babble of voices broke out behind him he slung the boy over his shoulder and, staggering under the added weight, ran for the embankment. Figures erupted from this hut and that amid answering yells; torches bloomed. But Jim was under the two trees now, stumbling across the pool of blackness and out on the far side to scramble up the crumbling slope.

He dug his moccasined toes into the soft earth, feeling his calf muscles knot and the dirt give way beneath him. But still he clambered, half dragging and half pushing the boy, who was doing his best to help. Below, a shot rang out, then two

232

more, in rapid succession, over the uproar of yells and running feet. As Jim gained the slope's top a bullet sang close by his ear and thudded into the earth beside him. Gasping for breath, he seized the boy and hoisted him up the sheer lip of the embankment, felt him clutch at the bushes above and knew the lessening of his weight as he wriggled half over the top. It was all but done. He bunched his muscles for his own leap—and the world exploded into a blaze of spinning lights as something crashed against the side of his head.

For what seemed an age he teetered there enveloped in noise, feeling his hands numb and his eyes glaze and his body tilt slowly backward. "Run Dan'l! Find Buckskin—" he tried to yell, but could not hear his own voice. Then the night whirled past and he was falling, tumbling and somersaulting, through a garbled, screaming uproar into a deep black well of silence.

Jim awoke to find himself bound hand and foot, face down in sand and brambles, with the world full of pain. Where was this place, and what had happened? Staring dazedly at the crushed leaves an inch from his eye, he realized they were visible in the first dim gray light of morning. Guttural voices came to his ears from somewhere off to the right, and the sound of a fire crackling and feet moving about. A whiff of frying fish brought the saliva flooding into his mouth. Dizzy with hunger, he struggled to clear away the layers of fog in his brain. A slight movement of his eyes brought a flash of deeper pain. Memory came back in a rush, and with it, sinking dread. He was still in the Umpqua camp, and it was morning. Had Dan'l got away?

Cautiously he lifted his head just enough to turn on his left cheek. The vicious throbbing that filled the whole side of his head at the movement sent him momentarily slipping back into that dizzy blackness; but in a moment he opened his eyes

233

once more. On the sand not two feet away lay Dan'l, prone and trussed up just as he himself was.

So all his efforts had come to nothing. Jim felt tired to his very bones. What a mess he'd made of everything, what trouble he'd set in motion the day he'd turned his back on Powder River and ridden westward to The Dalles! But no, the trouble had started long before that. Its roots stretched back to Absaroka, back to that grizzly—back, back to that long ago, fatal morning he'd run away from home. And now, today, the wreckage was complete.

He heaved a sigh that tangled painfully in his throat. Instantly there was a stirring nearby, a tremulous "Jim!" He raised his eyes to meet the wide, incredulous ones of the boy, who had wriggled around to face him.

"Oh, cracky, Jim, I thought you was dead!"

"Not yet I ain't."

"Oh, lordy, I'm so glad, oh Jim I'm so awful glad!" Dan'l's lips quivered, but Jim saw the kindling of new hope on his face.

He figgers I kin git him out of this, Jim thought. Even now. Even tied up like a trussed deer, with a bullet furrow in my skull. Blast it, them devils might as well've finished me off fer all the good I kin do him now—

It made him sicker than ever, the knowledge that he must lie helpless and watch the boy's hope fade away, the trust in his eyes cloud over with disillusion.

He'll find out what I'm worth, all right, Jim thought bitterly. It won't be long.

"They're eatin' breakfast, Jim, and gettin' ready to leave," the boy whispered. "How we gonna get loose?"

"I dunno, Dan'l."

"Do they mean to take you in the canoes along o' me?"

"I reckon so."

234

He knew so. He'd already figured out why he was still alive—they were saving him for the kind of thing he'd watched sometimes in Absaroka, when a swift death was deemed too good for some arrogant enemy. What Indians did to white men was nothing to what they did to each other when the occasion warranted. Well, he'd show the boy he could die well, anyway. Scalp Necklace's rigid training would not be wasted; these coyotes would get no satisfaction out of a Crow.

"You got a plan yet, Jim?"

"Not yet. I'll think of somethin'."

He closed his eyes again, cursing himself for a coward. He should tell the boy the truth, to let him go on hoping was only another form of torture.

A kick landed in his middle, and he glared up into the malevolent face of an Umpqua chieftain. He wore a red blanket striped with black, and a bone through each braid. He kicked again, viciously, snarling something in his throaty dialect and pointing behind him. Probably talking about those dead sentries, and painting lurid pictures of what was to come. Jim spat out some equally lurid remarks in Crow and ignored a third kick, harder than the others, which filled his head with that savage throbbing.

Next minute the Umpqua had beckoned one of the sullenfaced warriors, who without further ado slung Dan'l over his shoulder like a sack of meal and vanished in the direction of the river.

The suddenness of it shocked Jim out of his mental torpor. Abruptly he was raging mad, determined to get them both out of this fix whether it was impossible or not. His brain began to work frantically, and as soon as the chieftain had strolled away his hands were straining at their thongs. Now that Dan'l had been removed he could see the activities beyond, and realized that the camp was nearly ready to travel. The sky had lightened while he lay there unresisting, and daybreak was upon them. He had five minutes at the most.

He hadn't even ten seconds. At that instant the warrior reappeared, accompanied by another. The next Jim was hoisted between them and carted down the sloping sands to the river. There he was dumped headlong into the bottom of a canoe and left, bruised and throbbing.

For precious moments he was so blindly dizzy he could do nothing at all. Then at last he managed to roll to his side and drag himself to a sitting position. For his pains he got a moccasined foot in his face that sent him crashing back again. He lay still, the sweat pouring off him as he fought back nausea. So there was somebody else in the canoe. A guard. He'd have to think fast how to dispose of him.

Suddenly there came a shout from somewhere back in the cove. Before he could decide what it meant he heard hurrying footsteps and saw through slitted eyelids that one of the warriors was running full speed down the sands. The canoe rocked as the man seized it, pushing it under a mass of overhanging bushes as he hissed some message to Jim's guard. Then he vanished, and the guard dropped forward to kneel astride Jim, clamping a fish-reeking hand over his mouth.

Now what? Frantically Jim cast about in his brain for an answer. What was happening up there on shore? What *could* be happening to make them suddenly—

Then he heard it—a loud, familiar bellow. "By thunder, you better savvy where they're at! I'll take it out'n yer hide, you flea-bit, fish-eatin', child-stealin', trouble-makin' coyote! I got the law of this hull thunderin' valley behind me, understand? And the United States gov'ment behind that! By golly, I want that boy and the feller that come after 'im! I want—"

The bellow switched over to no less threatening Chinook jargon, and the chieftain's harsh voice answered protestingly in the same tongue. Several things took place simultaneously in Jim's brain. He remembered his own words sending Sally to Mullins'—"*Tell Jonnie . . . south'ard along the river . . . they kin foller if they want*"—and he heard the unmistakable sound of bourgeway boots crashing through the underbrush atop the embankment, and he knew he'd have a knife in his heart in another minute—and so might Dan'l—unless he could immediately give the show away past all concealing.

There was only one reckless thing to do, and he did it. At the instant the chieftain was swearing there had never been a boy, and that the Indian who had broken into the camp last night was unfortunately dead, Jim brought both his knees up hard into the crouching guard's belly and with a violent twist sent him over the side. Before the splash had settled he was struggling to sit up, yelling "*Meek!*" with all the power of his lungs.

The chieftain's voice had choked off. Now footsteps pounded down the sands, accompanied by a babble of noise over which Meek's roar rose triumphant. "Dead, is he? By golly, it's a mighty lively corpse can yell like *that!*"

The guard's head popped up out of the water, but Jim was ready for him, bringing his bound wrists down with smashing force. By the time the head came up again Meek was splashing through the shallows. With an instant and expert grasp of the situation he sent the guard under once more with a well-aimed toe, then yanked the canoe into the open.

On the beach the Umpquas were scattering in all directions, but Jim didn't watch what became of them. He gasped, "Cut me loose, Meek!" and an instant later was staggering across the graveled shallows to another clump of trailing bushes. Meek understood his intention and splashed ahead of him, but Jonnie had beat them both. He pushed out of the branches as they got there, and he had Dan'l in his arms.

"He's all right, he ain't hurt," he told them shakily. "Let's

237

have that knife, Meek. Them blasted varmints gagged 'im as well as tied 'im."

And so it was finished, and the impossible had been done, and Dan'l was sobbing with excitement in Jonnie's arms. And Jim, swaying from dizziness and that throbbing in his head, was too tired to wonder what Jonnie was thinking of him.

Meek drew Jim aside as the other men crowded around the boy and Jonnie. "Can you travel, Jim?" he asked quietly.

"Sure, let's git started."

"Man, you done a job last night. I never even thought of them varmints. It mighta been weeks—"

"I made a mess of it."

"The devil you did! That bullet mighty nigh made a mess of you, though. I reckon they didn't bother to feed you?"

"No."

"Then come on. I got jerky in my possibles, onct we git up to where we left the hosses."

They scaled the embankment in silence, the others following. At the top Meek turned to look at Jim, and spoke again. "I reckon they ain't but one way to keep ahead of you in these Injun troubles, boy, and that's to git you on my side. You're a prime tracker, Jim, and jest my meat fer chasin' wolves. Lemme know when you git over that there headache, and I'll have you sworn in as deputy. If you want it, you got a job."

Jim stared at him dazedly, remembering a shining vision of thudding hoofs and a fine brass badge. What a difference this might have made to him, only two weeks ago! The difference between going and staying. But now it was too late. The only thing left that he could do for his brothers and Sally was to get out—go far, far away where he could never hurt them again.

"Thanks, Meek," he muttered. "But onct we git the boy home I'm headin' east. Fer good."

Chapter XIX

Under a bright midmorning sun three days later, Jim, Jonathan, Dan'l, and Mr. Rutledge rode into the clearing beside the Tualatin. Meek and the others had already scattered for their own claims to spread the news that the boy was safely home; Jonnie had shouted it at the top of his lungs as soon as they were in earshot of the cabin. Almost before he reined his horse to a halt Sally was at his stirrup, laughing and crying at once as she pulled Dan'l down into her arms and held him as if she never meant to let him go. Mrs. Rutledge and the twins were only seconds behind her, and for a few moments the little runaway was all but smothered by the swirling skirts and joyous, tearful babble that surrounded him.

Jim looked on silently, thinking by how slim a margin this scene had missed being one of tragedy. His paint was gone long since, his fringed shirt covered the bronzed, scarred body of Talks Alone; the medicine bundle no longer swung on his braid but rested deep in the hidden darkness of his pouch. He was Jim Keath again, his face a little haggard from three days of wearing that savage throbbing down to a dull ache, but his mind more resolved than ever on what he knew he must do.

He waited until Dan'l was well launched on a breathless

recital of all that had happened in the past fearful week. Then he drew Jonnie aside.

"I'm leavin' now," he said quietly.

"You're doin' what?"

"I'm leavin'. Tell Sally ever'thing she said is true, and I know it. Tell her—"

"Why don't you tell her yourself?" Jonnie said.

"Thunder, I couldn't face her. She hates the sight of me."

Jonathan was silent a moment. From the group around Dan'l, Sally's voice floated to them clearly. ". . . can just thank our stars for Jim, that's all! If it hadn't been for him . . ."

"It don't sound much like she hates you," Jonnie said.

"You didn't hear her the other day, when I fust come back. She's dead right, too. Been better if you'd never seed me—"

"I don't feel that way about it."

"Well, you oughta."

"No, I oughtn't! Jim, lookee here. You headed out of here last week for good and all, you know you did. Yet you turned around and come back. Why? You tell me why!"

Jim thought of Laurel Hill and the new world he'd envisioned as he watched the wagons; of Tom dissolving wraithlike into the misty past and himself riding joyously down the mountain toward a future he'd finally glimpsed. Jonnie was making this mighty hard. There were things you couldn't explain, things you couldn't bear to talk about.

"No use tellin' you why, Jonnie. I just wanted to come back. And now I wanta go."

"You're lyin'. You don't want to go no more'n I do."

Jim spoke desperately. "Never mind what I want! You seen what I done to the boy—I got to get out, go far away from him, so's he'll fergit all about me. Looks to me like the only thing I kin do!"

240

"It looks to me," said Jonnie slowly, "like runnin' away again."

Jim shook his head violently, his thoughts in a tangle, his whole will concentrated on hanging on to that one clear decision. "I'm goin', that's all," he muttered, and turned away.

But Jonnie caught his arm. "All right," he snapped. "But you ain't gonna go without tellin' Dan'l. Not again, you ain't!"

Before Jim could stop him he raised his voice. "Dan'l! Come over here. Jim's got somethin' to say to you."

Dan'l detached himself from the group around him and ran eagerly across the grass. Then he was standing there, waiting and Jim had to say something.

"Dan'l—" he began, half choking on it. He looked down into the snub-nosed, inquisitive small face with its wide, clear eyes, and knew he had to make him understand the whole thing, once and for all. He dropped down on his haunches before the boy, seizing his shoulders.

"Dan'l, you ain't never gonna run away agin," he said softly, fiercely. "You understand that? You're gonna fergit ever'thing I ever told you about the Crows, and Absaroka, and all the rest."

"Forget it? Why?"

" 'Cause it's got nothin' to do with you. This here's yer home, this valley. They's big things happenin' here. Powerful big things, Dan'l! You gotta be in on 'em!"

"Jim, what d'ya mean?"

"I mean you mustn't ever want to be a Injun any more! By gor, it ruint me but it ain't gonna git to you. It's folks like you gonna make the country over, you know that? I seen it happen t'other day right afore my eyes. Up on the mountain—"

He told the boy about Laurel Hill, about the wagons plunging down. He had forgotten Jonnie and the others now, he thought only of the thing he'd glimpsed and the terrible importance of making Dan'l see it. The boy's eyes darkened with interest as he listened, but they were bewildered, too.

"Well, shucks, just gettin' some old wagons down a hill— that ain't so much. It ain't half as much as what you done t'other night! Sneakin' me away from them Umpquas and up the bank—"

"Oh, thunder, it ain't the same at all!"

"Why ain't it? You're as brave as them. Lots braver."

Jim gave him a frantic little shake. "Now listen. You gotta listen to me. You gotta change all them idees! Them wagons'll be all over the plains afore we know it. Lookit the folks in this valley a'ready! Why, they'll be plowin' fields in Absaroka! They'll be buildin' schools, and towns—"

"I don't care about all that!" cried Dan'l. "I only want to be like you!" The wide eyes swept over Jim's braids and feather. "*You* didn't change! You're just the same. And I'm gonna be just like you!"

Jim's hands slid from the boy's shoulders as he slowly straightened, looking down into a small, inflexible face whose expression of stubbornness he remembered too well from that snowy evening high above the gorge.

Jim turned slowly to Jonnie. So that's what you meant, he thought. He won't believe me less'n I prove it. I got 'im into this and now I gotta git 'im out. I can't run away and leave him to fight it by hisself—the rough way, the way I done. I gotta stay—and show 'im.

He looked again at Dan'l. "All right!" he said. "Then go ahead and *be* like me. Here's how I'm gonna be."

With a swift motion he had his knife out, then he seized a braid. One ruthless slash and it dropped, slithering and glossy, at his feet; an instant later the other followed. He snatched the coup feather out of his hair and flung it down beside the braids. Then he stood there, breathing hard and shaking, everything in him in an uproar at what he had done.

242

"Take a thunderin' good look," he said. "That's the last you'll see of a Crow around this here claim. Now go on in the cabin and git some sleep. I've had my say."

Slowly Dan'l obeyed, moving away toward the cabin like one in a dream. For the first time Jim became aware of the others. He didn't meet their gaze—not even Jonnie's. Reaction had set in now; he couldn't stand to look at what lay at his feet. He had done the right thing for Dan'l. But what of himself? Of his helpers? Suddenly Sally darted forward and scooped braids and feather into her arms, then whirled toward the cabin.

"Hold on!" Jim grated. "Whar—whar you takin' them things?"

Slowly she turned back. "I'm gonna put 'em where they belong," she told him softly. "The braids in the leather box, so's we'll always remember 'em. And the feather under the clock with Pa's medal."

The understanding in her voice, the strange weightless feeling of his slashed-off hair—it was too much for him to handle. He turned blindly and headed for the woods. It was all right, he need not leave the valley now, he could stay with his own people. And still—

He knew only that he must be alone awhile, to straighten the whole thing out and get hold of himself.

Jonnie, searching cautiously through the willows upstream ten minutes later, spotted him sitting on a flat stone by the water's edge, his head in his hands. Jonnie hesitated, touched by the weariness in the pose, and by the shorn black locks, which parted themselves sleekly down the back of Jim's head as if the braids were still there. What had they meant to him, Jonnie wondered. Something far deeper than anyone had guessed until the moment he had slashed them from his

243

head. That was a moment Jonnie knew he would not forget —nor would any of them who had seen it.

Jim had heard him, and turned.

"Want me to leave you be?" said Jonathan.

"It don't matter. Come on."

Jonnie went on, but stopped abruptly as he reached Jim's side. Jim was holding that little heathen buckskin sack. "Want to talk about it?" Jonnie asked.

Jim shrugged. "I'm just—tryin' to figger out whar this comes in. It's the only thing left," he said desperately. "But it's the biggest thing of all—"

Jonnie sat down very quietly beside him. "Jim, what is that?"

Jim hesitated, as if crossing some final inward barrier. But at last he spoke. "It's my medicine, Jonnie. It's the only luck I got. And it's powerful strong. It's saved my hide a hun'erd times—it even brought me here! But it's Crow medicine. It won't know me or help me now. By gor, I dunno what to do without it."

Jonnie sat rigid. Oh, lord a'mighty, he thought, we've changed him all we could, but inside he's just the same. He's still a Injun.

"It—brought you here?" he repeated cautiously.

"The song did—the medicine song. It was in my dream."

Then the whole thing came out, piece by piece, and haltingly. It was hard for Jim to tell this, Jonnie could see that. It was deep and private, locked away securely in Jim's Indian heart and only brought out now because the very foundations of his life were being shaken. Jonnie tried to be worthy of the trust, not letting his feelings show, keeping his pity and scorn and helpless anger all to himself.

But as the tale went on, as Jim quit explaining what medicine dreams were and began to describe his own, Jonathan's anger faded, and astonishment filled his mind instead. "You spoke English to that grizzly?" he broke in softly. "When you was a Crow three year a'ready you dreamed in white man's talk?"

Jim nodded, his hands tight on the bundle. "I dunno whar I knew them words, Jonnie, seems like it was mighty long ago. 'The Lord is my shepherd—he makes me lie down in green pastures—he leads me beside still waters—though I walk through the—"

Jonnie was on his feet, shouting with relief and joy. "Oh, crimeny, Jim—oh, lord a'mighty—*I* know where you knew 'em, I know all about it! And I thought you was really Injun, clean through—!"

Jim slowly rose to face him. "What are you talkin' about?"

"About them words, Jim! It's all so blasted simple now—" Jonathan broke off, fighting to calm himself. He pulled Jim down again upon the stone. "Now listen," he said quietly, trying to keep his voice from trembling. "I'm gonna say 'em to you—and say 'em right. 'The Lord is my shepherd; I shall not want. He maketh me to lie down in green pastures; he leadeth me beside the still waters. He restoreth my soul; he leadeth me in the paths of righteousness for his name's sake. Yea, though I walk through the valley of the shadow of death, I will fear no evil; for thou art with me; thy rod and thy staff they comfort me. Thou preparest a table before me in the presence of mine enemies; thou anointest my head with oil; my cup runneth over. Surely goodness and mercy shall follow me all the days of my life; and I will dwell in the house of the Lord forever.' "

The words hung in the still air, vibrant with beauty and courage.

"That's your medicine, Jim," Jonnie said softly. "The Bible. The twenty-third psalm. Mother allus read it to us when we was sick, remember? That's why you thought of it in that dream—you was sick then! Feverish from starvin' and cuttin' yourself with that knife! That's all a medicine dream is, from where I sit, Jim—a nightmare. You had yours about that grizzly—and it ain't no wonder! But what they was Injun about it you could put in your eye. You been a white man all along, clean through."

Still Jim sat silent, though understanding now lay clear and steady in his eyes. Then deliberately he ripped open the buckskin bundle in his hands, and with a gesture of revulsion flung the whole thing on the ground.

The late afternoon sun was slanting through the shallows before Jim straightened his cramped legs and stood up, aware once more of his surroundings and that it was time to go home. He was ready now. The afternoon had been like a miracle, illuminating the last dark corners of his mind. He had never felt so free, so completely without fear.

The future rose glowing before him—he would teach Dan'l how to shoot and ride. He would plow and reap and work with Jonnie, ride the length and breadth of the valley "hunting wolves" whenever Joe Meek called—and he hoped it was often. He grew warm with pride when he thought of the shining brass badge, the valley looking to him for law and protection. Nothing could touch him now, the tangles were ended. He and Jonnie had talked over every plan and hope and optimistic dream, and he was supremely confident that they would all come true. Never again would Absaroka cross his mind. He'd forget it entirely.

He stared down at the scattered grizzly teeth, in spite of himself seeing the thin brown line of horses and Indians file over the hills, seeing the hidden streams and the birch thickets where the deer played, and the copper-brown faces of the brave young men he'd grown up worshiping as heroes. Then Jonnie's hand reached down, gathered the scattered teeth and the piece of buckskin, and tucked them in his pocket.

246

"I reckon," said Jonnie, "these oughta go in that leather box too—so's we'll always remember. Them Injuns wasn't so bad, Jim. Look what they done for you. Made you fast and strong and brave. Mighty brave. The medicine even brought you back home. We don't want to forget 'em."

"Jonnie, I never could anyhow."

"I know. I seen you tryin'. Don't try."

Jim nodded. Here was the closeness he and Jonnie had known so long ago—regained at last, and deeper than ever. Once again they "knew each other's heart." He smiled, realizing the phrase had come to his mind in Crow. No matter. It was good that way.

He drew a deep, contented breath and started cabinward, then turned back, brushing awkwardly at his hair. It felt so strange, chopped off like this, hanging over his cheeks. He frowned and studied Jonnie's, then moved past him to the riverbank. Kneeling, he scooped up water and wet the dangling locks, clawing it back over his ears with his fingers. When he arose with a somewhat sheepish grin and turned to be inspected, Jonnie's laugh was good to hear.

"By golly, if that don't make a difference! You know somethin'? We look alike again."

They pushed on through the willows, climbed the path to the clearing and walked slowly, happily, up the sloping grass. Yonder across the glades the sun was setting; the woods showed black against a brilliant sky. But more brilliant by far in Jim's eyes was the yellow oblong of the doorway just ahead of him. There were no ghosts remaining in that cabin now, no memories he could not face. All was settled and at peace. He swept one lingering glance over the woods, the whispering river—all the riches that were his. Then he followed his brother through that lighted door.

Jim Keath had come back home again, at last.

NEWBERY AWARD BOOKS
AND NEWBERY HONOR BOOKS
AVAILABLE IN PUFFIN

Blue Willow, *by Doris Gates*
Dobry, *by Monica Shannon*
Fog Magic, *by Julia L. Sauer*
The Golden Goblet, *by Eloise Jarvis McGraw*
The Good Master, *written and illustrated by Kate Seredy*
The Hundred Penny Box, *by Sharon Bell Mathis*
Journey Outside, *by Mary Q. Steele*
Miss Hickory, *by Carolyn Sherwin Bailey*
Moccasin Trail, *by Eloise Jarvis McGraw*
Rabbit Hill, *written and illustrated by Robert Lawson*
Roller Skates, *by Ruth Sawyer*
The Twenty-One Balloons, *by William Pène du Bois*
The Secret of the Andes, *by Ann Nolan Clark*
The Summer of the Swans, *by Betsy Byars*
The White Stag, *written and illustrated by Kate Seredy*